THE
SIXTH FORM

Books by Tom Dolby

THE TROUBLE BOY

THE SIXTH FORM

Published by Kensington Publishing Corporation

THE
SIXTH FORM

TOM DOLBY

KENSINGTON BOOKS
http://www.kensingtonbooks.com

KENSINGTON BOOKS are published by

Kensington Publishing Corp.
850 Third Avenue
New York, NY 10022

Library of Congress Card Catalog Number: 2007934365
ISBN-13: 978-0-7582-2258-9
ISBN-10: 0-7582-2258-0

First Printing: January 2008
10 9 8 7 6 5 4 3 2 1

Printed in the United States of America

For Drew

I

FALL

CHAPTER 1

Before he met Todd, in those first few weeks at Berkley Academy, Ethan Whitley sought refuge in the cool calm of the art studios, amidst the smells of dried paint and eraser shavings. The heat had surprised him; Massachusetts in September was balmy, sweltering, mosquitoes buzzing around brackish pools, verdant lawns that spread for acres beyond the brick facades of Berkley's Colonial campus. The advanced studios of the Stevenson Art Center were air-conditioned, a rare luxury for a school that prided itself on its Spartan, character-building accommodations. When he was working alone in these rooms, Ethan imagined that they protected him from all that lay waiting outside.

As he worked, he would think ahead to the next hour or two, safely tucking his portrait in his cubby, shuffling across the linoleum floor, walking upstairs, past the library, its fifty thousand volumes tempting him, across the inlaid marble of the school's foyer, through its atrium of white columns and vaulted ceilings, out the French doors of the main building. His fellow classmates—he didn't know their names; they were as anonymous as strangers in Grand Central Terminal—would lay sprawled on the grass under a cluster of birch trees like a clothing advertisement, a triple-page spread, their chlorinated blond locks falling lazily over their eyes, tanned legs, scratched in the right places (sports injuries, not clumsiness), skin free of blemishes. They lived in a world where people made witty remarks to each other, and no one worried too much about things like money or popularity or sex.

He was shocked then to find himself one evening, three weeks into the school year, sitting in a taxicab, a rattling old station wagon, barreling into town with Todd Eldon, a boy who lived on the floor above him. Five days earlier, Todd had burst into Ethan's room with the force of a raid—*Hands up! We know you have no friends, and we're going to do something about it!*—and asked him to summarize the week's English reading, the first section of *Jane Eyre*. Since that evening, the friendship had progressed so effortlessly that Ethan had nearly forgotten those horrible weeks prior, the sitting alone in his room after check-in, staring at the Jackson Pollock poster he had tacked to the wall above his bed, dreading the mealtime ritual of finding people to sit with, making conversation, smiling politely even when everyone who was done got up to study or goof off in the dorms.

Now Todd rifled around in his messenger bag and pulled out a nearly empty pack of cigarettes, its crumbs of tobacco littering the backseat. "Need to get more on the way back," he muttered.

Ethan felt his brow furrowing in disapproval, and he forced his visage to soften. He didn't smoke and had always suspected that people who did were not to be trusted. The cab pulled into the gravel driveway of Wilton's tearoom, one of a handful of places where students could eat in town, and Ethan reached for his wallet. Todd waved him away, signing the charge slip with a scribble.

The boys entered the tearoom and Todd greeted a young woman who was wiping down several of the tables, introducing her to Ethan as Laura. The room felt cozy, with yellow walls, ancient red tea canisters on high shelves, antique tables and chairs of varying sizes, a potted palm next to a fireplace. A group of girls from school, Fourth Formers, were chattering at the front table, occasionally giving the boys flirtatious glances; a local woman and her two children sat in the far corner. A sideboard held an assortment of desserts—fruit cobblers, pies, bread pudding, chocolate, pound, and carrot cakes. Ethan breathed in the deep warm aroma of vanilla and cardamom.

Madame Beauchamp, the old French lady who owned the tearoom, led them to a table near the window looking out on the back garden. They followed her, the wake of her old lady perfume trailing behind.

Laura came over and handed them menus. On the back were all the varieties of tea; on the front were the food selections. Ethan read the menu—soups, salads, sandwiches, scones—and then looked hungrily over at the cakes and pies on the sideboard.

The little that Ethan knew of Todd already made him feel inadequate. Todd had an older brother who had gone to Berkley, had apparently had numerous girlfriends (surely he had already had sex), played sports, and had grown up in New York City. Being from California, Ethan was embarrassed to admit that he had only been there once.

The door of the tearoom opened, bringing with it a burst of cool air, and in stepped a woman with flowing blond hair and light freckles on her cheeks. She wore a white dress and was carrying four boxes, the type used to carry baked goods. She was older than a student, but she didn't quite look like a teacher, either.

"Just in time!" She brushed past the boys and placed the four boxes down on the counter of the open kitchen, smiling at Madame Beauchamp. "Carrot, cheesecake, blueberry cobbler, and a strawberry rhubarb. All fresh from the oven."

Madame Beauchamp took the desserts and placed them on the island in the small kitchen, opening up the top box and examining its contents. "*Délicieux,*" she said.

The woman with the blond hair turned toward the boys and smiled.

"You guys look like you'll be wanting dessert."

Todd and Ethan stared at her. Ethan wondered why this woman, this exotic creature, was speaking to them.

"You're—hold on—Todd, right?"

Todd nodded.

"I've seen you here before. And who's your friend?"

Ethan felt a blush blooming in his cheeks as he looked up (he had noticed her dress, its neckline, the pale skin on her breastbone; his eyes darted away from this area, as though he had touched a hot teakettle and been burned). "Ethan Whitley," he said.

"Well, hello, Ethan Whitley," the woman said. "I'm Hannah. Ms. McClellan. You can call me Hannah."

Ethan was confused; he thought he had seen her around. "Are you a teacher?"

"That's what they tell me. I make some of the desserts here, too. Sort of a hobby I do on the side. Gets me out of my head."

Ethan wondered why she was inviting them to use her first name. Perhaps the younger Berkley teachers, the ones right out of college, might do this in private, but no one on the Berkley faculty who was Hannah's age—she had to be at least thirty— would ever allow this.

She sat down on a chair at the counter, facing the boys. "Ethan Whitley . . . you're new, right? Did I read some of your short stories last year that came in with your admissions packet?"

Ethan's blush deepened. "It's possible. I submitted a few."

"I loved them. They were really gorgeous. The one about the mother. I hope you keep writing."

"Thanks," Ethan croaked.

"Anyway, have some dessert. It's on me." She winked at Madame Beauchamp. "What do you guys want?"

"I usually get the carrot cake," Todd said.

"Um, blueberry cobbler?" Ethan said.

"Give them extra big pieces," Hannah said to Laura. "They're growing boys." She smiled again. "I haven't made as much of the blueberry cobbler lately. It's hard to find good local blueberries this time of year."

"It's my favorite," Ethan said. His mother used to bake it for him and his father when he was growing up. But not recently—recently she hadn't been doing much cooking at all.

"I'd better get going," Hannah said. "Laura, if they want it, give them seconds."

Looking back, Todd would sometimes think it had all happened by accident. He was behind in the reading—he was always behind in the reading—and Ethan was the closest guy in the dorm who was also in Ms. Davis's English class. Taking him to the tearoom a few days later had been partly a tactical move: Todd had discovered several weeks ago from his friend Izzy that Laura, the waitress, was selling the best weed in western Massachusetts. There were only so many times he could go to the tearoom alone; Ethan would be the perfect cover. Laura had taken some convincing, but once he assured her that he was a city kid, that he wasn't going to get her in trouble, she agreed to sell to him. It wasn't practical, after all, to go home each time he needed to replenish his stash, and the student he had bought from in previous years, an Upper East Side brat-turned-drug-dealer, had graduated.

Todd knew he shouldn't be smoking—not as a member of the cross-country team, and not with college applications looming in the coming months. But he hated running. Sometimes during practice, he would will his lungs to collapse on him, pushing himself harder and harder, savoring the sharp pain his breathing cavities exerted on his body, knives cutting him inside, blades steeped in nicotine and sinsemilla. Afterward, there was no camaraderie. His fellow runners weren't like the football players, who would shower together in the field house after practice, exchanging taunts and laughing all the way to the dining hall. His teammates were lonely creatures, climbing up the hill toward the dorms each evening, retreating to their rooms, one by one, in preparation for dinner. If he had to be alone, he wanted to be high; that was one of the few things he could do without anyone else. The weed helped him shut out the silence, the drudgery: of classes, of college applications, of feeling so alone.

The plan had gone flawlessly that evening, as Todd went inside again while they waited for their cab, saying he had forgotten something. He slipped Laura five twenties, and she handed him a small package, just out of Ethan and Madame Beauchamp's sight.

After arriving back on campus, Ethan and Todd headed to the snack bar. Now that he was with Todd, Ethan felt confident about entering the gossipy haven that was dominated by Sixth Formers each evening from seven until ten. He hoped they would stay awhile, hang out, talk with some girls.

"I need to find Alex," Todd said, looking around for his girlfriend, Alexandra Roth. He was suddenly in a panic, as if his future livelihood at the school depended on it. Todd could not be seen entering the snack bar with Ethan Whitley (the puzzling Ethan Whitley, a blank slate, a cipher, for some; for others, one who was suspect—a bit too well read, a bit too smug: *California*, after all? Who came from *California*?). Ethan felt a glum sensation as Todd ignored him. He imagined himself being demoted back to his place in the social strata, as if he had been given a glimpse of what it would be like to be popular, to be granted the attentions of someone like Todd Eldon, and was now being informed that actually there had been an error, that he was not meant to have been at the tearoom at all, that he had been mistaken for someone more popular, someone better-looking. He looked around the snack bar: all the usual suspects. Athletes in one corner, stoners in another, the African-American and Asian cliques at their own tables, the artsy crowd (they hadn't embraced him, either—even the outcasts weren't taking new admissions, though he was an artist himself) scattered in the middle. Books and papers everywhere. Empty bottles of soda and paper plates littered with the remnants of hamburgers and grilled cheese sandwiches. Todd located his friends across the room and motioned for Ethan to follow him.

He bought two Cokes at the counter and brought them to a table where Todd was sitting with Izzy Jacobsen, Miles Nolan, and Kevin Bradshaw; they were part of what Ethan had heard referred to as the "banker boys," guys whose fathers had made their money in investments. Todd introduced Ethan to everyone and pulled out a chair for him. After he sat down, Alex appeared behind Todd and wrapped her arms around him. He squirmed uncomfortably, releasing himself from her grip.

Alex smiled at Ethan. "Hi." Her cheeks glowed from the brisk night, a warm peach color. Ethan had noticed her before, in the hallways, near the mailboxes. The girl with the brown pageboy cut and the large eyes, the one who wore Doc Martens with Laura Ashley dresses. He felt a green pang of jealousy. Todd was that guy, the type who existed in books or movies or his imagination, who had everything a teenager wanted (everything, in fact, that Ethan wanted): friends, a girlfriend, as much money as he needed. There was so much he could learn from Todd, but what did Todd want from him?

Alex turned to Todd. "Should we go?"

Todd shrugged and got up, grabbing his fleece pullover.

Ethan felt his gut flip: nervousness, then annoyance. He wanted what Todd had, not only emotionally, but physically, in the deepest, most visceral part of him. He imagined what they would do together: a romantic walk back to the dorm, perhaps a visit to the studio to show Todd what she had been working on (now Ethan remembered her name from one of the paintings in the main hallway's exhibition of student work). They would hold hands, and then in some dark corner, he would kiss her, pressing his body to hers, pushing his erection against her pelvis.

"I'll catch you guys later," Todd said to everyone, and the two left the snack bar.

"Lucky bastard," Izzy Jacobsen said, as he scratched his crotch. "That guy gets laid more often than I jerk off."

The following evening, Todd made a call from the pay phone on the fourth floor of Slater Dormitory. Though this arrangement afforded Berkley's students little freedom, it was one of the few options they had to make contact with the outside world. Cell phones had been banned years ago after several students' phones went off during class, the chimes of Beethoven's Fifth sending them directly to the deans' wing. The only permitted alternatives for communication were pay phones or e-mail. In this case, Todd needed to talk to his father directly.

He was about to hang up when Don Eldon picked up on the fourth ring. They hadn't spoken in several months, and Todd hadn't seen him in over a year. From a practical standpoint, it didn't matter. His mother, Jackie, had plenty of money to take care of him and his brother, and their father was busy keeping his development ventures in Florida afloat (Todd had to admit that he never understood exactly what it was that his dad did each day). Jackie had never been clear with Todd or his older brother, Brian, about whether it was raising two children, her flourishing literary success in the field of romantic suspense, or a combination of the two, that had driven him away. Miraculously, she had been able to crank out a bloodcurdling best-seller every year while supervising the changing of diapers and the scheduling of play dates. She had become a publishing sensation, and her husband was still a failed real estate broker with a drinking problem. When Todd was five, Don Eldon did what Todd figured most men would do: he left. Jackie had filed for divorce, instructing her lawyers to make sure the man didn't get a penny of her hard-earned book advances.

"Yeah?" Todd's father said, over the din of a baseball game playing on the television.

"It's Todd."

There was a pause as he turned down the game. The pauses: Todd had forgotten about them. They took forever, were like that peculiar feeling of being on a family car trip and never knowing when you would arrive.

"Hey, kiddo. What can I do for you?" his father finally said.

"I wanted to talk to you about my college applications."

Todd heard his father sigh. "Todd, you know I can't contribute to that. Your mom's got plenty of money set aside for you and your brother."

"It's not about paying, Dad."

"What's it about then?"

"There's a statement that's supposed to be written by your parents—you can do it separately, if they're divorced—but it's supposed to be about what your parents think of you, why they think you should go to that college, stuff like that." Todd nervously scratched away at a Harvard sticker that had been plastered on the wall next to the phone.

"Todd, your mother is the writer in the family. I think she would be much better handling that sort of thing."

"Okay," Todd said. "I just thought I'd ask."

"No problem, kid. Let me know if you need anything else."

Todd hung up without saying good-bye. His hands were shaking. Was it too much to ask his father to write a five-hundred-word recollection of his younger son? Todd thought he had written a statement for Brian. Or had his mother simply mailed in one on both their behalf? It would be like Jackie not to want to admit to an admissions officer that Don Eldon played no role in his sons' lives.

It didn't matter anyway. What Todd needed to focus on were his grades; his college adviser had assured him of that. He wanted to get into a good school (Brown was his top choice), not simply for himself, but to show his parents he could do it without them. He feared that they saw him as a failure; he had never had the marks or gotten the recognition Brian had when he was at the school. His brother had been the model Berkley Boy: photo editor of the yearbook, head proctor, starting player on the lacrosse team, winner of the school spirit award in his Fifth and Sixth Form years. Not that his father would have noticed; he hadn't even shown up for Brian's graduation, only sending a card and fifty dollars in his absence.

As a replacement, Jackie had pathetically brought along as a date her best friend and literary agent, Nick. He was nice enough—Todd had known him since childhood—but he was the most effeminate man Todd had ever met, and he knew that wouldn't fly on the Berkley campus.

When he recalled Nick's visit, the cream suit he had worn, complete with lavender pocket square (he sent out a silent prayer: *please, don't let her bring him again*), Todd was reminded of a story from the 1940s that was often told to the younger students. Theodore Bainbridge had been a fey Fifth Former who liked to read poetry; Whitman was his favorite. He would recite it in the halls, carry it with him to the dining hall, quote from it in class. His dorm mates, who were more excited by athletics and females, decided they would teach him a lesson one afternoon; poetry, after all, was far too precious an affectation for a Berkley Boy (it was fine, perhaps, to attract the opposite sex, but that was the extent of its usefulness). A trio of hockey players hanged Theodore by his silk necktie one afternoon as a prank before heading out to practice, suspending him in front of his doorway. He screamed and shouted for them to let him down, but they ignored his cries, laughing all the way to the rink. Theodore, they assumed, would get himself down easily. Someone would see him; the point would have been made. When they returned three hours later, his body was limp, his face the violent purple of an eggplant, the door scratched and battered where he had tried to kick his way free with his hard-soled lace-up shoes. The boys were never apprehended, as it wasn't discovered until fifty years later that what had been ruled a suicide was in fact not so.

CHAPTER 2

Why boarding school? Why now? Ethan had prepared numerous answers to these questions, expecting that he would be asked to explain himself the moment he arrived at Berkley as a transfer student to the senior class, known as the Sixth Form. The hubris, he now realized, of assuming anyone would care! His fellow classmates were burdened with the minutiae of high school life: athletic uniforms that were unflattering (everything was always too baggy, or too tight), unusual growth spurts (Evan Douglas had gained four inches over the summer), absurd rumors (a Fourth Form girl had become a kleptomaniac and was said to have hundreds of tins of lip gloss in her bedroom—if she liked you, she would share), haircuts (Robbie de Sola had clipped off his beautiful dark locks), students who hadn't returned after summer break (where were they?), summer flings (Tina Palmer had done it in her parents' Southampton bedroom with a townie).

Ethan knew people arrived at the school at various junctures for different reasons: They needed an extra year of credits before college and would help beef up the hockey or football team (or occasionally, the music or drama program). They had been kicked out of another, equally prestigious institution (there weren't really any better schools than Berkley—it had always been ranked in the top five, according to those who knew about such things), and had been admitted as a last-minute favor, usually with the help of a letter from a member of the board of trustees. They had been dissatisfied at home.

Though Berkley was generally not the type of school where young people in trouble enrolled—those institutions were further down the ladder, more akin to military academies and the like—a fair number of young people in trouble still ended up there. Or perhaps, Ethan would wonder, as he heard stories of his fellow classmates sharing cigarettes in the shower at 2:00 a.m., or stumbling drunk down the hallway in the middle of the afternoon, still in school uniform (coats and ties, always, for the boys), the trouble found them after they arrived.

But nothing so thrilling as having been expelled had happened to Ethan. He wasn't a rebel, or a slacker, or a drug addict—he could only faintly recall the last time he had broken a school rule. (It would have been in the sixth grade when, unable to catch, he had been so afraid of playing touch football that he hid in the school library during PE for an entire semester. It had garnered him an F on his report card, the only one he had ever received. An F! His parents laughed it off: he, a professor of engineering and she of literature, were not the type to care about such quotidian matters as grade point averages. They were of the rare breed who only cared if their child was learning.)

His parents' house in Palo Alto was ten minutes away from campus and it had been too easy to fall into the same patterns he had followed since grade school: walking home directly after classes, not socializing with his peers, spending hours in his bedroom reading, finding himself alone on a Saturday night. His social life had improved, certainly, in his first three years of high school; he shuddered to think about what he had been like as a freshman (geeky glasses, pimples, faint mustache—why hadn't his father noticed it was time to teach him to shave?). He had been on a few dates with girls; he had friends whom he would see occasionally, though he suspected they felt the same sort of ambivalence toward him that he felt for them. He could have managed his last year of high school at home, but he and his parents knew he needed to move on.

The other element was his mother's illness that had enveloped their little house. The official word was that she was in remission, though there was always the danger of the cancer metastasizing. Ethan suspected that she and his father hadn't been telling him everything in recent months. He wanted to be there for her, but he also longed to escape the reality of it. It had been discovered seven years ago, the epithelial carcinoma on the outer surface of one of her ovaries. He knew these details by heart, from his mother reciting her condition, early on, at the dinner table after each appointment with her oncologist. At first, Judith treated it distantly, as if it were a work of literature they were discussing, or a trip they would be taking to a foreign country: the different methods of treatment, the chances for survival (*A doxorubicin liposome injection? How fascinating!*). Lately, though, she had become bored, and she appeared to want to shield her son from the details as much as possible. She would go to her chemotherapy, lying in the infusion center for hours with a needle in her arm; the doctors would cut away at her organs (every time she was hopeful, though her optimism gave way to pragmatism, as each operation was not wholly successful). She didn't give up: there had been radiation, clinical trials, experimental therapies. Judith Whitley, an internationally recognized expert on feminist literature—her critical study of Simone de Beauvoir was considered a classic—was wasting the last years of her life being shuttled from appointment to appointment. Ethan couldn't believe that this was what it meant to be in remission.

While he was afraid his mother's condition might further deteriorate, his parents had felt it was more important to get him out of the house. And so he was cast out, armed with promises of regular phone calls and the understanding was that were anything, God forbid, to happen, he would be notified immediately, and could fly home. From the mountain of catalogs, Ethan had picked Berkley, the school with the enormous arts wing, the place where the director of admissions had assured him that he would fit in. He remembered a conversation he had had with his mother about it, as he readied himself to file his late application the previous spring. He would be lonely, he would miss his parents, he would feel the perpetual heavy stone of despair in his stomach.

"There is no logical way you can convince yourself that this will be easy," his mother had said. "Sometimes you just have to do things without thinking about them."

While studying several evenings later, Ethan received a phone call at the dorm. There was always the possibility of news about his mother's health, a prospect that sent a quiver to Ethan's gut as he padded down the hall's worn carpet in his moccasin slippers.

"Ethan? It's Hannah, from the other day at the tearoom." He faltered for a moment. Hannah, the teacher? He wondered why she was calling him, how she had gotten his number. She must have looked it up in the school directory. Being called like this made him feel naked, exposed. He leaned back against the hardness of the wall, felt the greasiness of the phone's receiver in his palm.

She continued speaking. "I'm making my blueberry cobbler again, the one you liked. I thought maybe you'd like to come by my place tomorrow and have some."

"Sure, that would be great," he said, though he wasn't certain it would be anything resembling great. He thought of a way out of this awkward invitation, of the prospect of visiting this woman alone at her house. "I could bring Todd."

There was a pause on the line. His eyes ran along the hallway, quiet at this hour. The corridor master's doorway was half-open, but no sound came from his study.

"I have a better idea," she finally said. "Why don't you come alone?"

He started out for Hannah's place around six the next evening, just as his classmates were finishing sports and heading for the dining hall. He had followed her directions past the school cemetery and across the golf course. The course surrounded the school property, and was a buffer of green between the main campus and the lake. Ethan had never walked across it before; the freshly cut grass was spongy beneath his sneakers.

After reaching its end, he walked down a short wooded path toward Hannah's house, white clapboard trimmed with green and black. In front of the house was a little garden; a set of well-worn wicker furniture sat on the porch. Ethan wondered what Hannah had done to be assigned such a nice place. Most of the younger Berkley faculty—and many of the older ones as well—lived in small apartments, not homes that could comfortably house a married couple, not to mention a child or two.

Ethan stepped up to Hannah's front porch, carefully wiping his feet on the doormat as he knocked several times. She opened the door, a bright bundle of energy and light. He examined her outfit; she was wearing stylish jeans and a white minidress top, making her look like she could be in her late twenties. It was something she could never wear to class, an ensemble that surely wouldn't meet the scrutiny of the head of the English department.

"Hurray! You came!" she said, pulling him inside and shutting the door. "Come in, come in!"

Ethan looked around the hardwood-floored room as he took

his coat off and let Hannah hang it on a hall stand. To the left was a kitchen area with a stove that gave off the aroma of spices and sweet things baking. Toward the back, in front of an entire wall of bookshelves (painted white, but meticulously trimmed in birch bark), was a rough-hewn oak dining table that seated four, a potted cluster of ivy in the middle. On the right was the living room area, outfitted with two giant club chairs, a sofa upholstered in a navy and cream toile, and a leather trunk that served as a coffee table, all arranged around a fireplace. Two doors on either side of the wall of bookcases led to other rooms. Through a doorway in the middle was a staircase to the second floor, presumably leading to Hannah's bedroom.

"This is it," she said. "Where all the madness happens. Have you eaten dinner yet?"

Ethan shook his head.

"You must be starving! Do you want me to make you something? Before the cobbler, that is."

Ethan didn't want to impose. "What did you have in mind?"

"How about a *croque monsieur* and a bowl of soup?"

Ethan cocked his head at her, confused.

"It's a ham sandwich, with melted cheese. You'll like it." She paused, smiling at him. "What would you like to drink? I just brewed some iced tea."

Ethan shrugged. "Sure."

Hannah brought him a glass of iced tea and fixed him a bowl of vegetable soup from a pot that had been simmering on the stove. She motioned for him to sit on a stool at the island in the center of the kitchen.

"So you like to cook," Ethan said, after taking a sip of iced tea. Stupid, stupid, he thought.

"It takes my mind off the writing. Off grading papers." She motioned to several stacks of student essays that were sitting on the table near the wall.

"I hope I'm not keeping you from your work."

"Not at all," she said, looking up from the ingredients for his sandwich. "I enjoy the company."

Ethan's eyes dropped down to her hands as she created the meal for him, slices of ham and Gruyère cheese on top of two pieces of bread, a dab of Dijon mustard, copious amounts of butter. She worked feverishly, her hands shaking slightly, as if this were the last meal she would ever serve.

To avoid staring, Ethan examined the elaborate iron rack that hung over the island and displayed an assortment of pots, pans, and baskets. He smiled as he realized that woven into the iron were actual tree branches and brambles, making it look like a forest was growing in her kitchen.

Once she was done assembling the sandwich, Hannah methodically placed it on a small metal tray, which she slid into a toaster oven. "Are your mother and father coming for Parents Weekend?" she asked, as she wiped her hands on a dish towel.

The yearly event was a week away. Ethan's father had been scheduled to give a paper at an engineering conference in Chicago; when Ethan told him that it would conflict with Berkley's annual weekend for parents to visit, his father offered to cancel, but Ethan refused to let him. His mother would have come, but she was on deadline with an essay for an academic journal, and Ethan didn't want to get in the way of her work. He had played down the importance of Parents Weekend to them, though he knew that nearly everyone else's parents would be there.

"No," he said, taking a spoonful of soup. "My father has to go to a conference."

Hannah started washing her hands. "What about your mother?"

"She can't make it," Ethan said quickly.

"Who are you going to show around the school?" she asked.

Ethan shrugged again. "No one, I guess." He looked down, as his face warmed. He couldn't wait for that weekend to be over.

"Too bad," Hannah said.

He turned slightly on his stool to look out at the rest of the room. The sun had set, and the view of the golf course through one bank of windows and the lake through the other had turned into masses of blue illuminated by pinpricks of light. Without the glow of the school in the distance, he and Hannah could be anywhere.

She handed him his sandwich, the melted cheese dribbling deliciously onto the plate.

"You may want to let this cool for a moment," she said. "I'll be right back." She headed to the door leading upstairs. Ethan stepped down from the stool and took a proper look around the room. He was drawn to the fireplace's mantel, where there was a collection of framed pictures; many were black-and-white photographs of people he imagined were Hannah's relatives. There were two pictures of a boy (one on a street corner; another in what looked like a forest), perhaps a few years younger than he was, in small silver frames. Strangely, they were the only photographs in color. He wondered who the boy was, what he was doing on Hannah's mantelpiece.

As he heard her coming downstairs again, he quickly went back to the counter and started eating his sandwich.

"Do you have any brothers or sisters?" Hannah asked him as she entered the room.

He shook his head as he analyzed the taste of the ham and the cheese and the Dijon mustard, tangy in his mouth.

"I want to have children so badly. Bundles and bundles of them. Couldn't you see kids running around this house?"

Ethan carefully wiped the corner of his mouth with his napkin. "I guess so." He didn't understand why Hannah was speaking to him so intimately when he barely knew her.

"So," she said, leaning forward, "I can tell you're not like the other guys here."

"What do you mean?"

"You're smarter, more serious."

He faltered, unsure of what to say. The idea that this woman whom he barely knew could so quickly dissect his personality was terrifying.

"Don't be upset about it," she said, patting his arm. "If it weren't for students like you, I don't know what I'd do. After a while, you realize this school just churns kids out like a machine. I want so much for you guys to experience things, but there's only so much time in the day. You know a faculty member actually said that to me once? 'We have to tire out the kids enough each day so they don't get into trouble at night.' Isn't that the most absurd thing you've ever heard?"

Ethan nodded, appreciative of her candor.

"The school just wants its students to learn enough so they can get into college, and so their parents keep paying the tuition. But I probably shouldn't be prattling on about such things."

"Don't worry about it—it's not like I have anyone to tell."

Hannah smiled. "It must be difficult, coming all the way from the West Coast."

"I guess so," Ethan said. "I do miss my parents." He paused. "It just seems—this is going to sound weird, but I guess I was raised differently from a lot of the kids here. I didn't grow up with as much money. Or at least, what my parents do have, they don't spend on the same things." Ethan took another bite of his sandwich, and felt a sense of relief. Since his arrival at Berkley, it was the first time he had admitted this to anyone.

Hannah started cleaning the kitchen, putting the soup into a plastic container and wiping down the countertops.

"So you could use some more cash?" she said, from over her shoulder.

He cringed at the boldness of her statement. "I guess."

She turned around, pink sponge in hand. "Why don't you come work for me?"

"Doing what?"

"See all those books?" Hannah pointed to the library on the

far wall of her living room. "They need to be organized. There are even more in my study. I can pay you, say, eight dollars an hour?"

"I don't know," Ethan said. "I'm pretty busy with everything."

"You don't play a sport, right? So you've got Wednesday and Saturday afternoons off."

It made him uncomfortable that she knew his schedule; then again, it was public knowledge, available on the athletic bulletin boards outside the dining hall. "Can I think about it?"

"Of course," she said, pausing to brush a crumb off her sleeve. "Take as much time as you need." She flashed him a quick, soft smile. "You know, it would be great to have you. I could really use a guy around here."

Todd was sitting alone in his room that night, stoned, when he heard a knock at the door. His eyes darted around the room as he made sure there was no incriminating evidence: no bong, no lighters, no stash. Any number of people could come knocking at this hour—his adviser, his corridor master, one of his teachers. And Berkley's no-chance policy was clear: get caught with drugs, and you would be expelled.

"Come in," he said, attempting to modulate his voice so he sounded clearheaded.

The door opened and Ethan stuck his head in.

"Jesus Christ, Whitley, I told you not to knock! Only faculty knocks on doors. You scared the shit out of me."

"Sorry," Ethan said, shrugging.

Todd could feel Ethan looking around the room, his eyes running over the liquor ads he had tacked up on one wall and the batik tapestry on another. As Todd lay back on his bed, Ethan started chattering on about some kind of job for Hannah. Todd found his attention wandering. He examined some stubble on Ethan's chin, a dark spot he had missed shaving. Todd thought about how he only had to shave once a week; even then his whiskers only sprouted in pale blond patches.

Ethan poked him. "Are you high? You seem totally out of it."

"Yeah, sure, you want some?" Todd giggled.

"I'm okay," Ethan said.

"I got plenty. And I can get more from Laura."

"That girl at the tearoom? You shouldn't be buying from her. The lady who owns the place could get in a lot of trouble."

Typical. Todd couldn't understand why Ethan was so concerned about propriety, about rules. He narrowed his eyes at his friend. "What do you care?"

"I just think you're taking a big risk," Ethan said.

"Isn't that what life is all about?" Todd asked. "Taking risks?"

"I don't know," Ethan said. "It doesn't seem worth it."

Todd swung his legs around and sat on the edge of his bed. "At least come have a cigarette with me."

"I don't smoke."

"Just try it."

Todd led Ethan down the hall to the bathroom. He opened the window a crack and sat on the tiled sill near the showers, expertly pulling out two cigarettes from his pack, lighting them both, and handing one to Ethan.

Ethan took a puff and attempted to exhale, the smoke sputtering out of his mouth in ridiculous clouds.

"Next time, we'll do the real stuff," Todd said. He felt a shiver as he thought about getting stoned with Ethan. What would he be like if he were high? Todd imagined Ethan stoned as a more advanced version of him, a relaxed Ethan, an Ethan who would open up to him.

"I don't do drugs," he said.

"That'll change soon."

Ethan looked at him, clearly worried, his long eyelashes fluttering slightly.

"Relax. Don't you want to experience more in life?" Todd asked.

"Why does experiencing life have to mean doing something illegal?"

"It doesn't," Todd said. "But sometimes it's more fun that way."

Ethan nodded. A long ash dangled from his cigarette.

"Your ash," Todd said. "You need to tap it out."

Ethan awkwardly flicked the ash into the shower's ventilation grate.

"There's something I wanted to ask you," Todd said. "You can say no if you want."

Ethan nodded.

"I need help with my college essays. Would you be okay reading them for me, maybe giving me some tips?"

"Sure," Ethan said. "No problem."

"Can I do something to repay you? Anything you want."

"I don't know," Ethan said. He attempted another drag on his cigarette, this time inhaling more skillfully. "Actually, there is one thing. I have to do this assignment for art class. We have to draw someone, do a portrait. I don't have anyone to sit for me. Everyone else is having their friends do it, but I wasn't sure who to ask."

"Sure, I'll do it," Todd said quickly. He liked the idea of Ethan drawing him. "When would it be?"

"Maybe the week after next? After Parents Weekend, definitely."

"Are your parents coming?"

"No," Ethan muttered. "They can't make it."

Todd looked at Ethan with what he was sure was an expression of pity, though he quickly tried to temper it.

"Do you want to come to New York with me?" Todd asked. "I'm staying at my mom's for the long weekend." Todd mentally ran through the preparations he would need to make; Ethan could sleep on the pullout couch in his room. They could go drinking together. He felt as if he were about to pour liquor and sin into this pure vessel. He, Todd, was tainted. He had long ago been sullied by the pot, the alcohol, the cigarettes. He had the sense that even if he did clean up his act, the dirt would remain.

Todd saw Ethan's eyes widen as he comprehended the invitation. "To New York? With you? I, well—sure. Yes. New York. That sounds great."

Ethan then did something that, for him, was unusual. After exhaling a long stream of smoke, he grinned.

The next evening, as they did on most nights, Todd and Alex headed for their usual spot, the *Bones* office underneath Slater Dormitory. As one of the publication's senior editors, he had a key, and he knew the room would be free at this hour. The two slipped into the dorm's side entrance unnoticed, and unlocked the door to the small room. He shut the blinds and pulled out the blanket he kept in the closet, laying it down on the floor.

He knew there should be more to it than the physical, and in the beginning, there had been. He and Alex had been in love, or so he had thought when they had started seeing each other late last spring, as much as he had a concept of what love was. Now the fun they had been having together had been replaced by the pressure of obligation. It was difficult, though, to give up something that was so easy and comfortable.

The worst part about it, Todd realized, as Alex moved up and down on top of him and his bare backside dug into the scratchy blanket, was that he wasn't completely there. In his mind that night, as he was inside her, he was having sex with someone else.

Later that night, Todd nearly collided with Ethan as he ran up the stairs to his room on the fourth floor of Slater.

"Did you do the English reading?" Todd asked, though he knew what Ethan's answer would be. Ethan had probably already finished *Pride and Prejudice* and written the required essay on it. Todd, as usual, had fallen behind. He asked Ethan if he could meet him in his room after they both took showers.

Todd had a routine to his ablutions, a ritual he would complete after having been with Alex. After checking in with his corridor master, he stripped and wrapped a towel around his waist, avoiding the disgusting stickiness around his crotch. The bathroom on the fourth floor only had two single shower stalls, and both of them were occupied. He could wait, or he could go down to the group shower on the third floor. He felt something pull at him. Ethan would be there now.

Todd walked down to the third floor and entered the bathroom. He hung up his towel on a worn metal hook and stepped into the shower room. Ethan was soaping himself at the middle head. Todd turned on the other nozzle and Ethan looked up.

"Oh," Ethan said, squinting without his glasses. "Hey."

"No hot water upstairs," Todd said.

Todd started lathering himself, but he couldn't help looking at Ethan's body. He knew that was what guys did, checking each other out like dogs. It was important to know how he measured up. It wasn't just penis size. How did his muscles compare? Did he have more or less hair than his peers? Who had the body of a boy, and who had the body of a man?

Todd let his eyes graze over Ethan; without his glasses, Ethan wouldn't know he was looking. For someone who professed little interest in sports, his friend was surprisingly muscular. He had mentioned that he liked to work out when he could, and claimed to do one hundred push-ups and sit-ups each morning. He had the body of a man, Todd decided: dark bushy tufts under his arms, with prickly hairs that led down from the V of his chest, past his navel, and toward his pubic area. Todd's own body hair was blond and sparse, and it shamed him, made him feel like a child.

Todd felt his face grow hot, even under the running water, as he stared at Ethan's groin.

He realized, with shock and disgust, that he was hard. He turned away from Ethan, faced the wall, and waited for him to finish his shower while he tried to make his erection go away. He focused on the cracks between the tiles, on the mildewed grout, on the drain in the corner that was sucking down the soapy water. Anything not to think about it. Anything but this. Not in front of Ethan. Anything but this.

Todd couldn't get it out of his mind: that night, as he lay on his bed in his boxers, the lights off; in chapel the next morning; while he was peeing. Perhaps it wasn't a physical thing. While Ethan was a good-looking guy, he didn't possess any of the natural surety and grace that Todd's other classmates did. Though he was well built, his body was ill-proportioned, as if it had been created from assembling a series of disparate parts and calling them a man. No, Todd's attraction to Ethan had little to do with looks. Todd sensed something else in him that he felt missing from his other friendships: Ethan was to him the person he hoped he might someday become, a person who wasn't merely book smart, but who wanted to understand the world, to go below the surface. Perhaps this was because Ethan had two professors for parents; Todd wondered if people grew up smarter in an environment like that. While his own mother was a writer, she had never been intellectually inclined, preferring the bubbling company of others to the solitude of a book. Todd wanted to absorb some of the intelligence, the wisdom of Ethan Whitley, simply by hanging around him, by soaking up his aura. Maybe that was what it was about. He wanted Ethan to become his friend, to draw him into his life, to fill that gap that had been empty for so long.

He realized, though, that getting close to Ethan was a bit like chasing a scared animal. He could hold out his hands, and it would go running away. If he pretended not to care, nothing would happen, either. It was a matter of coaxing, bit by bit.

CHAPTER 3

The following Saturday afternoon, after the normal half day of classes, Ethan arrived at Hannah's, ready to work. He had wolfed down a turkey sandwich in the dining hall and was craving something sweet. The memory of Hannah's blueberry cobbler from several days ago had stayed with him, permanently erasing any recollection he had of his mother's sad concoction. Hannah's cobbler had been spicy, tinged with nutmeg, cardamom, cinnamon, and a hint of ginger; the rich, buttery crust had littered the top with its sweet wreckage, covering the layer of plump blueberries.

He rang the doorbell, but there was no answer. It was chilly outside, so he let himself in, sat down at the kitchen counter, and continued his reading of *Pride and Prejudice*. In the quiet of Hannah's living room, Ethan could hear the turning of each page. He looked out onto the golf course, where a few students were playing on the third hole. From this vantage point, he felt invisible. He could go into Hannah's bedroom, go through her drawers. He could find out things about her.

Ethan got up to take a look around, keeping one eye on the driveway where Hannah would park her car. He gravitated again to the fireplace's mantel. There was a photograph of an older woman he thought he recognized from somewhere, though he couldn't place her. He looked again at the pictures of the boy; they were the most contemporary of all the images. (Why, he wondered, were there not pictures of anyone else? No parents, no friends, no one, Ethan guessed, from the last fifty years or so.) But of the boy, these were recent photos. He had pale cheeks and dark brown hair, similar to Ethan's own; his face was defiant, nearly a sneer, as if he were issuing a challenge to the person taking the photograph. It could have been Ethan's imagination, but he appeared to have some of Hannah's features: a thin, delicate nose, wavy hair. Perhaps he was a younger brother, or a cousin. Ethan looked again at the background of the photo taken on a street corner, picking up the frame and studying it closely. It didn't look like an American city.

As he examined the photograph, Ethan heard Hannah's car pull in from the road, its tires chewing on the gravel. He quickly wiped off any fingerprints with the sleeve of his sweater, replaced the frame on the mantel, and went out to greet her.

"I was out of supplies," she said, stepping out of the car, a burgundy Peugeot convertible. "I hope I didn't keep you waiting long."

Ethan helped her unload several sacks of groceries—sandbags of flour and sugar, two dozen eggs, three gallons of milk, baskets of blueberries, pears, apples, raisins, loaves of bread—from her car. They brought them into the kitchen, placing them on the counter. Ethan helped her put away the groceries as Hannah explained how she wanted her books organized. There were several hundred of them in the shelves in the living room, and even more in her study.

"I want them all in order," she said. "Nonfiction by subject matter, fiction by author."

Ethan examined the shelves. They were all mixed up: fiction, biography, history, criticism.

"How do you find things now?" he asked.

"I know where most things are, more or less. But I hate not being able to find something quickly when I need it. When I moved in, I couldn't deal with sorting it all out. Too many memories." She took a volume from the shelf, a copy of Proust's *In Search of Lost Time*. "This, for example, I remember reading this in Paris, when Alain and I first met."

"Alain?"

"My husband. Ex-husband, I guess."

Ethan nodded.

"God, I love that city—the tea shops, the flea markets, the book stalls on the river. I miss it so much!"

"What were you doing in Paris?"

She paused. "I think that's a story for another time."

Ethan wasn't sure how to respond, so he started sorting through the volumes. The project could take several weeks, but he didn't mind. He liked being part of her world, seeing what she read, what inhabited her imagination. The books varied in size and shape. Some were contemporary fiction, with colorful covers. Others were older copies of the classics. Mixed in were pulp fiction, books on painting, theater, opera.

The sun started setting, and Ethan realized he had been working for almost four hours. The time had gone quickly, and he was pleased with his progress. It was only sorting books, but it gave him a feeling of accomplishment. He was doing something separate from his studies at Berkley, something no other student was privy to.

Hannah had been working in her study, tapping away at her laptop. She came into the living room and sat on the armrest of one of the club chairs. "Are you hungry?" she asked. "Shall I make us some dinner? I have an apple pie for dessert."

"I should really be getting to the dining hall."

There was a look of longing in her face, as if he might disappoint her terribly if he left now. "This'll be more fun. And I promise it will taste better."

"Oh, of course," Ethan said, blushing. He knew she was an excellent cook. But how had sorting books turned into an invitation for dinner?

In twenty minutes, the meal was ready. She had made a salad and pasta with fresh pesto and chopped tomatoes.

"This looks amazing," Ethan said.

"It's nothing," Hannah said, as she poured herself a glass of red wine. "Help yourself to a soda." Ethan got himself a Coke from the refrigerator, and the two of them sat down to eat.

"You know," Hannah said after a few bites, "the students at Berkley aren't the same anymore. They used to be wonderful. We would hang out here all the time, after classes, whenever."

Ethan nodded, not sure what she was getting at.

"You and Todd are more like the kids I used to be friends with." She pulled her blond hair out of its ponytail, shook it out, and then reattached the band she had been using to hold it together.

Ethan noticed how attractive she looked with her hair down. Her eyes stood out: blue, flecked with hazel, like the speckled wing of a butterfly. He imagined her as an angel in a Renaissance fresco.

He looked down at his plate and continued eating.

"I'm sorry," she said. "I'm probably embarrassing you."

"Don't worry about it," he said, through a bite of pasta. "I'm not—I don't feel too similar to any of them, really. Even Todd. I wish I were more like them. They're so relaxed about everything. Like they've got it all together."

"There's a saying, 'You don't want to peak when you're sixteen.' And you don't want to peak at seventeen or eighteen, either. All these kids—the ones who seem so cool, especially—they're not the ones who are going to make a difference in the world.

They're having their moment now, and then they're going to get ordinary jobs, and marry ordinary people, and have ordinary families. You're not like that. You want something more from your life."

Ethan nodded. "I don't know. Sometimes, with Todd, it's like nothing bothers him."

"Please," Hannah said. "He's as insecure as they come. Underneath all that bravado, he's just like you."

Her frankness surprised him, though perhaps she was right. Maybe the only difference between Todd and him was confidence. And confidence could be learned, couldn't it?

Ethan realized he had inhaled his food.

"How about a piece of apple pie?"

He nodded a yes.

"Good," she said. "We can't have you getting too skinny, can we?" She patted him on the shoulder as she got up.

The pie sat on the kitchen counter, its crust sprinkled with powdered sugar that crawled across its surface like a tiny trail of white ants. Ethan excused himself to use the bathroom while Hannah put on a pot of tea. Her first-floor powder room smelled of scented soaps and bath salts. He noticed that the set of blue towels on the rack was monogrammed with the initials *H.M.R.*

When he returned to the kitchen, Hannah had cut herself a thin slice of pie, and a fat one for Ethan.

"They say you should never trust a thin chef," Hannah said, coming back to the table with their plates. "I'm hoping I'm the exception to that rule."

Ethan kept eating until he had finished every last crumb.

After leaving Hannah's house, he cut across the golf course toward his dorm, the autumn breeze crisp against his cheeks. He was the only Berkley student experiencing this taste of the outside world, of life beyond the brick gates of the school. He had wanted to say something to Hannah when he left her house, to let her know what this job meant to him, how much he appreciated that she seemed to understand him. But he hadn't been sure how to put those feelings into words. He took one more breath of the fresh night air and ducked into the back entrance to his dorm.

As Ethan made his way up to the third floor, he had none of the familiar anxieties of where he was going to hang out on a Saturday night, whether he would have people to talk to. In a burst of warmth, he felt his life sprawl forward in a great parade of possibilities: meeting his true love in a bookshop in New Haven, working as an artist in New York, visiting friends who lived in Connecticut, Vermont, New Hampshire. Some of these things might happen; some of them might not. It didn't matter, for it was suddenly all there for the taking, as if the world had offered itself to him, as if he had found a door, and needed only to open it to be let in.

CHAPTER 4

That evening, Todd decided to end things with Alex. They met in their usual spot in the Caldwell Memorial Garden, on an oak bench next to a trellis overgrown with wisteria. There had always been something he liked about this garden. It was bordered by tall hedges, so he could sit in it undisturbed; sometimes even, if he were feeling bold, to sneak a cigarette. Broken pieces of statuary were arranged among the foliage; when the school's land, having previously been the site of a grand nineteenth-century estate, was converted into a seminary, the priests had destroyed all the statues on the grounds, breaking off their heads, arms, legs. Dozens of classical icons—likenesses of Venus, Adonis, swans and goats, gargoyles, a head of Athena, one of Medusa as well—seemingly worthless at the time, had been dismembered and buried across the property. The school had unearthed most of the statues, everything that could be discovered on the formal grounds, and had donated them to a museum in Hartford, where they had been properly restored and preserved. But occasionally in the woods, students would come across a decapitated female torso, or a giant lion's paw. The broken pieces were totems, markers of where they were in the forest. Here in the garden, there were a few examples that had been saved: a torso of Adonis, nestled next to a bush of yellow roses; a gargoyle's head, bewitching as it gazed over a plot of pink petunias; a swan next to the trellis, nearly intact save for a broken wing.

As Todd sat with Alex in the chilly night air, he explained to her that with college applications and keeping his grades up, he didn't have time for a relationship. He knew it was a lie, and he sensed that she did, too. He was no longer interested in sleeping with her; everything that had been so exciting six months ago had vanished. Alex was the coolest girl he had ever known—pretty, smart, a dry sense of humor. But something was missing, some essential ingredient Todd imagined relationships to have. He thought about all the girls he had dated: there had been a string of them, starting when he was thirteen years old, all attractive, some smarter than others, all of whom wanted a piece of him. One by one, he had broken up with them. He would retreat into his boy-world of hanging out with Miles and Izzy, watching sports and playing pinball, until another girl captured his attention. Things would go swimmingly until his interest waned again.

Alex suddenly looked very small, like a wounded bird, all her Greenwich-born prep school bravado having left her. "If you want to take a break, that's what we should do," she said quietly.

He didn't want her to cry. He couldn't stand it when she cried. "I'm sorry," he said. "I wish I felt differently." The words felt like cardboard coming out of his mouth.

He took a deep breath, relieved her reaction had not been tears and hysteria. As they walked back to the snack bar together, a safe distance of several feet between them, Todd felt a weight, an anxiety that held the black shade of depression, leaving him. The future was like an open field, white, snowy, clear.

The following Saturday was Parents Weekend. Todd sat waiting for his mother on one of the leather couches in the entryway of the main building. Jackie was driving up from New York that morning; most parents had arrived the previous night, and most had taken their children out to dinner, but his mother had needed to attend a cocktail party, which had prevented her from coming until now. Todd supposed he should be grateful she would be there at all.

He looked out nervously at the main circle. Todd wanted to intercept her before she did anything embarrassing. He hoped she hadn't gone too heavy on the fancy jewelry.

He jumped up when he saw her clicking her way across the rotunda of the main entryway. Outfit: conservative, a navy blue suit. Jewelry: understated. Hair: swept up in a French twist, a few blond strands falling around her temples. Todd felt himself relax, ever so slightly. Finally, after all of his and his brother's years at Berkley, his mother had gotten the message that prep school was not a fashion show, at least not the kind she was accustomed to in New York.

"Hi, Mom," he said shyly. From five feet away, he could tell she had not gone easy on the perfume.

"Darling," she said, kissing him on both cheeks. "The roads were incredible this morning! Soaking wet. You're lucky I made it here alive! Let's get some coffee. I'm famished."

They walked down the hallway together toward the dining room. Todd tried to pay attention to her, and not to what he imagined were the stares coming from everyone around him. It was true; he knew he should accept it. Among the Berkley parents—the WASPy, the frumpy, the fat, the simply strange—his mother was the most glamorous.

Jackie charged into the dining hall like an old pro, grabbing a tray for both of them. "Just coffee for me," she said. "Black."

"Don't you want a piece of fruit or something?" Todd asked. "You should eat."

"Fine, I'll take an apple," she said.

To his right Todd noticed that his English teacher, Ms. Davis, was filling up the large mug of tea she carried with her everywhere she went. She turned around just as Todd was about to leave the service area. *Please*, he thought, *please don't talk to us*. It was too early in the morning to deal with his teacher and whatever her agenda was that day.

Ms. Davis and her bright green eyes had already spotted them.

"Todd!" she said, smiling at him and his mother. "Is this your mother?"

"Yeah," he mumbled.

Jackie extended her hand and introduced herself. "Are you a teacher of Todd's?"

"English," she said, firmly returning the handshake. "And I understand you're a writer yourself?"

"That's right," Jackie said, smiling.

"We had a wonderful reading last night. Did Todd tell you about it?"

Todd cringed. He had skipped the reading, even though Ms. Davis had told the class they should attend.

"No!" his mother said. "What type of reading?"

"A nonfiction writer, a recent alumna of the school, actually."

Oh no, Todd thought, *here it comes*.

"She read from her new memoir about being a boarding school student and exploring her lesbian identity."

"How wonderful!" Jackie said brightly. Todd realized that his mother could read his teacher like a book herself. It was common knowledge that Ms. Davis was seeing Ms. Hedge, the art teacher.

Come on, please let it end here, he thought.

Todd's mother leaned forward with a conspiratorial glint in her eye. "You know, it is so wonderful that the gay community has an outlet these days."

Todd reddened. It came back to him, something his mother's

agent had lovingly called her at a dinner party after a few glasses of wine: "the World's Biggest Fag Hag." He remembered, too, what she had said in return: "I accept the honor completely."

He touched his mother's arm to indicate that they should get going.

"Will we get to sit in on one of your classes today?" Jackie said to Ms. Davis.

"Yeah, third period," Todd said.

"Fabulous! I can't wait."

Todd pulled his mother to the farthest corner of the dining hall, where he would be sure not to run into any more of his teachers (or worse, his friends—word had reached him that his friends had informally voted her "the hottest mom alive").

"I can't believe I'm here again," she said, taking a sip of coffee and eyeing her son's white toast with suspicion. "I remember six years ago, when we moved your brother into his dorm. Brian was so nervous! I was nervous, too. Now it all feels familiar. And this will be the last time I get to do this." She leaned forward and straightened Todd's tie.

"I wouldn't get too broken up over it," he said.

"Come on, now," she said. "I'm sure you're going to miss this place."

Todd slouched in his seat, yanking on his tie and undoing his mother's handiwork. Would he be sorry when he left at the end of the year? He would miss the comfort of it, the fact that he knew where everything was; he had his friends, who gave him the well-worn satisfaction of an old pair of shoes, the feeling that, while they were not perfect, they wouldn't disappear on him one day, or decide they no longer liked him. Before he had arrived at Berkley, his mother helping him pack carefully from the list the school provided, he had been anxious. He was, back then, only three years ago, a bed wetter, a secret about which he had never told anyone. It was an intermittent problem, occurring on and off ever since his father had left them. It wouldn't happen for months, or even years, at a time, and then it would strike for a few days, or a week. Todd had become used to trudging down the hall of his mother's apartment in the middle of the night to the washing machine, throwing in the messy bundle of sheets. Jackie would wake quietly, appearing at the threshold to the little laundry room like an angel, silently taking out new sheets from the linen closet, helping him make his bed again. The two of them were complicit in their deception, so that no one—not Brian, not the housekeeper, or the chef—would ever know that Todd (at age seven, at ten, at fourteen) was soiling the bed. Jackie had done everything to prevent it—she had taken him to a psychiatrist, set alarms for him in the middle of the night, encouraged him not to drink water before bedtime. On a family vacation, the problem had struck unexpectedly, and Jackie found herself calling housekeeping at the seaside villa where they were staying in Positano and requesting garbage bags that she cut open into larger panels and placed under Todd's bedding.

Then the problem would go away. He had always been a deep sleeper, so deep sometimes that nothing could wake him up. He felt as if he weren't responsible for his own behavior, that his body was acting of its own accord.

The problem never lasted so long as to be a cause for serious concern, just long enough to create discomfort, to give him anxiety at the thought of overnights at friends' houses; his mother would pack him identical sets of pajamas, just in case. When he left for Berkley, ready to enter the Fourth Form (his school in New York, like many, had gone to the ninth grade), he was worried. Would he, at age fifteen, be caught one morning by his classmates in a puddle of his own urine?

It had never happened. Not once. He was proud of this, that something at Berkley had solved the problem, that while other more masculine fluids might stain his sheets, never again would he have to do a load of laundry as the sun was rising.

He looked at his mother, considering her question. "I don't think I'll miss it. I want to get the fuck out of here."

Jackie sighed. "That English teacher seemed nice."

"She's cool. A little too political, but basically okay."

His mother started rifling through her handbag. "I do wish you would appreciate the fact that you're here. I never got to have an education like this."

Todd groaned. He could feel one of her speeches coming on. Several times a year, his mother would remind him how hard she had worked to ensure that he and his brother got the best schooling, how the tuitions she paid now were more than she had made in her first job working as a secretary. *Sure,* Todd thought, *but they're about one-fiftieth of one of your book advances.* He supposed he shouldn't be ungrateful about it. Those books had made everything possible.

But his mother didn't offer a lecture. Instead, she asked him the question he was dreading even more. "What about Alex? Is she around?"

"Yeah, she's around."

"Will I get to see her? She's such a sweet girl."

"Mom, we broke up."

"Oh, darling!" His mother leaned over in an attempt to hug him. He winced as he noticed that her voice had just gone up by several decibels.

"Don't make a big deal about it," he hissed, pulling away. "It's nothing."

"Has it been hard?" she asked. "I never would have known."

"Mom, just forget it. I don't want to talk about it."

"Well, you look great, I have to say. There's color in your cheeks, your complexion is clear, you look healthy." She leaned forward and whispered, "How's the smoking? Are you still smoking cigarettes?"

"Sometimes," he said.

"Well, you shouldn't. They're so bad for your skin. But whatever you're doing, keep at it. It's working." She extracted a small pocket mirror from her purse, surreptitiously examined her teeth for remnants of apple, and then began reapplying a shiny tube of lipstick to her mouth.

Todd winced as he realized, from his mother's pose, from her demeanor, from her tone of voice, that she was addressing him in exactly the same way she spoke to Nick.

Later that day, Todd was sitting with Jackie at the tearoom. The small restaurant was bustling with students and their parents; the crowd overflowed into the entryway, and Laura couldn't seat people fast enough.

In her usual inquisitive fashion, Jackie had grabbed a booklet describing Wilton's offerings, though Todd was hesitant to remind her that this might be her last chance to shop for hand-dipped candles or overpriced antiques. He noticed she was perusing a section on the history of the town. It had been founded in the late seventeenth century after the Salem Witch Trials as a refuge for those who might be suspected of practicing the craft. For a hundred years, Wilton was a home for misfits, those shunned by society. Because of its remote location and spectacular landscapes, however, it was eventually discovered by the wealthy from Boston and New York as a bucolic respite from city life. As Wilton's past as a haven for eccentrics was long forgotten, it continued to be populated by adventurous city dwellers who visited the town with a sense of stoic reserve, as if they had been coming here for centuries, as if they were not simply enjoying their leisure time, but rather enacting an ancient filial duty, that edict that stated Thou Shalt Not Spend One's Weekend in the City.

Ethan was supposed to join Todd and Jackie for lunch before the three of them pushed off for New York. Todd felt nervous, he realized, because his mother would be meeting Ethan for the first time.

As Todd and Jackie glanced over their menus, Ethan arrived in a burst of cold air and commotion, his tie crooked and his hair mussed.

"Mom, this is Ethan," Todd said.

"Hello," his mother said, in a tone that Todd knew she reserved for maladjusted teenagers and the elderly.

Someone had taken the third chair from their table. After mumbling an awkward hello, Ethan went to find another one.

"Is that a friend of yours?" Jackie asked, once Ethan was out of earshot.

"Mom, it's *Ethan*. Ethan who's coming to stay with us for the weekend? He's in my English class?" In Ms. Davis's class earlier that day, Ethan had arrived late, and had raced off as soon as the bell rang. Since Jackie had wanted to quiz Ms. Davis on feminist interpretations of *Pride and Prejudice* (even Todd, who was behind on the reading, could tell that his mother was out of her depth), he had not been able to introduce his friend to her until now.

"Of course! I'm sorry, I totally forgot."

At that moment, Hannah appeared in the doorway, alone.

"Well, look who's here!" she said, looking down at Jackie and Todd. She stuck out her hand. "I'm Hannah McClellan."

"Jackie Eldon." Todd's mother greeted Hannah.

"It's so nice to finally meet you! Todd has told me so much about you."

Todd couldn't remember if he had told Hannah anything about his mother, if she knew more about Jackie than anyone else did at Berkley.

"Thank you," Jackie said. "That's so sweet." Todd could see there was no recognition in her face.

"Hannah is an English teacher here. She makes the desserts for the tearoom," Todd said.

"Todd and Ethan have been great," Hannah said. "I've even got Ethan working for me."

Jackie gave Hannah a confused look.

"He's organizing her library," Todd explained. He sensed Hannah would be annoyed that she was a virtual stranger to his mother.

"Don't let me keep you from your meal," Hannah said.

"Of course not," Jackie said. "It's always lovely to meet Todd's teachers."

The three of them zipped along the roads of Massachusetts and New York in Jackie Eldon's emerald-green Jaguar, alternating Vivaldi and classic Bowie on the CD player. Ethan savored the scent of fresh leather, admired the wood paneling on the doors. Even if they decided they could afford it, he couldn't imagine his parents owning a car like this one.

Todd didn't seem to be fazed by the luxury of his mother's ride; she had to tell him twice not to put his feet on the dashboard. He spent half the trip turned around and chattering at Ethan until, at Jackie's insistence, they finally switched places at a rest stop off the Taconic.

Ethan sat next to Jackie (she had said he should call her that) and tried to relax. He imagined New York was full of women like her. He had the strange urge to read one of her novels.

"So tell me," Jackie asked Ethan, as they cruised along the woodsy parkway, "do you have your eye on anyone at school?"

"Mom!" Todd barked from the backseat. "Leave him alone."

"Darling, we'll be spending the whole weekend together. I think we should get to know each other."

"You don't have to answer if you don't want," Todd said to Ethan. "Besides, we're not spending the weekend together. Ethan and I will be doing our own thing."

"No, it's fine," Ethan stammered. "I, uh, well, there's this one girl . . ." It was Alex Roth, but he couldn't say that. There was no way he could talk about having a crush on Todd's ex so recently after they had broken up.

"Who is she?" Jackie asked, teasing.

"Yeah," Todd said, "you've never told me about this."

He decided to name someone else, someone from his art class. He would say it was Julie Moore. She was from Boston, was applying early to Harvard. She wasn't going out with any-one, and would serve as a plausible decoy.

"It's Julie. You know, Julie Moore?"

"Ethan, Julie Moore is way out of your league. She dates jocks."

"Todd, stop being such a pain in the ass!" Jackie said. "Okay, so, Ethan, what are we going to do to get Julie's attention?"

"Mom, you're crazy."

"Oh, come on," Jackie said. "I'm just having fun." She put her hand on Ethan's knee as she spoke to him. "My son can be such a spoilsport sometimes!"

Ethan squirmed in his seat. Thank God for seat belts, or else Jackie Eldon would see him sporting wood in her Jag. "Well, I don't know," he said. "There's this Halloween dance. I thought maybe I'd try to, you know, dance with her or something."

"She's out of your league . . ." Todd continued in an annoying singsong voice.

"Dancing is good," Jackie said. "I prefer champagne and jew-elry, but then again, I suppose you are in high school."

"Mom, it's totally different for us," Todd said. "You don't know how it works."

"Explain it to me then," she said.

"Please," Todd said. "You're being ridiculous."

"I am not being ridiculous!" Jackie waved one of her mani-cured hands at her son in the backseat, and the car swerved onto the shoulder of the road. She started laughing hysterically as she righted the car.

"Mom! You're going to get us killed."

"Don't worry, I just renewed my insurance." Was the woman crazy? Ethan wasn't used to adults who didn't take things seriously. "Come on," she said. "How do you get a girl to like you?"

"Mom, just drop it. Why do you care so much anyway?"

"Well, of course I'm interested in your life. But there's another reason. My publisher has asked me to write a young adult novel. And, if I'm not mistaken, you two are young adults."

"You're going to write about teenagers?" Todd laughed.

"What's wrong with that?" Jackie said. "I mean, for Christ's sake, I've had two of them. Tell me. How does it work these days?"

"I don't know," Todd said. "It just happens. You start off as friends with a girl and then, you know, one thing leads to another, and then you're a couple."

"'One thing leads to another.' God, is there no romance anymore? What about dating?"

"Mom, we go to boarding school. We can't go on dates. We have to be in our dorms by ten."

"What about that tea place? Can't you take a girl there?"

"That's not really dating. That's just hanging out."

Relationships, dating, being a couple: it had all seemed so complicated back at home. Just when he thought he had figured out how it worked at a day school, Ethan had been hit with an entirely new set of rules at Berkley. But it seemed not so much about rules as it was about summoning an essential range of emotions. Ethan feared that even if he did follow the guidelines to the letter, it wouldn't be right, the girl he had chosen would feel something lacking, would turn away, and he would never know what he had done wrong.

The walls of the Eldon apartment's private vestibule at 1040 Fifth Avenue were upholstered in tan suede panels, a Picasso drawing of a female nude greeting visitors as they got off the elevator.

The floors were ebonized to a deep black shine and covered in Persian rugs. To the right were the dining room, living room, kitchen, and servants' areas; to the left were the private rooms, a quiet cream-carpeted hallway that led to Todd's, Brian's, and their mother's bedrooms, Jackie's study, and the library. The art adorning the walls was not the type of local artists' work that Ethan's parents had decorated their house with, but statues and paintings and antiques of the quality he would see in books and museums (was that really a Miró, he wondered, in the living room?). Family photographs (Todd, age four, with his parents, Todd and Brian together, Todd grinning after losing a tooth) were carefully arranged on the glossy black piano in silver frames. Flowers everywhere, enormous multicolored arrangements in the public rooms, and then simpler arrangements, perhaps put together by the housekeeper, in little nooks, on bedside tables, in the powder room: small vases of fresh roses, a single lily. As his friend glided around the apartment like a museum director rushing through a priceless collection on his way to an appointment, Ethan marveled at the abundance of brass and gold and silver; everything stopped short of being overdone, but was decadent, still: chandeliers and candlesticks and picture frames and doorknobs and switch plates. Hand-painted fabric murals in the dining room, a scene from the French Riviera. Ivory *craquelure*'d walls in Jackie's study, like fragmented eggshells, a giant ebony Chinese desk its centerpiece. Framed covers of her numerous best sellers were the only nod to her professional persona as Jacqueline Sterling, a writer hard-bitten by glamour, someone who maintained a steely outer facade, a mask of foundation and Chanel. Those novels, hoarded by women all over the world, their foil-stamped covers tucked secretly into handbags, were what had made this life possible.

After they had gotten settled into Todd's bedroom (hunter-green walls, collection of vintage toy soldiers, flat-screen television set), there was a meal waiting for them, wild salmon filets cooked by Jackie's chef. During dinner, she let them drink wine, a California chardonnay; the evening went by in a blur as Ethan accepted glass after glass from two different servers who had been employed for the evening. Jackie and Todd's lives swirled around him while Ethan quietly observed: phone calls were accepted, Todd and his mother argued about where they would spend Thanksgiving, Jackie rushed to the kitchen to get a new knife for herself, as hers had a spot on it. Ethan found himself taking small and deliberate bites of his food—never before had he been so worried about talking with his mouth full—as he watched this thrilling world unfold, full of discussions of travel and real estate and parties in exotic locales. Unlike their time in the car, when Jackie had attempted to talk to them as teenagers, here in her own dining room she seemed perfectly content to treat Todd as an adult. Ethan was surprised to hear his friend opining, albeit gruffly, on everything from the quality of Jackie's latest driver to the relative merits of Aspen versus Vail.

After a dessert of low-calorie raspberry sorbet (Todd told Ethan that Jackie had banned all full-fat products from the household), the boys stumbled back to Todd's room. Ethan was feeling buzzed—more than buzzed, drunk, really—and he flopped down on the foldout couch that had been prepared for him.

"Don't crash yet," Todd said. "Let's smoke." The thought of doing anything after this many glasses of wine seemed inconceivable.

"Smoke cigarettes?"

"No, I got some weed."

Ethan blanched at first, though the idea actually excited him. "Where?"

Todd motioned for him to come down the hall. "Out on the terrace."

Ethan followed him toward the living room. As he passed the door to Jackie's bedroom, the light coming from under it made him sad for a moment, as he thought what it must be like to be a single woman of her age; Todd said that though she had received several proposals, in the twelve years she had been divorced, she hadn't yet met a man whom she wanted to marry.

Todd opened the French doors leading outside. Ethan had taken a brief look at the wraparound terrace earlier in the evening, but now he could really get a sense of the view: from up here, they could see across Central Park to the West Side and all the way to New Jersey.

Todd fired up the pipe and inhaled quickly. He handed it over and Ethan took a sharp, choking hit. He started coughing.

"Go easy, don't burn your lungs," Todd said, taking another hit himself. "That's probably enough for now. Just see how it works for you."

Todd clearly knew what he was doing, and Ethan realized that he trusted him. As the pot seeped into his consciousness, he had a sudden desire to spill out a litany of secrets, secrets that lay far below the history of his middle-class existence, secrets he had never told anyone: the fact that in his entire seventeen years, he had only kissed a girl once, just a warm, wet peck on the lips during a game of truth or dare at summer camp in the San Juan Islands when he was thirteen—there had been a horrible *smooch-ing* sound that had made the others giggle, thereby sealing his fear of locking lips with anyone over the next four years. The fact that he had once stolen a pornographic magazine from a bookstore in Palo Alto, a giant megachain that he was later horrified to realize was equipped with surveillance cameras, and that the entire thing was *on tape* and therefore indelibly seared into the collective memory of the community at large (for six months, he avoided even walking in front of that store). The fact that, during an argument with his mother about something stupid (now he couldn't even remember what it was), he had told her he wished she were dead, a statement to which Judith Whitley had said nothing, only shaking her head and leaving the room.

He stayed silent as these vignettes went racing through his

brain. A cool breeze came from across the park, and Ethan looked out again at the expanse of foliage, the squares of light in the distance, the flickering reflections on the Hudson between the buildings.

"This is amazing," Ethan said.

"Yeah, it's good shit."

"I don't mean the weed, I mean your whole life. Everything. This apartment. Your mom. It's out of a dream or something."

"I don't know, you get used to it."

The two gazed out at the view. A paranoia briefly struck Ethan—he was smoking, he was breaking the law, he might become a drug addict!—and then he relaxed. He remembered himself a year ago, where he had been (nowhere, really), living at home, and thought of all he had experienced since then. He was at a school, part of a group of people who were considered in the top one-tenth of one percent of the population (if even that much) in terms of education, opportunities, possibilities. He was invincible; anything could happen this year. And here he was, in actuality, on top of the world.

He started babbling, the words coming out of his mouth without control. "It's so weird, it's like you take it all for granted. I can't even imagine what it would be like. I . . . well, I guess I would give anything to live like this. Not forever. Just for a little bit. Just to see what it was like. I guess." He realized he sounded stupid. "I don't know."

Todd laughed wryly. "Be careful what you wish for."

Ethan frowned for a moment, then decided to push from his mind the idea that Todd's life could be anything less than remarkable. As a set looks far from spectacular when one is actually onstage, Ethan wanted to sit, if only for a little bit longer, in the audience.

*   *   *

51

After they finished smoking, Todd led Ethan through the dark hallway. His mom had gone to bed and the chef had left for the evening. The two of them brushed their teeth, mint toothpaste masking marijuana, Todd turned off the lights, and they climbed into their respective beds. He couldn't remember the last time he had hosted an overnight guest; for a moment, his familiar anxieties returned. He felt his heart pounding from the lingering high. There was a glow surrounding Ethan, a light emanating from him. He heard Ethan rustling his sheets, repositioning himself for sleep.

"Ethan?" he said. Todd turned on his side toward the foldout couch, brushing his cheek against the plaid flannel of his pillow-case.

"Yeah?"

"I'm glad we became friends."

"Me, too," Ethan said. "G'night."

"Night."

If there had been any doubt before, Todd was now sure he was stoned, because as he drifted off to sleep, he imagined himself walking over to Ethan's bed and climbing in next to him, their bodies intertwined, skin touching skin, electric, thin cotton T-shirts, soft underwear. His eyes opened with a jolt: he was still in his bed, Ethan was on the couch, and nothing had changed.

CHAPTER 5

The next week, Todd finished dinner early and arrived at six o'clock at the Stevenson Art Center, where Ethan was waiting with his sketch pad and board. The studio was empty, as most people were still at dinner. It was already dark, and the room was lit with washed-out fluorescent light.

"Sit over there, near the skeleton," Ethan instructed him.

Todd sat on a creaky stool in front of an anatomical model that the intermediate class was drawing for Halloween. His right foot was shaking slightly; he tried to steady it against the hard metal of the stool.

Ethan began to sketch Todd. "I'm going to do a few versions," he said, flipping his pad to a fresh page after several minutes.

He worked diligently, and for a quarter hour, all Todd could hear was the scraping of Ethan's pencil against the rough paper. He tried to keep still, but the more aware he was of Ethan watching him, the more nervous he became. Keeping a normal expression on his face became an unnatural act. It was like posing for a photograph. If the picture wasn't taken soon enough, the smile became an act of will, an expression that represented not happiness but pain.

After Ethan had completed several versions, the door opened, and Ms. Hedge, the gray-haired art teacher, came in. Todd let out an inaudible sigh. Trailing behind her was Alex.

"Hi, Todd," Alex said. "What's going on?"

"Ethan's sketching me," he said. "What are you doing here?" As he said it, he remembered: Alex was in the intermediate studio art class. He knew he needed to treat her more civilly.

"Ms. Hedge is looking at my portfolio," she said.

The art teacher came over and stood behind Ethan, appraising his work. "It's coming along well," she said, smiling at Todd.

Ethan mumbled a response Todd couldn't hear. Todd loved how intent he was on his work, how he didn't want anything to intrude.

"It's so nice of you to pose for your friend," Ms. Hedge said to Todd, giving him a knowing look. He was crazy, mooning over Ethan like this. He looked over at him, bent over his sketch pad, brow creased in concentration, cowlick of hair touching the frames of his glasses. He was nothing like the guys Todd had grown up with; they were masculine, tough. Ethan was the type of boy who would have been picked on, who would have spent his entire adolescence buried in a book. But Todd liked that he wasn't the same as the other guys at Berkley. Todd didn't want to be different himself, but in Ethan, he admired the quality.

Why did Alex have to be here? It was as if she knew his every movement, every nuance of his day. Alex hadn't altered her schedule to avoid him since he had broken up with her; she had adhered to his even more stringently. As he kept one eye on his ex-girlfriend, her pert ass encased in a pair of designer jeans, feet shod in a pair of trendy hiking boots (as if she would ever go hiking), he hated that she was in the studio.

Ethan announced that he was finished, and Todd could take a look. It wasn't a bad likeness, though Todd was bothered that his expression was curled into a permanent frown, brows narrowed, wrinkles visible on his forehead. "I look confused," Todd said. "Why did you do it that way?"

"I don't know." Ethan shrugged. "I just drew what I saw."

Over the past several weeks, Ethan had continued sorting through Hannah's library whenever he had a free moment, though he was easily distracted. He had started reading snippets from her book collection, looking at the opening pages, author photos, acknowledgments. It reminded him of one of his favorite things he used to do when walking home after school, stopping at a used bookstore on University Avenue and browsing for hours through the shelves. Unlike those books, whose anonymous owners Ethan would never know, Hannah's books carried stories of their own that went beyond the words on their pages. Dozens of her volumes had the name *Hannah McClellan* written in the upper right-hand corner of the first page; in some, the last name *McClellan* had been crossed out and replaced with *Reinard*, which had then been crossed out and replaced with *McClellan*. Curiously, several volumes of French children's books were labeled with the name *Bertrand Reinard*. One of these, a copy of *Le Petit Prince*, had a photograph tucked into it, a color snapshot of a boy sitting in a restaurant, the type of photo one takes for fun, not planned or posed. Ethan immediately recognized the boy in the picture as the one from the mantel. He wanted to know more about the names, about the photograph.

One afternoon, Ethan stood in the doorway of Hannah's study and held out the photo. "What should I do with this? It slipped out of *The Little Prince*."

Hannah was typing away at her laptop. She turned toward him and looked at the photo he was holding up. An expression of alarm crossed her face, but she quickly composed herself. "Oh dear, I was wondering where that went," she said, without offering any explanation. She carefully took the photo from him and put it in a desk drawer. He felt, in the look she had given him, as if he had done something wrong, as if it were inappropriate for him to be handling the snapshot.

Ethan wished he could ask her who the boy was, but he knew from her reaction that she didn't want to tell him.

The following Saturday was the annual Halloween dance. As soon as Ethan arrived at the dining hall, he cursed himself for not having picked out a costume. When he ran into Todd, his friend scrutinized his jeans and sweater and promptly dragged him back to the dorm so they could rummage through his closet.

Todd was dressed as Zorro, the Masked Man, complete with a hat, long cape, rubber boots, gloves, and a mask. As they entered Todd's room, its rancid guy smell hit Ethan, a mixture of sweat, mildew, and Right Guard. Perhaps Todd did the same thing as Kevin Bradshaw, spraying his dirty shirts with deodorant instead of washing them.

"I have an old mask in here somewhere," Todd said. He seemed a bit wobbly as he rifled through his closet; Ethan wondered if he was drunk. "We'll get a cowboy hat from Cren. You can go as the Lone Ranger. We'll be a team, Zorro and the Lone Ranger."

Todd headed out the door to the room of George Crenshaw, a beefy young man from Texas.

"I won't be able to wear my glasses with that mask on," Ethan said, but Todd was already gone. He never went anywhere without his glasses, not even running. He supposed he could get by without them for one night.

Once Ethan was suited up, the two of them went back to the dining hall. Todd led Ethan into a circle of guys and girls dancing. They moved along with the group, engaging in the sort of low-commitment gyrations that were popular at Berkley dances;

no one was specifically connected with anyone else, everyone was moving with the crowd, as if they had all been swept into a collective frenzy.

After about ten songs, Ethan was hot and tired; he was grateful when Todd motioned for them to go to the snack bar. He bought a large cup of soda and took it to their table.

"Sit next to me," Todd said. Concealed by his cape, Todd pulled a small airline bottle of vodka from his pocket. He took a gulp of the soda, and then poured the bottle into the cup, swishing it around. After taking a sip, he passed the cup to Ethan, who took a swig of the antiseptic formula, the alcohol burning his throat.

"Why didn't we do this at the dorm?" Ethan whispered.

"I had some at the dorm already. I couldn't find you then."

The two finished off the drink together and went back out to the dance floor. Enveloped in the music, Ethan was drifting. In his mask and cowboy hat, no one could recognize him. Buoyed by the vodka, he didn't need to worry about anything: college applications, girls, his mother and her disease.

As Ethan danced in a daze, he noticed a cute girl dressed as a fairy. Though his vision was blurry, he was pretty sure it was Alex Roth. He wanted to talk to her, so he moved a little closer.

She looked his way, and he smiled. Her glittery wings flapped at him.

He gave a half wave. "Do you like the music?" he shouted. The deejay was playing Abba.

"What?" she said.

"Do you like the music?"

"It's okay."

Now he was standing next to her, swaying back and forth in tandem with the organza folds of her costume. He was dancing well, or at least he thought he was. He could smell the sweet mixture of her perspiration and body lotion.

"Do you want to get something to drink?" he asked. Since when did he ask girls if they wanted to come to the snack bar with him?

"I'm okay dancing," she said, giving him a saccharine smile.

Of course Alex Roth wouldn't want to go to the snack bar with him. He didn't know how to act around someone like her; though he was fascinated by Alex, she scared him. She was popular, she was from Greenwich, she played sports. They had the art thing in common. But that wasn't enough, was it?

Ethan looked up and saw he was standing directly below the portrait of Louisa Berkley that hung above the dining hall's walk-in fireplace. He couldn't make out the image clearly, but he could tell from the light flashing on it that he knew it from somewhere. He remembered: the photo on Hannah's mantelpiece. At first he imagined Louisa Berkley staring down at him, smirking at his social inadequacy. Then he imagined her commiserating with him in his unhappiness. He decided he liked that vision of her better.

Ethan licked his lips; he wanted a cigarette. Over the past few weeks, he had gotten used to sharing butts with Todd in the shower after check-in, to sneaking behind the tennis courts while everyone was at the snack bar. He knew he shouldn't be smoking, but how much damage could a few do, anyway? His mother had never smoked, and she had gotten cancer; it didn't matter what you did, you could still get it anyway.

He wondered where Todd had gone. Ethan's eyes darted around the dance floor, but he didn't see his friend. He wasn't in the snack bar, either.

Chastened from his rejection by Alex, Ethan decided to head back to the dorm. Outside, the air cooled the vodka-induced heat on his face. He didn't want to go inside, not yet. As he passed the cemetery, he saw a glow from the tip of a cigarette. He let himself in the side gate and walked among the headstones. In the middle, next to the crumbling monument under which Louisa Berkley was buried, was a stone bench. On it, a figure in a black cape and mask stubbed out its cigarette in the grass.

"Greetings, my masked brother," Todd said. He giggled and held up a soda can. "I got a refill."

Todd handed it to him and Ethan took a sip. Once again, the delicious burn warmed his chest. He sat down next to Todd. He took another swig and wiped his mouth on his sleeve. There was a rustling on the far side of the cemetery.

Ethan asked Todd why he left the dance.

"It was lame," Todd said. "I wanted to be alone."

Ethan shifted his body away from Todd. "I can leave, if you want."

"No, no, stay, it's better. I like having you here. You know, someone to talk to." Todd paused. "Besides all the dead people. Hell, you're probably on top of Louisa Berkley's feet."

"That's creepy. Don't talk like that."

"What do you mean? It's nothing. It's just bodies."

Ethan looked at his friend. He wasn't sure why he was about to say what he did, but it just came out. "Todd, my mother is sick. She has cancer."

"Oh, shit, I'm sorry," Todd said. "That was really uncool of me."

Ethan said nothing.

"I'm such an idiot, talking about dead bodies."

"She's going to die," Ethan said quietly. "But she's not dead yet."

"I'm sorry, Ethan, sometimes I don't know how to act around you."

"Don't stress about it."

Todd looked up. "Maybe it's the full moon." He let out a small burp. "Or the vodka. They make me want to do strange things." Todd took another swig from the can and handed it to Ethan, who gulped down a mouthful.

"Easy there, don't kill it."

Ethan started feeling flushed again, not an unpleasant sensation. All he could see of Todd was his mouth, his lips. In his mask, Todd could be anyone. In his own mask, he could be anyone, too.

"Come here," Todd said. "I want to show you something." Todd pulled his face close to Ethan's, so close that Ethan could feel Todd's breath on his cheeks. "Try to relax."

Lit only by moonlight, Todd gently held Ethan's chin, opened his mouth, and kissed him. Ethan sensed Todd's tongue probing around in his mouth like a slug, but he felt powerless to do anything. He wasn't even sure he wanted to push Todd away, for this was Todd, his friend whom he could trust, his friend who had invited him into his home, his friend who was now kissing him. When Todd pulled away, Ethan jumped up from the bench and ran back to the dorm. It was the first real kiss he had ever gotten in his life, and it was from a guy. It was nothing like what he wanted: it was—grotesquely, as if he had created his own nightmare—the exact opposite of what he wanted. It didn't feel like he imagined a girl's kiss would; far from the passionate experience he had always envisioned, it was little more than two people's body parts touching each other. Aside from the sliminess, apart from Todd's exertion, he could have been kissing a doll, or a piece of fruit. After shedding his costume and changing into some sweatpants, Ethan hurried to the bathroom and brushed his teeth, wanting to get rid of the alcohol, of the remnants of Todd's saliva. (In grade school, once, a bully had held Ethan down and spat a glob of phlegm into his mouth—he had immediately run home and brushed his teeth for half an hour. He supposed, remembering that incident now, that Todd's offering wasn't quite so bad.)

There was still another ten minutes until check-in. Ethan went back to his room and lay down on his bed, only turning on his desk lamp. He tried to forget about what had happened, tried to pretend Todd had been a girl, tried to imagine that this was an everyday occurrence, but he couldn't.

After Ethan had bolted from the stone bench, Todd felt queasy. The alcohol, the full moon, the graveyard: they all spiraled together in his mind. To do this right after Ethan had confided in him about his mother made Todd feel like an insensitive letch. But he had wanted so much to connect with his friend, to show him how he cared for him; instead, he had done completely the wrong thing.

He hoped no one had seen them. There had been some movement on the other side of the cemetery, probably just a senile faculty member walking his dog. He didn't know if Ethan would ever speak to him after this, if he had ruined their friendship with one simple action. Todd raced up to his room, the muscles in his legs quivering. As he rinsed himself off in the shower, he wondered if he was being silly. He liked Ethan; he had wanted to kiss him. He hoped desperately for it to be as simple as that.

After toweling off and returning to his room, though, he knew it wasn't. A hot burst of shame surged over him, though he was naked in his darkened room, the October breeze drifting in through the open window. The kiss was such a revelation that he felt conflicted. He wanted more, but he also wanted to run away: to get back together with Alex, to reconcile with her, to acknowledge that this was all a mistake. Maybe he was attracted to girls and guys, destined to be one of those sexual chameleons who refused to be labeled. He considered the possibility as he threw on a pair of pajama bottoms. Going back to Alex would be safe and secure, but stifling, a prison. Going in the other direction, whatever that might be, was the only option.

* * *

61

Ethan stayed in his room for the rest of the evening, and Todd didn't come to visit as he usually would on a Saturday night. The next day, he was in the library studying when Todd sat down across the table from him. Todd looked frightened, ashamed, his usually clear complexion mottled and red. He glanced around to make sure no one could hear them.

"About last night," he whispered, "I'm sorry, I was drunk. I guess I thought you were someone else. I really had a lot to drink."

"Don't worry about it," Ethan said. "Let's just forget it."

This was the pathetic state of his life. The most exciting thing to happen to him all semester was that his best friend had kissed him. Ethan considered himself a liberal thinker. His parents had gay friends whom they would invite to dinner. There wasn't anything wrong with it; it just wasn't for him. Could Todd really have been drunk and confused? Ethan bit down on his tongue as he tried to concentrate on his reading. After making it through a page, he raised his fingers and let them graze over his own lips, letting them linger there, just for a moment.

CHAPTER 6

November passed quickly, each day darker and colder than the last. Todd invited Ethan to come home for Thanksgiving with him, and they spent a week together in Manhattan. While Ethan missed his parents, he knew it didn't make sense for him to fly all the way to California for only seven days, not with all the papers and projects he had to complete by semester's end. Ensconced in Todd's apartment, the two of them worked on their college applications and final papers, Todd in his bedroom, Ethan in the library, the dazzling view of Central Park out the window—even the trees, mostly barren, a few with lingering dashes of fall color, were beautiful to him, an architecture that framed the patches of dark green. Jackie's chef would bring them lunch on a tray, or they would go out to New York places Ethan had only seen in movies: Greek coffee shops, Jewish delis, Serendipity for ice cream sundaes. Ethan sensed that Todd had planned much of this for his benefit, for someone who hadn't spent much time in New York; he knew Todd was too cool to do some of these things on his own. Jackie didn't mind if they drank at night, as long as they took the bottles down to the garbage room; she was more concerned about her staff knowing than the actual fact of it. In staying with Todd, Ethan felt as if he had collapsed into a giant feather bed of privilege. When he returned to his parents' home, he wondered, would he miss the magnificent art, the freedom to wander through the halls by himself and examine, up close, no museum guard watching, sketches by Matisse, a painting by Pissarro, even a small, exquisite Seurat?

He couldn't forget, of course, the awkward incident from last month—it was still out there, drifting, but what did it really mean? Ethan didn't want to know, and part of him had stopped caring. It was Todd's business, and it shouldn't change their friendship. He hadn't meant to hurt Ethan—Todd was, in fact, respectful now, very respectful, of Ethan's privacy. Though Ethan didn't lock the door while he showered in Todd's bathroom, Todd never, ever went in, though it would have been perfectly reasonable to grab a hairbrush or a tissue. After all, they had already seen each other naked, and what was the big deal about that? But still—Todd had gotten a message from Ethan, however unwittingly it had been sent: *Hands off.*

For Thanksgiving, Jackie took the three of them—Todd, Ethan, and Brian—to a trendy new restaurant on the Upper East Side. Todd had informed him that morning that he would need to dress nicely, which he hadn't realized. His friend declared they would borrow a blazer from Brian, a plan that left Ethan unsettled. He didn't really know Todd's brother, hadn't exchanged more than a dozen words with him as he passed him in the hallways of the apartment during that week. Brian was so mature, the four-year age difference between them seeming like a decade. A big guy, a fully formed adult—albeit one who still behaved like a teenager—Brian seemed in perpetual motion, even more so than Todd himself, always with his cell phone, texting his friends, scratching himself in odd places, completely comfortable, not noticing that anyone, least of all his brother's houseguest, could be watching him.

Todd knocked on Brian's door that afternoon, and was greeted by his brother with a punch on the arm. Ethan stood back in the hall.

"Fucker!" Todd said. "That hurt." He rubbed his biceps. "We need to borrow a jacket."

"Sure, whatever." He looked at Ethan. "I guess you are a bit taller than little T here."

Ethan noticed Todd wincing as Brian tossed him a jacket from his closet. It didn't fit perfectly, but it would do.

That evening, the four of them sat at dinner in a restaurant that occupied the first floor of a town house in the East Eighties, lingering over a seven-course meal. The chef had recently been granted three stars by a noted guide (Ethan hadn't caught the name), a fact that Jackie continued to marvel over as "extraordinary." They were now on the main course; it resembled turkey, though if Ethan had not read on the menu that it was indeed turkey, he wouldn't have been certain. The whole arrangement felt strange, not having a man escorting them. It was as if Todd and Brian were surrogate dates for their mother. Jackie seemed perfectly at home, accepting several *amuses-bouche* from the chef and a personal congratulations on her latest novel from the owner.

As her fourth glass of wine was poured, Jackie turned to Ethan. "So, Todd and Brian have told me all about their classes. What about yours? How about that Hannah teacher, what's her story?"

"Oh," Ethan said, blushing, "she's not really my teacher."

"More of a friend?" Jackie looked at him playfully.

"I don't know if I would say that. I don't really know her. I mean, I help her with projects sometimes."

"She's a strange one," Brian said.

"What do you mean?" Jackie said.

"She's, I don't know, mysterious. She lives in that house, all alone. And she's hot. Mom, have you met her?"

"Last month, I think," Jackie said, as she nodded to a waiter that her plate could be cleared.

"She's like—it's like she doesn't belong there. A single woman in her thirties? She shouldn't be living in a small town like that. How's she going to meet anyone?" Brian chuckled.

"What's so funny?" Todd said.

"When I was a senior, there were these two guys in the dorm who would talk about her constantly. What a hottie she was, how much they wanted to fu—" He looked at his mother. "You know, sleep with her."

"Thank God my children have learned something about how to speak at the dinner table," Jackie said, giving Ethan an amused glance.

"So what happened?" Ethan asked, as he felt his speech quickening. "Did they?"

"I don't really know," Brian said. "Let's just say . . . the interest may have been mutual. But you know how gossip is. You hear things, and then it passes." He took a sip of wine. "I think she's a bit nuts, though."

"Nuts?" Todd asked. "Come on, she's cool."

Ethan felt grateful Todd was coming to Hannah's rescue, so he didn't have to.

"Whatever," Brian said.

"That's what's so great about you kids being at that school," Jackie said, with an air of finality. "You get to meet all different kinds of people. I support it."

It was so much more than people, Ethan thought, as he surveyed the dining room—men in suits, women in fur coats, a scene he would never imagine as Thanksgiving eve; it was everything. He remembered calling his parents earlier that day to check in with them. When his mother asked where they would be eating that night, Ethan had lied and said Jackie was preparing dinner, though inwardly, the thought made him laugh.

* * *

Todd wondered that week if he and Ethan would run into any of his old friends from St. Bernard's. Though he was rarely in touch with them during the school year, he found that as soon as he returned home, he would fall into the predictable patterns of hanging out, going to bars in Yorkville, drinking beer bought at Korean delis, and smoking cigarettes in the park. He didn't know, though, if his friends' world would mesh with Ethan's. Theirs was one of nightclubs and designer handbags and expensive drugs; for some of them, their comings and goings were even noted by gossip columns and party photographers. They were on their cell phones constantly; they always had somewhere better to be. To them, Ethan would be a veritable country bumpkin. But even if he did live up to their scrutiny (he could be, Todd imagined, the smart kid—every group of friends had one, didn't they?), Todd didn't want to share him with anyone else.

On Friday night, the two of them were out at a bar on First Avenue that was known for not carding. Todd had palmed his Amex off on the waitress, a lithe girl not much older than they were. He noticed Ethan flinching. It mystified Todd; Kevin and Izzy and Miles, all of whom had healthy bank accounts, would gladly accept Todd's largesse, while Ethan, who never seemed to have much money, insisted, nearly all the time, on paying his own way.

This time, Todd told Ethan to put his wallet away. "It's easier," he said, as he motioned to the waitress weaving her way through the drunken masses. "She'll keep a tab."

The place was packed with prep school kids, a sea of fisherman's sweaters and fleece pullovers and oxford cloth shirts, and Todd wasn't surprised when, forty-five minutes after they had arrived, he spotted Brooks Stewart, a friend from grade school. Brooks was tall, nearly six foot four, with a shaggy mop of hair, and had the sort of body that swayed back and forth when he walked, as if he might be blown away by a gust of wind. Now Todd felt guilty that he hadn't called him.

"Hey, man—I didn't know you were home!" Brooks gave Todd a robust slap on the back, nearly spilling Todd's beer.

"Yeah, sorry I haven't called," Todd said, attempting his best imitation of earnestness. "I've been crazy with, you know, college applications, and stuff."

"I thought maybe you were out of town."

Todd realized that Ethan was patiently looking up at Brooks, so he made the necessary introductions.

Brooks shook Ethan's hand, and then looked back at Todd. "Do you want to join us in the back? We're playing a game of quarters."

"I don't know," Todd said. "We should be getting home."

Todd looked at Ethan. Brooks Stewart was a savvy guy. In the ninth grade, he had always figured out which girl Todd had a crush on before Todd had even told him. He pulled Ethan back into the crowd, afraid of what his old crew might think about his friend. (Yes, New York made everyone faster, brighter, wittier, more beautiful, and he had seen that happen to Ethan as well. But still.) He and Ethan had a DVD to finish at home, and that sounded more appealing to Todd than a drinking game.

He wondered, too, if his mother sensed something between them. He noticed an ease about Ethan's presence that was unlike her; he heard her telling acquaintances on the phone that "Todd has his friend *Ethan* staying with him this week." There was something about the way she said his friend's name, as if in those five letters were a plethora of secret codes, as if his mother understood how he felt.

Whatever Jackie thought, Todd loved having Ethan there, waking in the same room as him every morning, eating their cereal together in the kitchen, hair messy, sleep in their eyes before they took their showers. It was difficult for him not to be able to reach out. Todd tried to think of Ethan as the twin brother he never had, as a peer. But some nights, that wasn't enough, and he would long for Ethan to take the place that Alex once had in his life. The trouble was, he didn't fit there.

On Saturday afternoon, they were hanging out in the kitchen when there was a phone call for Ethan. It was Hannah. Though he knew it was a strange thought—who, after all, would want a teacher to call?—he had been hoping she might. It was comforting to hear her voice, like chatting with an old friend; this idea, of friends like Todd and her, pleased him—he was collecting them slowly, one by one, like perfect glass marbles.

"I miss you boys," she said. "When are you coming back?"

"Tomorrow. We're taking the bus."

"Don't take the bus. I have to go into the city anyway. Let me pick you up."

Ethan gazed out the window in the kitchen, to the park, to the cabs streaming down Fifth. He couldn't imagine a Berkley teacher in this world, this cosmopolitan place Todd called home. "Are you sure?"

"I'm caught up with all my work. I've been writing college recommendations for the last three days."

"What are you doing in the city?"

"I have to visit an old friend."

He wanted to know more, but he was afraid to ask.

"Will we be able to fit everything in your car?"

"Ethan—don't worry, we'll make it work."

The next day, Ethan waited with Todd in the black-and-white marble-floored lobby of Jackie's building. They hadn't told her that they weren't taking the bus, knowing that as a seasoned boarding school parent, she might find Hannah's offer strange (and yes, Ethan thought, it was strange—but she had picked

Todd and him, had decided to bestow on them special favors, and who were they to refuse?). Todd had been pleased, seemingly seeing it as nothing more than a chance to hitch a ride back to school without sitting on a bus for three hours. He had asked Todd the night before if there was some kind of rule against being driven by a teacher; Todd said he didn't know of one.

Hannah pulled up at the curb in Jean-Paul, the name she had given to her little Peugeot. Todd's doorman helped them cram their duffel bags into the tiny trunk. They both squeezed into the car, with Ethan in the front seat and Todd on the small seat in the back.

"Let's do something fun," she said, as they cruised down Fifth, past the Plaza and FAO Schwarz.

"Like what?" Todd asked.

"Anything. Go to a museum. Catch a show."

"Don't we have to get back to school?"

"We have nine hours till check-in," she said. "As long as I get you back before then, we'll be fine. I know—I have a friend we can visit."

The three of them zipped downtown, parking in front of an art gallery that was on the first floor of a warehouse building in Soho. Ethan was surprised when Hannah didn't lead them to the gallery's glass door, but rather up onto a concrete loading dock. She rang the buzzer for the third floor.

"Yeah?" came a voice from the intercom.

"Ben, it's Hannah."

They were buzzed in. Ethan and Todd followed Hannah up three flights of stairs. The steel door was open when they reached the landing.

"Hey, hey!" a man said. "What a surprise." He wore cowboy boots, a leather jacket, and worn jeans that rode low on his skinny hips. He had short dark hair and eyes that were a little too close together, as if he were perpetually suspicious.

"Is this a bad time? I'm sorry I didn't call first."

70

He and Hannah embraced, and she planted a light kiss on his mouth.

"No problem. I was just headed out to run some errands, but they can wait. Come on in." He looked at Todd and Ethan. "Who are your friends?"

Hannah introduced them. "They're students of mine. We're on a little field trip, of sorts." She turned to the boys. "Ben is a brilliant short story writer. His last collection was nominated for a ton of awards."

"Please. I've only written two books. And I didn't win," Ben said.

"Still, it's amazing!" She turned to the boys. "I'm so proud of him."

Ben motioned for them to sit down. The loft was enormous, its brick walls adorned with abstract paintings and rows and rows of books.

Ben took off his leather jacket, revealing a white T-shirt and a tattooed strand of barbed wire around his right biceps.

"Can I get you guys anything to drink?" Ben asked. "A glass of wine?"

"Wine would be lovely," Hannah said.

He took an already-opened bottle of red from the kitchen counter and began to pour it into glasses.

Ethan tensed up at the idea of drinking with a teacher. "I really don't think we should—"

Hannah waved away his concerns. "Ethan, relax. We're off campus. No one will ever find out."

Ben brought the glasses over and placed them on a coffee table strewn with books. The three of them sat down on a large burgundy leather sofa with gilt legs.

"Cheers," Hannah said, holding up her glass. "To being in New York."

"To a few more hours away from Berkley," Todd said, before greedily taking a gulp.

Ethan took a small sip. The amount of alcohol he had consumed in one week astonished him. And now he was drinking
with a teacher. But maybe Hannah wasn't really a teacher. Maybe
outside of Berkley, she was just another adult. From where he
was sitting now, he could smell her—that feminine, girlish scent
of body lotion, the slightest hint of perfume and perspiration.

"Man, I can't believe you guys are in high school," Ben said.
"Makes me feel so old."

"How old are you?" Todd asked.

"Todd!" Hannah said. "That's rude."

"No, it's fine," Ben said. "I'm twenty-nine."

Ethan counted out the years in his head. Twenty-nine seemed
decades away. He wondered about this guy Ben, who lived in this
enormous loft and drank red wine during the day. It all seemed
so decadent, so louche. *Stop it*, he thought, *stop being so judg-
mental.*

"How do you guys know each other?" Ethan asked.

Sly smiles passed over Ben and Hannah's faces, a shared intimacy that wasn't about to be revealed. "Long story," Ben said.
"Have Hannah tell it to you on the way home." He turned toward Hannah. "So, what are you doing in the city?"

"You know, the usual, saw a show of Henry Moore sketches at
the Met, did a little shopping . . ."

"You went to see David." Ben leaned back in his chair, clearly
satisfied he had reached this conclusion so early.

"No, I didn't."

"Hannah, I know you. There's no way you came to New York
and didn't try to see him."

Ethan noticed Hannah blushing, a tinge of pink in her usually
pale cheeks. He felt sorry for her.

"I walked by his apartment in the Village. You know how his
place is on the first floor, and you can see right into the living
room if the lights are on? He's changed the furniture around, I
think."

"He's seeing someone." It struck Ethan as cruel of Ben to say this.

"Really?" She took a sip of wine. "Oh, what does it matter? It was the summer before last. It's ancient history."

"What were you doing in New York then?" Ethan asked. "I thought you always taught summer school."

"Well, aren't you the nosy one," Hannah said, turning toward him.

"No, I'm not trying—I'm sorry," Ethan stammered. "I'm just curious."

"It's okay," she said, looking at Ben. "*Someone* shouldn't have brought it up."

"Sorry," Ben said. "You know I can never keep my mouth shut about anything."

"Well," Hannah said, winking at Ethan, "we'll just be sure not to tell you any of our secrets anymore."

Ethan asked if he could use Ben's bathroom.

"Back there." Ben motioned to a door next to an unmade king-sized bed strewn with pillows and a red velvet bedspread.

Ethan went into the bathroom and shut the door. Hanging above the toilet was a calendar. It was off by several months, but that wasn't what startled Ethan. It was that August's photograph was a black-and-white portrait of a naked man. Ethan flipped over the cover. *Portraits: Male Nudes,* it read.

When he returned to the group, Todd and Ben were both lighting cigarettes.

"Want one?" Ben motioned at Ethan to an ivory box on the table. Ethan took one, looking nervously at Hannah.

"Oh, what the hell," Hannah said, choosing one for herself. She accepted a light from Ben, and exhaled a column of smoke into the air.

Cigarettes on the table, naked men in the bathroom. It was strange, but Ethan liked it. Maybe this was what the life of an artist was like. He wondered if this was what Hannah had wanted them to see.

By sundown, the three of them were on the Hutchinson River Parkway, headed back to Massachusetts. Todd felt glum as the reality of returning to Berkley started to set in. The buzz of two glasses of wine had now faded and turned into a mild headache.

Ethan broke the silence that had fallen over the three of them. "That guy was really cool."

"How do you know him? You can tell us now, right?" Todd leaned forward from the backseat.

"We were lovers," Hannah said. "Right before I moved to Paris. I was twenty-five, he was eighteen."

If Ben was now twenty-nine, that meant Hannah was thirty-six.

"But isn't he, you know . . ." Todd asked, his voice trailing off.

Hannah kept her eyes on the road. "Yeah, he's gay, no big deal."

"Does he have a boyfriend?"

"I don't know. Why? You want to date him?" She glanced back at Todd, a teasing look in her eyes.

"No!" Todd said, mortified. "I was just curious."

"You know what they say about curiosity."

Ethan snorted, but Todd was silent. He hoped he didn't give off the appearance of being that way. It had been exciting meeting Ben, the way he had shaken Todd's hand when saying good-bye to him, giving it an extra squeeze and saying, *Hope to see you again sometime.* Ben was more than ten years older than Todd, but Todd still found him intensely attractive. He wanted to kiss the jutting hipbone that protruded over his jeans, to nuzzle his face in Ben's chest.

Now he looked at Ethan from the backseat, his friend's face

illuminated by the dim lights of the road. He had thought of Ethan as a man. Compared to Ben, he was still a boy.

That evening, as Todd got ready for bed, he kept thinking about the encounter—Ben's masculine energy, his cowboy boots and tight muscles. Maybe Todd could get Ben's number from Hannah and call him over the break. The idea filled him with desire, a perverse tickle in his stomach that signaled excitement and dread.

CHAPTER 7

Given the constant stream of final papers and projects, exams, and college applications, Ethan didn't see Hannah much over the next two weeks. He would pass her in the hall—he was usually rushing off somewhere and she was burdened with a stack of student papers or blue books—and they would exchange a quick hello, but that was the extent of it. One afternoon, he walked by her Fourth Form English class. As he heard her voice resonating down the hall, he stopped and pretended to read a poster on the bulletin boards outside the English department office, allowing himself a peek through the windows that looked out onto the corridor. Hannah was asking for a comparison of Esther Greenwood in *The Bell Jar* to a similar male character in literature. A student named Chas Marshall, a bookish fifteen-year-old, raised his hand to answer the question. He picked Holden Caulfield (a predictable choice, Ethan thought), and went on about their similarities and differences.

"Chas, that's wonderful!" Hannah said when he was finished. "Mmmm . . ." She leaned back in her chair, her eyes closed, as if the boy had just fed her a chocolate truffle. "This is the kind of close reading that I want you all to do!" she exclaimed, as her eyes popped open. "Nice work, Chas."

Just at that moment, her attention turned to the windows looking out on the hallway, and her eyes met Ethan's. He quickly started walking away, humiliated that she had seen him, and yet, at the same time—what was it he was feeling? Jealousy, though he didn't know why. Had he imagined he was the only student on the Berkley campus who got to spend time with her, was commended by her, was an audience to her performances? Chas Marshall might have been a scrawny, pimply fifteen-year-old, but Ethan still wished he had been sitting in his seat, that he had volunteered the same response, however mediocre, and been the object of her praise.

The day before school let out for Christmas break, Ethan trudged across the snow-covered golf course toward Hannah's house. The ice crunched under his feet and the cold air stung his cheeks as flurries of wind blew across the lake. Black ice was what it was covered with now, ice so clear it looked black. He imagined diving into that ice, being trapped under it, the other world it might contain.

Hannah had invited him over for hot chocolate, and he was relieved to take a break from studying for his philosophy final the next day; he had reached the end of his review of Nietzsche and his eyes were growing blurry.

The house floated in the moonlight. Through the windows, Ethan could see Hannah's living room was lit only by candles. He knocked on the door and she let him in.

"It's a little dark in here," he said, taking off his coat.

"I was meditating earlier. It's easier when it's dark." Hannah nervously smoothed the folds of her skirt. She looked as if she had dressed up for the occasion.

"That's weird," Ethan said.

Hannah cocked her head at him. "You'd get a lot more out of life if you didn't put down everything that seems different to you."

Ethan cringed at his rudeness. "You're right," he said. "I'm sorry."

She poured a mug of cocoa for him and he took a delicate sip, wincing as it burned his tongue.

"Careful, it's hot." She paused for a moment and then drank from her own mug. "I've got something for you." She handed Ethan a package wrapped in lavender tissue paper. "Merry Christmas."

Ethan felt his ears go hot. "For me? I'm so embarrassed. I mean, I didn't bring anything for you."

She sat down on one of the wicker stools at her kitchen counter and motioned for him to do the same. Ethan's knees touched hers as he held the present in his lap.

"Don't worry about it," she said. "Just being my friend this semester has been enough." She patted his forearm. "Open it."

Ethan tore open the package.

"You're supposed to read the card first!" she said. He pulled the card from its envelope. It was simple cream-colored stock with a wreath printed on the front. *For Ethan*, it read on the inside. *An artist, a scholar, and a friend. Love, Hannah.*

"Thank you," he said. He felt awful for not bringing her anything. How was he supposed to know she would be getting him a gift? He didn't even buy Christmas presents for his friends, let alone his teachers.

He continued tearing open the wrapping paper. Inside were two paperbacks. One was a collection of poetry by Arthur Rimbaud. The other was *Breakfast at Tiffany's*. He ran his hands over their matte covers, felt the sharp edges of their spines.

Ethan was reminded of getting presents from his parents. His mother, having no sense of what was appropriate for a teenager, had given him *To the Lighthouse* when he was fourteen. (He thought of how she had looked at him while he opened it, how his eyes had betrayed his confusion.) In Hannah, he saw the same look of expectation, of excitement at the prospect of shared knowledge.

"They're two of my favorites," Hannah said. "The Rimbaud is everything I love about Paris. And the Capote is everything I love about New York. You haven't read them, have you?"

Ethan shook his head. It made him uncomfortable that she was being so nice to him.

"Hannah—I feel terrible. You've been amazing. I know what I'd like to do. I'd like to give you one of my paintings. You can come to the studio and pick one out."

"That would be lovely," she said. "An Ethan Whitley original." She looked at his empty mug. "Do you want some more hot chocolate?"

"I should be getting back," he said. "I still have that exam tomorrow."

"And then you're leaving on the bus at noon?"

Ethan nodded.

"Three weeks without you guys is going to be tough."

"Won't you be with your parents for the holidays?" He realized he knew nothing about Hannah's family. He simply assumed she had parents, somewhere to go for the break.

She shook her head. "They're not around anymore. My father passed away a few years ago, and my mother died in childbirth."

"I'm sorry," Ethan said.

"I'll probably spend some time in New York with friends, hang out with Ben. We always do a big Christmas goose."

Ethan didn't know why he cared, but he was relieved Hannah wouldn't be spending the holiday alone.

"I nearly forgot," she said. "Your check. I still owe you for the last bit of work you did on the bookshelves."

"You really don't have to—" Ethan faltered. "You don't have to pay me. I enjoy doing it."

"You sweet thing. Look—take this." She handed him a check, which he carefully folded into his wallet. "I'm sure it will come in handy over the holidays."

Ethan moved toward the door, and Hannah opened it for him. She leaned forward and gave him a quick hug. "Be safe," she said.

As he walked back to the dorm, Ethan thought about Hannah's gift, the card tucked neatly inside the front cover of one of the books. Hannah had written *love* on the card. People wrote *love* on cards to their friends all the time, didn't they? He pulled it out, and examined it again in the moonlight, his gloved hands holding it clumsily by the corners. *Love, Hannah.* He smiled to himself. Someone liked him, someone as sophisticated and worldly as Hannah. It felt like the beginning of a life populated by artists and writers, people who lived in places like New York City, people who meditated by candlelight and read the classics and wrapped gifts in lavender paper. People who used the word *love*, freely and without reservation. Yes, he thought, as the blood rushed in his ears and the snow crunched rhythmically under his feet, it was the beginning of a new life.

Ethan was nearly finished with his first semester at Berkley, and his college applications were in the mail—a host of Ivys (Yale was his top choice), Stanford, a few backup schools. Tomorrow, after taking his philosophy exam, riding on the bus to the airport, and making an eight-hour trip across the country, he would be seeing his parents. He wondered if they would sense a change in him. In some ways, he felt different, more ready to face the world, as if he were going home with a wealth of experiences. In other ways, when he thought about the often solitary life he was leading—the constant reading, the endless papers, his lack of a girl-friend—he felt small and insignificant.

He headed up the narrow path to the dorm, the cemetery on his right, the headmaster's house on his left, looming like a ghostly ship. He would go back to Slater and study some more, would get an early night's sleep in preparation for his exam. No, that wouldn't do. Things were going well for him, and there was no reason he had to continue being the same old Ethan as before. He would go to the snack bar and hang out with Todd and his friends.

The ramshackle sound system in the snack bar blared "Satisfaction" from one of Todd's mixes. His friend was sitting at a booth along the back wall with Izzy and Kevin. Ethan got himself a cup of senior coffee and joined them. He didn't like Izzy—not only was he not a nice person; he could be an outright asshole—but he felt sorry for him. Todd had told Ethan several nights earlier that Izzy's brother Joshua had become partially paralyzed while dropping acid last summer after senior parties. He had decided to climb a lighting tower at an outdoor concert and had fallen into the crowd. Now he was taking a year off from college to do physical rehabilitation, along with a hefty dose of drug and alcohol counseling.

"Brought some of your reading with you?" Todd said, motioning to Ethan's two books.

"No," he said. "Han—Ms. McClellan gave them to me. Sort of a Christmas present."

"Ooh, a Christmas present from Ms. McClellan," teased Izzy. "What else did she give you?"

"Nothing," Ethan said, blushing. "It's not like that. We're just friends."

"Sure you are," said Kevin, his eyes lighting up. "I heard she likes 'em young." Ethan flinched at Kevin's comment. Hannah was one of the teachers people liked to gossip about. It wasn't only Brian's half-baked story; he had heard so many outrageous tales over the past few months, none of which he imagined were true: that she was descended from British royalty, that she used to model, that she was once married to a man who owned his own country, that she was a showgirl at the Moulin Rouge before tragically sustaining a knee injury. He wondered which, if any, were the truth.

"Those are just rumors," Todd said. "Hannah would never do anything like that. Jesus, I mean, she's thirty-six!"

"She doesn't look thirty-six," Kevin said. "She looks pretty fuckable to me."

"Come on," Ethan said, "that's gross." He paused for a moment. "I don't mean gross. It's—well, it's disrespectful."

"So she *is* your girlfriend!" Izzy said.

"She's not," Ethan said. "But you can think whatever you want."

"What'd she give you?" Todd asked.

Ethan held up the two books.

"*Breakfast at Tiffany's?* Isn't that a movie?" Kevin asked.

"It's a novel, you dumb fuck," Todd said, punching Kevin in the arm. "Are you going to read that over the break?"

"I was going to start with the other one. I've never read Rimbaud."

"Can I borrow it?" Todd asked. "It's one of my mom's favorite movies."

"Um, I don't know. I probably shouldn't, since it was a present—"

"A present from your girlfriend!" interrupted Izzy.

When was this going to stop? He never should have come to the snack bar, at least not with his new books in hand.

"It's fine," Ethan said, handing Todd the Capote. "You can read it over the break. Just be careful with it. Don't, you know, dog-ear the pages or anything."

Izzy was smirking.

"What?" Todd said.

"Didn't know you were into books written by faggots," Izzy said, as Kevin started laughing.

Todd was speechless for a moment. "What does that matter?"

"Dude, I'm kidding. Relax!" Izzy laughed, and Todd was mollified as he put the book in his bag. Ethan doubted Todd would read it. Somehow, giving him one-half of his present made the whole thing less of a big deal. It was just a teacher recommending some stuff for him to read over the break. But Ethan preferred it when Hannah's gift felt like something special, something that was his alone.

After check-in, Ethan continued reviewing for his exam. As he read through his notes, his mind wandered back to Hannah's card. The card! He had left it in the copy of *Breakfast at Tiffany's*. He shot out of his room and ran up to Todd's, taking three steps at a time.

Todd was lying on his bed, listening to music on his earphones.

"The book," Ethan said, panting. "The book I gave you. I need—I left something in it."

Todd opened his eyes and turned off the music. "It's in my bag."

Ethan exhaled, relieved. Todd hadn't seen the card. He dove into Todd's satchel, where the book was nestled in with a pile of papers, and pulled out the card.

"Did anyone see this?"

"I'm sorry, I shouldn't have looked at it, but it slipped out."

"Did you show it to anyone else?"

"No, of course not."

"It's kind of embarrassing."

"What's embarrassing about it? It's just a card."

Ethan pushed aside a pile of clothes and sank down on Todd's desk chair. Maybe it was just a card, a card like any other, a card that meant very little.

Still, as Ethan went back to his room, he tucked it protectively into the pocket of his jeans, where it could stay safe from the rest of the world.

On the second day he was home from school, Todd decided to call Ben Atwater, Hannah's writer friend. He had procured Ben's number from her, claiming he wanted to interview him for *The Bones*.

Ben's phone rang four times before someone picked up. "Yeah?"

"Hi, um, Ben? This is Todd Eldon, Hannah's friend."

There was silence on the line.

"We met a few weeks ago, when Hannah came to visit you?"

"Oh yeah, what's going on, man?"

"I wanted to give you a call . . . I'm staying at my mom's in the city. I thought maybe it would be cool to hang out or something." Todd suddenly had the sensation that he might throw up. He took a breath, and it passed.

"Uh, sure, what exactly did you have in mind?"

Todd had to think quickly.

"I'm going shopping in Soho tomorrow. Maybe I could just stop by?"

They agreed that Todd would give him a call when he was in the area. After Todd hung up, he felt stupid. Why would Hannah's friend want to hang out with him? He was seventeen; Ben was twenty-nine. There was nothing Todd could offer Ben that he couldn't get anywhere else. Nothing except his youth.

The next day, Todd took the 6 train downtown, getting off at Spring Street and emerging into the busy crowd of Christmas shoppers. He called Ben on his cell, having carefully programmed in the number the night before.

Ben's voice sounded groggy, though there was rock music playing in the background.

Todd walked down Wooster Street, the blood rushing in his legs. When he reached the building, he ran up the three flights of stairs and arrived out of breath at Ben's floor.

Ben opened the door with a grin. "Doing some shopping?" he said, holding open the steel portal to his loft.

Todd realized he wasn't carrying anything. "Yeah, I was going to do some later," he said.

"Come on in. Do you want anything? I can make coffee . . . or do you want a beer?"

"I'll take a beer," Todd said, even though it was two o'clock in the afternoon on a Tuesday. Maybe it would relax him. Todd stood awkwardly next to the stainless steel refrigerator as Ben opened two bottles of Stella Artois on the kitchen counter. He handed one to Todd, and Todd took a sip. "So Hannah said you guys used to be, you know . . ."

"Sleeping together? A long time ago. I was so young."

"But now you're, like—"

"Oh, what, queer? It's no big deal. I mean, sexuality is such a fluid thing, don't you think?" Ben motioned for Todd to sit down next to him on the couch.

"Yeah," Todd said. If it were fluid, did that mean he could change? Todd took a sip of his beer and then looked at Ben. "Can I ask you something?"

"Sure."

"What was the deal with Hannah and her ex-boyfriend?"

"You mean David? He's a friend of mine, an architect. They dated two summers ago, started living together while Hannah was working for a theater company—I think she was planning on taking some time off from teaching once fall came. Then he had an affair with another woman, a friend of a friend. I guess Hannah thought it was all more serious than it was, them living together and all. I think she wanted him to marry her."

"Oh," Todd said, as he felt his voice grow quiet. "That's terrible."

"It wouldn't have been such a big deal except that Hannah freaked out. She moved out, and then started stalking him all the time, following him to work, spying on him, sending nasty notes. The woman he had done it with was really scared. I mean, all she'd done was have a fling with an attractive guy, and suddenly she had incurred the wrath of this other woman."

Todd was suddenly surprised at how frank Ben was being with him. He felt as if he had entered an adult landscape, where no one thought of him as a prep school student, as seventeen years old, as Jackie Eldon's son. "So what happened?"

"I probably shouldn't tell you this. Just don't tell her I said anything about it, okay?"

Todd nodded.

"David eventually had to file a restraining order against Hannah, which seemed to be successful in keeping her away, though she still finds an excuse to walk by his apartment whenever she's in the city."

"She doesn't seem to have very good luck with men." It was the type of adult observation his mother would make. All he really knew about Hannah was that she had been married once.

"Hannah's a great girl, but she gets herself into these situations, and then she gets hurt. But I owe my life to her. She was so supportive of me when I came out."

"Yeah . . . I sort of wanted to talk to you about that," Todd said.

"What about?" Ben cocked his head at Todd.

"I think I might be, you know, interested in guys, and I wanted to ask your opinion about it." Todd's voice suddenly felt mechanical to him. *Ask your opinion?* It was as if he were floating three feet above his body, participating in and observing the conversation at the same time.

"What did you want to know?"

Todd took a deep breath. "How do I go about it?"

Ben laughed. Todd noticed his teeth, perfectly straight, but stained with tobacco. He wanted to lick the stains off, to wipe them clean.

"How do you go about it? Well, it's not exactly like learning to drive or something." He paused. "It's a good question."

"How did you do it?"

"I was in college, I knew that was what I wanted to do, so I went to one of the dances and met someone, and we went back to his room . . . is this what you want to hear?"

"Yeah, and then what happened?"

"Well, he had too much to drink, so he got sick, and then I left."

"And that was it?" Todd asked.

"We kissed and messed around a bit."

"So, like, how do you go about the messing around part?"

The conversation made Todd recall an annual checkup with his family doctor at age fifteen—it had been required in order to enter Berkley—when suddenly words like *penis* and *testicles* and *masturbation* were being used freely. They were not, he had always thought, words to be used lightly; they were forbidden, words that carried weight and meaning. And now here he was, talking about sex with someone who was an adult, someone he barely knew.

Todd continued. "I mean, is it like sex with girls? I've had sex with girls."

"I'm sure you have," Ben said, smirking at him. "But aren't you a little young to be coming out?"

"I don't want to come out," Todd said. "I need to know if it's right for me first." Was he asking for Ben to have sex with him? Maybe he should just go into Ben's bathroom and jerk off. Maybe that would take care of it. Filthy, dirty.

Ben took a pull on his beer. "Todd, aren't there youth groups or something, places where you could meet other kids your age?"

"I don't want to do that," Todd said. "It would be embarrassing." He thought about one gay kid in his class, Jeremy Cohen. Todd imagined these youth groups would be filled with little faggots like Jeremy, scrawny, lisping queens—kids who had been kicked out of their homes, kids who were beaten up at school (Jeremy was part of the gay-straight alliance at Berkley, a group that consisted of him and five girls, only two of whom identified as lesbians). Those kids didn't have a choice; they had to come out. Todd didn't look gay, and he didn't act gay. In the same way that you might conceal an awkward birthmark under your clothes, Todd could hide it until even he had forgotten it was there.

"I'm not exactly sure how I'm supposed to help you here."

Todd took another deep breath. If he wanted the low-hanging fruit, he would have to grab at it. Face rejection. Face the fact that it might be horrific.

"I want you to show me," he said. "I want you to show me how it's done."

"You're sure about this?"

Todd nodded. He had never been more sure of anything in his life.

Ben put his beer down on the coffee table, leaned forward, and kissed Todd on the mouth. His breath tasted like cigarettes, not the faint tang of one cigarette recently smoked, but a long-seated odor of nicotine that had seeped into his gums. Todd felt Ben's tongue explore his mouth, and he sensed his own erection growing. His heart was thumping, and he tried to steady himself.

"You're shaking," Ben said. "Maybe this isn't a good idea."

"I'll try to relax." He made himself keep breathing. His mind kept jumping back to Ethan, to the memory of kissing Ethan. This was nothing like that. Ethan's mouth had been stiff, rigid. Ben's was supple, flexible, welcoming.

Ben led Todd over to the bed. It was happening so quickly, so easily. Was this what sex was like between men? Were they even about to have sex? Would Ben just stick it in him, or would it happen the other way around? Was that something people did on a first date? Was this even a date?

When it was over, Todd lay on Ben's bed, the sheets wrapped around both of them (he wondered, why the modesty now?). He had reached orgasm almost immediately; Ben had taken a little longer. He felt guilty for being so quick about it: he thought his body might explode with pleasure, that it would turn inside out, semen and organs flying everywhere. It was a completely different experience—no, not just an experience, a completely different *universe*—than sex with Alex or any of his other girlfriends. With Alex, he now realized, he had been merely going through the motions—exciting, yes, but not the same.

For Ben, though, it seemed there had been something automatic about the process—having Todd go down on him (Todd had done it, like a girl, and now it made him sick, as he thought of his mouth on Ben's smooth, salty-sweet skin), jerking each other off—as if it were simply a matter of pushing the right buttons in a certain order to achieve a desired effect. He wondered if this was all there was to it. There had been no emotion—not the real feelings Todd had for Ethan, the way it might be if he did it with Ethan. There was that familiar swelling in his chest, what Todd pictured as love, or at least lust, but it was intermingled with an emptiness, the sense that all this would be over very soon, that it was fleeting, a trifle.

"Ben," he said. "Do me a favor?"

Ben pulled his arm out from under Todd's body and propped his head up on his elbow. Todd admired the dark hair in Ben's armpit.

"Yeah?"

"Don't tell Hannah. When you see her for Christmas, don't tell her, okay?"

"I'm not seeing her this year," he said. "I'll be staying with my parents in Philadelphia."

The late afternoon light threw shadows around the loft. Todd followed Ben's pale ass with his eyes as Ben got out of bed and headed to the bathroom.

"You'd better get going," Ben said, speaking to Todd over his shoulder. "I'm supposed to be at a cocktail party in an hour and a half."

"Maybe I could come with you?" Todd asked. He didn't want the experience to end so quickly. He hoped he and Ben could have dinner together, hang out some more during the break. He hoped they could become lovers. He imagined it happening like it did in his mother's books.

Ben snorted. "I don't think that would be a good idea."

Half an hour later, as the sun was setting, Todd left Ben's loft. It was as if he had died and come alive again, as if he had crossed a river and had made it to dry land. He felt shock, of course—who wouldn't?—but also joy. He wove his way among the crowds doing their last-minute shopping. He still needed to get his mother a gift, a gift for a woman who had everything. It could wait until tomorrow. For now, he wanted to remember this moment: of walking away from Ben's loft on Wooster Street, the wind blowing in his face, his cashmere scarf wrapped around his neck, looped in the style Jackie had shown him, the street-lamps starting to turn on, the resplendent displays in the shop windows, an abundance of gifts available for the taking.

The next day, Todd left a message for Ben, but received no return call. He phoned him every day until the day before Christmas, when someone else answered his line, a man.

"Ben's not here," the man said.

"Who's this?"

"This is Paul."

"Paul?"

"Yeah, Paul, as in Ben's partner Paul?" The man sounded annoyed.

Todd wanted the conversation to be over; it was too horrible.

"Who's asking?"

Todd opened his mouth, but no sound came out. He slowly placed the receiver back in its cradle. It didn't surprise him. It had all been so casual. It wasn't supposed to be easy: sex, love. Once again, his life had moved from the thrillingly new to the familiar dullness of disappointment.

He thought of telling Hannah about it, but realized she would probably become hysterical. She didn't even know he was interested in guys. No, he was definitely not going to tell her. He was definitely not going to tell anyone.

CHAPTER 8

Being back in California was a novelty for Ethan. Unlike on the East Coast, the light wasn't cold and gray; it had a yellow glow, refracting off the leaves in Ethan's front yard, warming the wooden shingles of his parents' house, the old gnarled tree, almost fairy tale–like in its charm, that grew around their picket fence.

He had landed in San Francisco late on Saturday evening; as the plane descended, the city was laid out as a glittering sea, twinkling diodes connected to each other like one of his father's circuit boards in his small workshop off the garage, a giant schematic where everything was connected. He met his parents at baggage claim. His father looked the same, distinguished in his salt-and-pepper beard and glasses, plaid button-down, undershirt peeking out of the collar, khakis a little too loose. Ethan thought his mother looked gaunt as she stood next to a luggage cart, though she was dressed in a colorful Indian skirt and top, the type of outfit, she joked, now trendy among young people, that she had been wearing for thirty years. Her hair—it had grown back in, but she kept it short—was a dull slate color. As the lovely brown had faded to gray through the years, it had always suited her; now, though, perhaps because it was so short, it made her look older than he had remembered. His father gave him a quick hug, and his mother gave him a longer one, holding on to Ethan with her bony frame until he thought he might not be able to breathe. "You have no idea how much I've missed you," she whispered to him. Ethan felt a lump forming in his throat; he wasn't certain if it was love, or guilt, or both. It wasn't fair of her to make him feel bad. She had wanted him to go away.

The house was also smaller than he had remembered. Even his bedroom—beige walls; desk and bureau bought from Sears; retro 1950s astronaut bedspread his mother thought was clever when he was fourteen—seemed to have shrunk. That evening, though he was exhausted, he examined the decorations he had accumulated during his childhood and teenage years, the posters of paintings by Gauguin and Toulouse-Lautrec; the stained glass flower he had made from a kit when he was twelve, now sitting on his windowsill; the feather and bead dream catcher hanging over his bed. He had forgotten how much of his own artwork had decorated his room. Studies of his hands. Landscapes. Self-portraits. A painting of the quad at Stanford.

He took off his glasses and rubbed the sore bridge of his nose. All this work, everything he had done before starting at Berkley, seemed immature, inconsequential. Had he really grown so much since leaving home? The thought scared him, because it meant shedding his past, deciding what to take with him, and what to leave behind.

His mother appeared at the door, her feet now shod in bedroom slippers.

"Is everything okay?" she asked. "I put fresh sheets on your bed this morning. And I saved some magazine articles I thought you might want to read—" She motioned toward his desk, to a neat pile of clippings. "Just some stuff on the new arts facilities at the university."

Ethan sighed. "Mom, I don't know if I want to go to Stanford.

I may want to stay back East." He couldn't imagine himself at Stanford; though he knew it was an excellent school, it seemed far too bucolic. He remembered living at home and seeing the students jogging, laughing, playing tennis. He didn't imagine he could ever be so at ease with life.

"That's contingent on your getting a good financial package. You know what the arrangement would be if you were to go to Stanford." It had been drummed into him a thousand times: it would be free.

"Just let me consider the possibility before I have to make any decisions, okay?"

"Of course." She paused, appearing to examine his room. He hated it when she did this. She had probably been doing it once a week for the past four months. He wanted to go to sleep. Being in his own bed would be comforting. Empty, but comforting.

"So what time will you be getting up tomorrow?"

"Mom—I've been living on my own for four months. I'll get up when I get up."

"I'm sorry," she said. "I'm just so used to—"

"It's fine," he said. "I know."

"I keep forgetting—my colleague Johanna Frasier, she's the new Kingsley Chair in Comparative Literature, she has a daughter who graduated from Berkley Academy last year." His mother seemed delighted by the coincidence as she continued. "She's a freshman at Stanford now. She would love to take you out one night. Maybe you two could go to a movie or something."

Ethan seized up; he hated it when his mother meddled in his personal life. "I'm going to be really busy," he said, though this was a lie. "Why would this girl want to hang out with me? She's really ugly, right?"

"Don't be ridiculous. I met her at a housewarming party that Johanna had. She's very attractive. It might be fun for you."

Why was other people's idea of fun always so different from his own? He doubted his ability to relax with someone a year older than he was, especially a girl who was pretty. When he was around girls like that, he became tongue-tied. They distracted him, the way they ran their fingers through their hair, the tropical smell of their shampoo, the way they moved so casually in the world, as if they owned it. But maybe this girl would be different.

"What's her name? She has a name, right?"

His mother smiled. "Yes, she has a name. Her name is Vivian."

He groaned. *Vivian*. He couldn't think of a more typical name for the daughter of an academic. Still, maybe she was smart. That would be cool. He liked smart girls.

"Johanna's given her our number, so she should be calling you in the next couple of days."

"I guess I don't have a choice then."

"I just want you to have fun," she said. "Good night, honey. I love you."

She shut the door of his room.

"Love you, too," he said to the closed door, though he was sure she couldn't hear him.

That year, as she had every year since the divorce, Todd's mother had invited several guests over for Christmas dinner. It would be Todd and Brian, Jackie's agent, Nick, Nick's boyfriend, Eduardo, and her old friends Harry and Patricia Clark, a couple who owned a contemporary art gallery in Chelsea. Todd wasn't looking forward to five hours of drunken conversation with his mother's friends.

This was the first time he had been on his own in the apartment in several months, without Ethan, without Alex, without anyone he loved. The building held its share of secrets: the empty elevator that, at certain hours, was filled with the scent of stale perfume; the banker's wife of a certain age who would get on at one floor and get off on another before reaching the lobby. Was she crazy? Having an affair? Jackie would speculate, always. His mother was curious that way, which made Todd think she was probably also curious about him.

He wandered over to the wet bar in the library, sniffing at the bottles, opening the small wood-paneled refrigerator, and taking a quick gulp of chilled vodka. He had already spent part of the afternoon sitting on the floor in his mother's study and examining the basket of Christmas cards that had come from all of Jackie's friends. They were families he had grown up with, childhood friends of his and Brian's, socialites his mother knew through the endless string of parties she was always attending. In the photographs were weddings and babies and families (families with mothers *and* fathers, as if they wanted to dangle this fact in people's faces) standing in front of elaborately decorated Christmas trees. As Todd dressed for dinner that evening, wearing his nice wool slacks and carefully ironing a new shirt his mother had given to him that day, he realized that all of it made him feel horribly alone. He sensed it in his legs, pelvis, chest. If he didn't think about it, he might forget to breathe. Sometimes he wondered if this was what it was like to be dead, in limbo, waiting.

It wasn't that there was no one around—between his mother's chef, Jorge, the housekeeper, and Jackie's personal assistant, Tatiana, the apartment was filled with people from morning until night, to the point where Todd resented the lack of privacy. But there was no one he wanted to talk to. Of all his friends at school, he missed Ethan the most.

Compounding this problem was the fact that Todd hadn't made any effort to hang out with his friends in the city. He had paid for a ticket to a Christmas charity ball, but had backed out at the last minute, claiming he was recovering from the flu. He was afraid his old friends might pick up on something different in him, would sense that he had changed. It was as if what had happened with Ben had branded the word *faggot* on his forehead, and he couldn't erase it.

Warmed by the vodka, he had gone back to his room, where he had jerked off silently with some hand lotion from the Ritz, standing in front of the full-length mirror, examining his own body, turned on by it, but also thinking about Ben and Ethan, the three of them, not in the same fantasy, but an erotic flipbook of different images, rotating kaleidoscopically through his mind, moving so quickly that they morphed into one another, muscles, hair, cock, ass.

Afterward, he rushed to the shower, guiltily scrubbing away all traces of his misbehavior. It was wrong, he knew, this new fixation on guys. Maybe not wrong—intellectually, he knew it was not wrong. Just unacceptable. It didn't seem possible to reconcile it with the rest of his life. He was supposed to be a normal guy, a guy who could step out of a Ralph Lauren ad, or the Berkley catalog, or *The Preppy Handbook*. If he could change it, he would. But deep down, underneath everything, and with a sense of surprise, relief, and shame, he realized he couldn't.

On Christmas Eve, Jackie served champagne in the living room, as everyone sat around an enormous tree on silk-covered Louis XIV chairs. Nick and Eduardo had been the first to arrive. Nick, who was wearing a cashmere blazer and a burgundy ascot, greeted Todd with a hug and a kiss on each cheek. Had Todd unwittingly entered into some kind of secret brotherhood in which kisses were exchanged between men? For the first part of the evening, Todd avoided Nick, using any excuse not to talk to him or Eduardo. (Eduardo, after all, owned an antiques shop in the West Village, and what could be more faggy than that?) As the evening wore on, though, and Todd drank glass after glass of champagne, he started to relax. So maybe he was gay. That didn't mean he had to be like Nick. He could be more like Ben, the young writer who made his body ache.

Over dinner, as the wine and champagne continued to flow,

the group became more raucous. His mother had put the Clarks on either side of Eduardo, knowing they would be able to talk about art and antiques. She sat next to Nick. Todd was across from him, though he avoided looking him in the eye. Brian always got along fine in these situations; he appeared to zone out. Todd would give him glances (*we're in the same boat, bro*), rolling his eyes, but his brother didn't offer a response. Todd tried to focus on the conversation, answering questions when asked. He felt so utterly distant from the entire situation, he might have been a character on the wall murals of partygoers on their yachts, dancing, drinking, looking up at the stars.

"Come on, Nora, let's switch for dessert." Jackie poked at Nick.

"Oh Lord, I haven't used that name in ages!" Nick said.

"What name?" Brian asked.

"It's my drag name," Nick said, somewhat abashed. "We came up with it one Halloween."

"Not that he's done drag in, what, ten years?" Eduardo quickly added. *Don't offend the Clarks*, Todd thought. *Don't want to seem too gay*. Eduardo was an opportunist. Anyone with money could be a potential client for his little shop.

"Named after Dashiell Hammett. Remember?" Nick looked around the table for approval. The Clarks smiled wanly and Brian looked confused. "Well, *I* thought it was clever at the time."

"We all thought it was clever!" Jackie said. "So, what ever happened to her?"

"Oh, honey, she died. Tragic fire. Burnt to a crisp." Nick paused and looked at the star-covered ceiling, divining inspiration from the gods. "But, oh, the funeral! You wouldn't believe it. Incredible. Everyone was there. I mean, *everyone*. Double-page spread in Suzy."

Jackie giggled. Todd had no idea what Nick was talking about.

"Todd, you sit next to Nick. Brian, change with Eduardo."

"Brian, you can tell me about Dartmouth. The boys from Dartmouth were the sweetest," Patricia said, as her husband mumbled something inconclusive.

Following his mother's directions, Todd now found himself sitting next to Nick.

"Jackie, you haven't told us about your latest novel," Eduardo said. "Give us the scoop."

"Oh, you know, it's the usual," she said, keeping one eye on the Filipino woman who was bringing everyone plum pudding with crème fraiche. "Love, murder . . ."

"Death, disfigurement, dementia," Nick said, as if declaiming poetry.

"Murder! I don't know how you dream it up," Patricia said. "It seems so—I don't know—so foreign from our experience. I mean, I've never known anyone who was murdered."

"Oh, anyone can be murdered," Jackie said. "Anyone can commit murder!" She laughed and took another sip of wine.

"What's murder are her deadlines," Nick said.

"It's all too morbid," Patricia said. "I mean, in art, it's fine, but in life, to have to think about it all the time—no, thank you."

"Darling, spend a week inside my head and you'd feel differently. It's all around me. I'm obsessed by it." She paused for a moment, eyes closed, head tilted slightly up, as if atoning for her fixation. Her eyes opened again. "Would anyone like some port?"

After dinner, the guests mingled again in the living room around a blazing fire; everyone raved about the Christmas decorations, as Jackie beamed. There had been some discussion over the past few days between Jackie and Brian about how much it all had cost. New custom ornaments and garlands, lighting, the tree itself, a florist to trim it all: Jackie admitted the decorations had run around twenty thousand dollars. Brian proclaimed it a waste to spend money on such things; Jackie had shrugged, simply saying, "It's fun, and people like it. And when you have your own money, you can do what you want with it."

Now that all this extravagance was being appreciated, Brian was nowhere to be found, most likely smoking on the terrace. Though Todd wouldn't have minded joining his brother, he plopped himself down in an armchair on the other side of the room before realizing he was sitting three feet from Nick.

His mother's agent smiled at him, as if he had been waiting all evening for the young man to talk to him.

"It is a bit much, isn't it?" he said, as he motioned at the decked-out tree, glimmering in the corner like the set of a Broadway musical. "Your mother's never been one for understatement."

Todd shrugged. "No, I guess not."

"You must have your college applications in by now, right? Exciting time."

Todd nodded. "Due a few days ago. Had to run to the FedEx office."

Nick laughed. "Just like Jackie. Always waiting until the last minute. Not a bad thing, of course. Keeps you on your toes. Hell for your agent, though."

"Oh, I'm not a writer at all."

"I doubt that. Some of that Sterling talent has to have rubbed off on you. Do you have a favorite subject?" Nick paused, as Todd faltered. "Oh God, what a stupid question! I feel like I'm a hundred years old asking you that! You must think I'm a silly old queen!"

Todd equivocated, not sure what to say. Ignoring the last part of Nick's statement, he finally admitted he didn't have one. "I am interested in—well, this is kind of dumb—but I'm interested in cooking. I think I might take a class or something. I don't know. I just like doing it."

"I have some cookbooks I could send you. One of my authors was on the best-seller list this fall."

"That would be great," Todd said.

"Okay, everyone!" Jackie shouted from the other side of the room. "We're opening presents!"

Nick leaned in close to Todd. "It was so good to catch up," he said, as he patted Todd's hand and gave him a wink.

Todd wanted to offer a warmer response, but all that came was a tepid smile.

After Nick got up to join the others, Todd squirmed for a moment in his chair as he wondered what that wink meant: *I know something you're not telling me? I know the secret you're hiding?*

Several days after Christmas, there was a phone call for Ethan at his house. He had predictably settled into the routine that took place each year after he and his parents had their sober Christmas celebration, the three of them bundled up in cotton sweaters to keep out the December chill and sipping hot cider, a drink that to Ethan spoke of a level of good cheer he wasn't feeling. The realization had snuck up on him that the company of his parents was no longer enough; it seemed a cruel joke that this would occur to him during the holidays, a time when one's social network was already supposed to be established. Occasionally, he pictured Todd, having fun with all his friends, running around Manhattan. Even though he didn't fit in there, either, it would be better than being at home alone.

His parents were out, and the call had woken him from a nap. He had been sleeping in vast stretches lately, amounts of time inconceivable at school. In dreams, his loneliness was disguised; it came in the form of vicious beasts and cold walks in the woods. It was never so palpable, never the stark grayness it was in life, the sensation of an open wound in the chest, the shape of a curious puzzle piece, waiting to be filled.

He picked up the phone on the third ring and sat up in bed. It was getting dark outside, so he switched on a lamp.

"Ethan? It's Vivian Frasier. My mother gave me your number? I guess our moms thought we could catch a movie, something like that?"

"Sure," Ethan said, after clearing his throat. "That sounds great."

The two decided they would meet for a coffee the next evening and then choose the film they wanted to see.

Ethan went to empty his bladder, and then the phone rang again. It was Hannah. He was momentarily surprised to be hearing from her, but then he remembered: there was nothing unusual about her calling him wherever he happened to be.

"Hey, stranger," she said. "How've you been?"

"Fine," Ethan said. "Sleeping a lot, but fine."

"Just fine? No wild and exciting news?"

"Not really," he said. God, why was he so boring around women? He took a deep breath, hoping Hannah couldn't hear him. "I do have a date tomorrow."

"A date! With whom?"

"This girl. The daughter of someone who works with my mom. I've never met her."

"A blind date."

"Yeah, a blind date." It sounded like such an adult thing to be doing. Taking the cordless phone with him, he started wandering around the house.

"What's her name?"

"Vivian. Vivian Frasier."

"Wait—did she go to Berkley?"

"I think so."

"I never had her in a class, but the name sounds familiar."

"How are things with you?"

"You know, same old stuff. Catching up on reading, paying bills."

"How was your holiday?"

"Fabulous. Ben did a big dinner at his loft. Tons of people. Catered. It was gorgeous." She paused. He could hear music in the background, something that sounded like Gregorian chants. "Have you been reading your books?"

"My books?" The books she had given him. "Yeah, they're really good." He had flipped through the book of Rimbaud's poems, but hadn't started reading it in earnest. It had been sitting on his desk, a talisman of the good things in his life, but he had been afraid to open it. Unread, the book was sure not to disappoint; it kept its mystery. He knew there was no way he could return to school without having read some of it. Why did he feel compelled to please Hannah? Reading the books she had given him, accepting the knowledge she was passing on to him was a key to the outside world. It made him want to be back at Berkley, back at her little house, drinking hot chocolate by candlelight. As he sat in his parents' kitchen, perched on a bar stool near their olive-green tiled countertop, he wondered why he could never enjoy experiences while they were happening.

He heard Hannah's oven buzzer go off. "I've got to get a pie out," she said. "I just wanted to check on how you were doing. And I want to hear all about your date. Call me anytime."

When he wasn't napping, Ethan had been spending his time indulging in another guilty pleasure. At the airport in Hartford, he had bought a copy of Jacqueline Sterling's latest novel, *An Independent Woman*; he had shoved it furtively across the counter at the newsstand cashier, hoping she would quickly stuff it in a paper bag. He kept it hidden until he was on his plane and certain not to see anyone else from school. Guys weren't supposed to read books like this, but he was curious about what went on in Jackie's head, as much as a novel could tell him what a person was thinking. He remembered something she had said about her fiction, the first time he had stayed at her apartment: "My books are my children. When I'm finished with them, they make their way in the world." Ethan knew Todd didn't take his mother's work seriously; he had recounted a conversation they had had when he was fourteen years old and furious at his mother for some injustice. "Mom, you write trash!" Todd claimed he had screamed at her. "I most certainly do not," she had replied. "I write contemporary fiction."

Jackie's novel was the story of a rich woman who was thrown into the role of private investigator when her husband was mysteriously killed. The scenes were violent: there were bloodied corpses and characters killed with pills and poison, all set in the world of the wealthy. As much as Jacqueline Sterling's books would never be regarded as part of the literary canon, Ethan felt that this one transcended a mere airplane read. There was a somber note in her novel, difficult to detect, subtle enough that many readers might miss it. But Ethan felt it, and it gave him new respect for Jackie. He felt jealous that his friend had access to this fantastic creature, this woman filled with sadness and sophistication, and he didn't know it. Only Ethan realized that like his own mother, someday Jackie, too, in all her whirling energy, would be gone.

One afternoon during break, Todd was in his mother's kitchen, attempting to bake an apple cobbler. Hannah had given him the recipe, and he wanted to try making it himself. He couldn't figure out how to give it the lightness, the fluffiness he knew it demanded. As he watched it through the glass door of the oven, he saw the crumbs sink down into the messy glop of chopped apples, sugar, and cinnamon, forming something more like a sludge than a dessert. It would still taste fine, but it wouldn't look the same. If he ever made it for Ethan—he wanted to, someday—he would know the difference.

While Todd crouched in front of the oven, Brian popped into the kitchen to grab a glass of water. "You've been spending a lot of time at home," he said.

Todd offered a "hmmm" in response. He was afraid his brother could tell something had shifted within him. He was convinced his mom already knew. It would thrill her—a sick part of him sensed that. She would expect him to go shopping with her (not that he hadn't already spent a good portion of his childhood—a portion he wanted to forget, humiliating as it was—trailing behind her in department stores), would want to hear about his crushes, would want to tell him about the men she was seeing. He couldn't bear it. He had overheard her talking with Nick once, late at night, when they were deep in their cups, about how to give a good blow job. There was no way he was going to fulfill that role for his mother.

As for Brian, Todd wasn't sure how he would feel. He was tolerant, yes, in the way that anyone with a mother like theirs would be. But he didn't have any gay friends. He was in a fraternity at Dartmouth. He was a notorious Casanova (he had lost his virginity at age fourteen to a Swedish au pair working at his best friend's house; Todd hadn't started sleeping with girls until a year ago). Perhaps Brian's skirt-chasing was in his favor, as it was always the guys who weren't scoring who were most uncomfortable with homosexuality (how Todd detested that word: it was so clinical, as if it were a disease!).

His brother leaned against the sink as he drank his water. "What's with the baking? You've never done that before."

Todd thought he detected a sneer in his brother's voice. "I don't know. Something to do. Jorge doesn't seem to mind." Jackie's chef had always taken a liking to Todd.

"How are things? You've been really quiet lately."

"Just stressed. College admissions, all that stuff." Todd checked the apple cobbler again. It was still a sugary lavalike mess, but at least it had started filling the kitchen with its warm, sweet smell.

"Just wait it out. You'll be fine. Hell, I didn't think I was going to get in anywhere."

Todd knew that wasn't true. His brother had earned a nearly perfect grade point average at Berkley, had brilliant recommendations.

Brian started chattering on about a party he was going to, and did Todd want to come? Todd said he would think about it. His relationship with his brother had always been strained. Other siblings had a shorthand by which they communicated, a series of signs and signals, communications as simple as a grunt or a glance: Todd noticed this on airplanes, in school, among his friends. He had never felt that way about Brian. They didn't even look alike; his older brother was dark, with close-cropped brown hair. When they went to Georgica Beach in East Hampton, he would turn brown like a nut, while Todd burned after fifteen minutes, the pink freckles on his cheeks blooming like an archipelago of islands. It was as if they had had two different fathers, though Todd knew this was not the case. He could admit they shared the same eyes, similar noses; he could see the resemblance between both of them and their dad.

It was easier to notice, particularly, in pictures of the younger Don Eldon; Brian was often in the pictures, too. As the older son, he had spent more time with their father, which made Todd jealous. It was the peculiar case with younger brothers: there was always a history, a past before they were born, that could never be recovered or relived, no matter how many experiences they had, how many new pictures or home movies were taken. In those old photos, faded after years of being displayed, Todd could see the connection, something he would never share, between the three of them, standing in Central Park, laughing near the Alice in Wonderland sculpture, Brian hanging around his father's neck like a little animal, his mother looking as if she couldn't believe her good fortune at having such an attractive husband and child. His father would be grinning, lean and trim, a thick mane of hair, a bristly blond mustache. In those pictures, he stood proudly next to Jackie. Those were the days before she was famous, when she was just Jackie Eldon, a woman who was lithe and natural in a sundress, no makeup required, her face not a mask but an open canvas, waiting, expectant.

Brian had always gotten more attention from her. When they were little and would go to bed around the same time, Jackie always said good night to Brian first. He would tell her about his day in excruciating detail, about what had happened at school, the teachers he liked and the ones he didn't. Brian was the talented one, but he required more maintenance; Todd floated along on a cloud of mediocrity. Every night during their childhood, as Todd waited patiently in his bed, he would hear his mother talking to his brother through the closed door that separated their rooms. And every night, by the time Jackie had finished putting Brian to bed, Todd was already asleep.

CHAPTER 9

"You must be Ethan."

Ethan greeted Vivian Frasier and walked with her to the midnight-blue Jeep Cherokee that was parked in the driveway behind his parents' cars. He took a deep breath before stepping up into her car. Perhaps this had been a bad idea. The difference, somehow, between senior year of high school and freshman year of college seemed so great.

As they drove to University Avenue, Vivian said she "loved" Stanford, and enumerated the reasons why, none of which seemed terribly compelling to Ethan: she "adored" her friends, she was "crazy about" her professors, everyone was so "open," she was taking a poetry class that was "amazing." Ethan had always been suspicious of such superlatives, for they indicated a level of comfort with the world he suspected he might never attain.

Even though she had moved with her parents from Evanston, Vivian still looked like a California girl: she had blond hair and watery blue eyes that crinkled at the corners when she smiled. As they sat together over coffee, discussing Palo Alto, the university, life at Berkley, Ethan tried not to stare at the point where her white peasant blouse was tied in a crisscross pattern, revealing the slightest triangle of pale white breastbone. He fidgeted with his hands instead.

There was a pause in their conversation, and Ethan asked her which classes she had taken at Berkley. "Did you ever take an English class with Ms. McClellan?"

"No," she said. "I'm sure her classes are good, though she's a little crazy."

"How so?" He felt his brow furrow.

"Well," Vivian said, "there was a whole drama about her divorce. A friend of mine said she had to flee France to get away from her ex-husband."

"I thought he was cheating on her." He had heard this while hanging out in the room of Robbie de Sola, a classmate whose father was the president of a small South American country, and whose older sister had been at Berkley at the time. Then, hearing the gossip had made him feel sorry for Hannah; now repeating it felt as bad as perpetrating the injustice itself.

"My friend was her advisee. Ms. McClellan used to invite her over at night, regale her with stories of what a head case her ex was. But from what I've heard, she was just as bad."

"What do you mean?"

"A year or so after she arrived, she developed a crush on one of her colleagues in the English department. He wouldn't have been there, hardly had any teaching experience, except that his fiancée had taught for a few years before he arrived, and they wanted to be together. Ms. McClellan started harassing the woman and flirting with him like crazy. It was near the end of the school year, and they were getting married over the summer. The next fall, neither of them came back. People said she chased them away."

Ethan scoffed. "Come on. How would she do that?"

"There was something weird about a dog—she was taking care of their dog while they were on vacation. I guess they didn't know she was as jealous of them as she was. She told them the dog was sick, like seriously sick, so they would have to cut their trip short. Turned out it was nothing." Vivian took a sip of her soy latte before delicately wiping the foam off her upper lip.

A grin broke out over her face; Ethan could see she was enjoying this. "Oh! This one was the best. I think the woman was from Rome—she taught Italian—and Ms. McClellan kept telling her how easy it would be to get her deported." Vivian shook her head. "Crazy stuff."

Ethan blinked as he listened to the stories, wondering if they were true. "And all this is through your friend?"

Vivian nodded. "I know, I know—I shouldn't be such a gossip. But it's juicy, you've got to admit that."

"It's ridiculous. I don't think Hannah would ever do those things."

"'Hannah'?"

"You know, Ms. McClellan."

Vivian took another sip of her latte, giving Ethan a sly smile. "I don't know," she said. "I wouldn't be so sure."

Ethan wanted to change the subject. "Did you have a boyfriend when you were at Berkley?" he asked carefully.

Vivian laughed at him. "You make it sound like it's winning the lottery or something! Sure, I had a few."

Ethan started playing with his napkin, wincing at his ridiculousness, and she softened.

"No—I know what you mean. It's not easy. I think the girls there would probably be a little too, I don't know—maybe too immature for you?"

"Yeah, people seem to say that about me." He thought of his conversations with Hannah. (Hannah who harassed people! Hannah who threatened to get people deported! He couldn't let it go.)

"You'll meet someone," she said. "You never know. Don't think about it, and it will happen."

At the end of the evening, after catching a revival of *Sunset*

Boulevard at the Stanford Theater (Vivian mentioned that a film studies professor of hers had insisted his students see it over the break), they pulled up to Ethan's house. He was suddenly sorry the date was over. Before he got out of the car, Vivian gave him a peck on the cheek. "I had fun," she said. "Let's do this again sometime."

The next day was Ethan's eighteenth birthday. Because it fell in that awkward period of time between Christmas and New Year's, when everyone was either on vacation or recovering from the holidays, it had never been celebrated with much fanfare. He couldn't remember the last time he had a birthday party.

He insisted that his parents didn't go to any trouble; he knew they had more important things to worry about. His mother picked up a small, generic cake at the supermarket, but she had forgotten to buy candles. (The latest medication she had been taking made forgetfulness less a handful of isolated incidents and more a way of life.) That evening, after a normal dinner of lasagna, his mother placed the little cake on the kitchen table; it was studded with three crumbling candles she had found at the back of an odds and ends drawer. After it was cut, there were a few presents to be unwrapped: a sweater he imagined never wearing; two fiction anthologies; a gift certificate to an art supply store. He loved his parents, but it wasn't supposed to be like this; he was supposed to have friends, to have people his own age who would remember his birthday, who might even—dare he imagine it?—buy him gifts. Todd hadn't called, and neither had Hannah. And everyone else—well, who was he really friends with at school anyway? Were things any better than they had been a year ago? He tried not to care, as he willed it to be over, willed the new year to bring him something different. The day had been merely a reminder of everything that wasn't going right in his life, a sign that another year had passed and most things were still the same.

Several days later, he was sprawled out on the living room couch, trying to get into Rimbaud. There was a poem Hannah had placed a star by, one entitled "Romance." The second to last line was, "Nobody's serious when they're seventeen." He wondered what she had meant by marking the poem for him.

The phone rang; it was Hannah. "You never called me," she said. "How did your date go?"

"It was fine."

"Are you going to see her again?"

"I don't know. I'd like to."

"It's too bad she lives in California."

Ethan sighed. He didn't know if he should mention to Hannah what Vivian had said. He wanted to know everything about Hannah, to know her secrets. "Hannah, Vivian said some stuff about you that I was wondering about."

There was a pause on the line. "Really. Such as?"

"Nothing much; it was no big deal. She just said that there was an incident—something about another English teacher—a couple having to leave the school? I'm sorry—it's none of my business." He realized he would have to stay vague about the story in order to ask her about it at all; he couldn't accuse her of the type of behavior Vivian had.

"It's fine, don't worry about it," she said. "He was a friend of mine, but his girlfriend wasn't having it. She got a better offer to teach Italian at Andover over the summer, after they were married, so they both left Berkley. It had nothing to do with me."

"I guess Vivian got the story wrong."

"That's right," she said. "You can't believe everything you hear."

Despite her storytelling, and for lack of any female company his own age, Ethan still wanted to see Vivian again. He waited several days before calling her, knowing his vacation would be over in less than a week. Outside, rain rattled against the window screens.

"Ethan," she said, after he asked if she wanted to go out again,

"I think you're really sweet. But I'm sort of seeing someone right now. I wanted to meet you, because I heard you were a great guy. Maybe we can hang out again next time you're back home."

His face burned as he put down the phone. His mother was in her study working on an essay for an academic journal. He burst in, though it had always been family protocol to knock.

"Why did you do this to me?" he asked.

Judith swiveled around in her office chair and looked at Ethan. "Do what? Honey, what's wrong?"

"Vivian. Sending me on a date with her. She's seeing someone. And she's so far out of my league, it's not even funny." He stared down at the sisal carpet, worn from years of his mother's daily journey from door to desk.

"She is certainly not. Johanna said she was delighted to meet you."

"Mom, she has a *boyfriend*. The whole date was pointless."

Judith rolled her eyes as she pushed up the sleeves of her sweater. "Well, for God's sake, Ethan, I didn't suggest the date so that you could become her boyfriend."

"I'm not saying I wanted to. It's just that you set me up with all these expectations. And then she turned out to be beautiful—" He flopped down on the leather ottoman in the corner and threw his head in his hands, uttering a frustrated groan. "I am so sick of being who I am! Why couldn't I have been born as someone different? Why do I have to have two professors for parents? Everyone at Berkley is rich and successful, and I feel like a loser all the time."

"You are not a loser," his mother snapped. "You're being ridiculous."

His father stood in the doorway, checking what all the fuss was about. Ethan held back the tears he felt welling up inside him. He wasn't going to cry in front of his parents, not about this.

"You have a lot to offer, a lot that's different from the others at school," his mother continued. "You need to find a girl who will appreciate that."

"Hell, not just a girl," his father said, one hand on the door frame, the other waving expansively toward Ethan. "A woman. You need to find a woman."

Ethan looked up at them expectantly, as if they might tell him how he would go about such a thing, but they said nothing. His mother got up from her chair and his father retreated to the den as Ethan stayed perched on the ottoman, his head in his lap. Judith sat next to him and hugged him awkwardly, as if she could protect him, even though they both knew that whatever efforts she could now manage would be deficient.

II

HISTORY

From the school's official portrait of Louisa Berkley, it was clear that what its benefactor lacked in beauty, she made up for in composure. Though the likeness had been painted when she was in her mid-thirties, her hair was styled in a way that would have been fetching on a girl half her age. She gazed out into the dining hall like a silent film star: dark, mysterious, lonely, wearing a simple black dress, a single strand of pearls against her pale flesh, a white cameo brooch pinned at her breast, lips bright red. She looked like a matron dressed up for a costume ball, an aging flapper who had gotten lost on her way to the cabaret and found herself decades later sitting above a fireplace at a New England prep school. The hint of a smile, very nearly a smirk, indicated that she didn't care, that it was all a ruse, that she had better places to be. It was the look of a woman in love.

Born Louisa Katherine Cabot in 1883, she had been raised on Fifth Avenue, the only daughter of Edward Cabot, a prominent New York banker. Her mother had died in childbirth, and she was brought up by the household staff. When she turned eighteen, her father and his new wife threw her a coming-out party in their ballroom. The room was decorated with dozens of miniature silk hot air balloons, and Louisa was dressed in a cream-colored gown that had been corseted so tight, she could barely swallow a spoonful of soup. At the party, she met Frederick Joseph Berkley, the twenty-nine-year-old Yale-educated son of a Massachusetts industrialist. The Berkley family made guns; Frederick was the president of the arms company that bore his family's name. His father, an eccentric inventor, had been responsible for a number of innovations in the field of firearms, including, most notably, the Berkley Repeating Rifle. The Berkley Arms Company had been tremendously successful during the Civil War, when it sold guns to both the Union and Confederate armies. As the two of them danced a slow Boston waltz, Louisa had listened, wide-eyed, to these facts, mentally recording notes, imagining what it would be like to marry him. Later in the evening, Louisa slipped the bandleader a sheet of ragtime music, and led Frederick Berkley in a cakewalk that scandalized all her guests. Frederick, who was tired of the usual run of society girls, was mesmerized.

Nine months after their initial meeting, Louisa married Frederick Berkley, and the two moved to his family's estate outside the small town of Wilton, Massachusetts. She gradually adjusted to the pressures of managing a household and the responsibilities of country life, though she made regular trips to New York, frequenting nightclubs and dance halls with her young friends, going to see popular plays, and dining out, as well as spending several summers abroad. By the time she was twenty-one, Frederick pleaded with her to settle down and start thinking about having children. She wanted to please him, so she stopped going into the city, instead ordering what she needed from department store catalogs and catching up on local gossip through letters from friends. Like an observer watching from afar, she could see herself becoming more and more the industrialist's wife, and she fought this impulse violently. Louisa believed she loved Frederick, but she refused to be subjugated to a mindless country existence. She had no formal education, but she knew she couldn't turn off her conscience at will. It disturbed her that the house had been financed by bloodshed. Every automobile, every fur coat, every loaf of bread or leg of lamb represented guns and bullets purchased, soldiers and civilians shot and killed. As a form of reparation, she did things she imagined would help society. She gave generously to the town library and the local schools; she insisted that Frederick make large donations to museums, the opera, and the symphony. She commissioned works by local craftsmen, in an attempt to boost the economy; she had her salon painted in a French pastoral scene, complete with silk balloons floating through the sky, just as they had at her coming out party. Her tastes in entertainment were eclectic; she held séances and poetry readings in her living room, sponsored lectures in the town hall on topics like suffrage and the importance of education for young women. She funded a local theater troupe's production of *Salome*. Frederick indulged her whims, but kept stressing the need to produce an heir to carry on the Berkley legacy. Finally, after nearly a year of trying, she became pregnant and started readying the house for the arrival of what she hoped would be a boy, a little body running around the three empty floors of the Berkley manor.

And then, nothing.

The first miscarriage had happened when she was in her second month, nothing more than blood on the sheets, sheets she promptly sent to the basement to be incinerated.

Then a second, and a third. Then a stillborn child. It was a little girl, born at eight months. She buried her in the town cemetery, planting a pink rosebush next to the miniature headstone. She started to wear black nearly all the time.

When her doctor told her he did not believe she would be able to bear children, she became hysterical, locking herself in her room for three days, screaming at the servants, and tearing at her bedcurtains. She was taken to a sanitarium in a nearby town, where she was put in solitary confinement for six weeks. She knew Frederick was disappointed. She had failed him by not providing the one thing he wanted from her. It didn't surprise her when he started traveling into the city more often, ostensibly for business, though she suspected him of having an affair.

When she was released from the sanitarium, her doctor diagnosed her with neurasthenia, prescribing continuous bedrest as a cure, which only exacerbated her sense of malaise. She would sleep all day, waking at night to wander the halls, barely able to eat, to read, to listen to music. Half the time, Frederick was away. The worst part was that she didn't care. When she did see him, he was a man she barely recognized.

Louisa would go through better periods, times when she would be up and about during the day, gliding through the house in a silk kimono, concocting elaborate plans to build additions to the property, to host a ball for her friends in New York, to travel to Europe with her father. None of it ever materialized; before her plans came to fruition, she would collapse into another hysterical spell. She had become a frightened woman. The world would not grant her a baby; she could only imagine what other tragedies it had in store.

During one of her particularly troubled periods, some of the local citizens were concerned about their benefactress. The town librarian, Mrs. Pennington, suggested that perhaps she would enjoy having someone read to her.

Fine, Louisa wrote, in a note responding to the woman's query, *but I don't want one of these nurses from the convent. Send me a boy.*

Cedric Hill, a bright young man from the local high school, was sent to read to her every afternoon, a job for which he was paid the extravagant sum of one dollar a day. Together, the two of them read everything from the *Wilton Record* to the *Times* to Tolstoy and Zola, Flaubert and Maugham, Wharton and James. Each day, their meeting gave Louisa something to look forward to, and she would prepare for hours, meticulously planning what she would wear, what room they would sit in, how her makeup and hair would be arranged. As her health and energy improved, they began walking on the grounds. The son of a gardener, Cedric taught her the precise names of the different flowers and plants, something she never had learned, having grown up in New York City. Louisa soon started to resume her regular duties as lady of the house, crediting Cedric with her recovery. She dismissed the local doctor who had originally confined her to bed.

It was rumored that she and Cedric, who was now a strapping youth of seventeen, were having an affair. When her husband was away, the staff created elaborate seven-course meals for the two of them. She took the boy to concerts and plays in nearby towns, and let him drive her Studebaker. In her bedroom, the doors locked and the house shut down for the night, they would make love, and she realized how cold and distant her relationship with Frederick really was. Whatever she had with Cedric—love, lust, or otherwise—was far more satisfying. In her rush to have children, she had robbed herself of these physical pleasures: the simple enjoyment of running her fingers through his straw-like hair that hung lazily over his eyes, touching his taut muscles, honed through years of working with his father. Cedric was happy to comply with her needs, and Louisa returned to her good self, the persona of a bohemian sensualist. They tasted wines together, ate exotic foods, took the train to New York for shopping and theater. Once, she ran into some of her old friends on the street. Years ago, she might have worried about what they would think, but now she shrugged off their glances. She was a rich woman with a young lover: what could be more wonderful?

As she heard more about Cedric's life, she learned that he was not getting a proper education from the local public school system. The one private school in the area, Wilton Academy, was located at the top of a hill on the outskirts of town. Founded in 1856, Wilton Academy was a school for feebleminded boys with wealthy parents. Its enrollment had been dwindling over the last twenty years, however, and it was on the verge of being shut down. Its land, which had previously housed a seminary, was nonetheless a prime spot for a boarding school, and Louisa felt that rather than opening a new school, she would make a large grant to reestablish Wilton Academy as a school of superior learning. Louisa had a new board of directors appointed, including her and her husband. Frederick, delighted his wife had found a cause to occupy her time, was happy to support her endeavors.

In 1918, several days before the groundbreaking for the school's new main building, Frederick was killed during a burglary of his Park Avenue pied-à-terre. The police noted that he had been shot by a pistol manufactured by his own company. They did not tell his wife that there had been a witness to the crime, Claudette Kelly, a chorus girl who had locked herself in the bedroom while Frederick attempted to fight off his attackers.

Louisa immediately announced that the school's name would be changed to Berkley Academy, in memory of her late husband.

After she hired him a tutor for the summer, Cedric went on to attend Yale University, just as her husband had nearly thirty years earlier. A letter of recommendation from her plus a generous donation ensured his acceptance.

The board of her own school, however, proved to be a cantankerous lot, full of bankers and businessmen and educators who had their own opinions of how the school should be run. Though Berkley Academy was almost entirely funded on her own money, Louisa became increasingly withdrawn from its day-to-day business. After several years, she retreated to a penthouse suite at the Plaza Hotel, receiving the occasional visitor, but turning most away. Her days were spent walking in the park, reading, and eating meals alone. She continued to contact Cedric while he was at school, but his visits became more and more brief, until finally he stopped coming at all, merely acknowledging her letters with a quick jotted postcard, or a snapshot taken of him at a football game or campus party. Eventually, even those missives stopped, and Louisa didn't hear from him for most of his senior year.

In 1922, Louisa Berkley jumped from the window of her penthouse suite, skirt billowing out like the wings of a bird as she traveled to the ground, breathless, her heart having stopped, missing the hotel canopy and landing at the doorman's feet, a crumpled, broken pile of black.

When her room was searched, authorities found a half-empty bottle of bootleg gin on her nightstand. Next to it was an invitation to Cedric Hill's wedding that had arrived that day with the post.

In addition to the statues of Louisa and Frederick Berkley that stand over their graves, there is now a bronze statue of Cedric Hill, the first Berkley Boy, near the main entrance to the school. Students are said to touch his nose for good luck before important exams. Over the years, the nose has been rubbed clean, polished and shiny like an apple.

III

WINTER

CHAPTER 10

In previous winter terms, Todd had always swum for Berkley's junior varsity team. While he was an adequate swimmer, he had never been a starter, was never one of the nimble-bodied young men who took to the water like fish, the ones who spent so much time in the pool that their hair was always wet or frozen. This winter, Todd longed to do something that would set him apart from his classmates.

Several days into the new semester, Hannah mentioned to him that business at the tearoom had been so brisk in the past few months that the arthritic Madame Beauchamp had increased her order of pies and cakes from seven to ten per week. Hannah didn't know if she could satisfy the increased demand, as her schedule was already strained by the current order. The old French lady had been hysterical when Hannah told her, as she insisted that her desserts were the best in the area. Sensing an opportunity, Todd asked Hannah if he could help, and the two decided that he would be the first student in Berkley history to do a winter special project in baking. They agreed they would donate their profits to the restoration efforts in the school cemetery, specifically to fix the decaying monument to Louisa Berkley that had been neglected over the years.

In the first few weeks, Todd learned from Hannah everything she knew about baking. Her expertise was staggering; Todd didn't know if he would be able to absorb all of her techniques. How to get the crust right, her method of frosting a cake, the best way to slice fruit. How a touch of lemon zest added extra flavor to a cheesecake, how a dash of salt brought out the taste of the fruit in a cobbler. He began to know her refrigerator as if it were his own—its shelves of exotic condiments, organic produce, rare cheeses, wines, a bottle of vintage champagne. He loved the transformative aspect of it, how raw butter and flour turned into dough, how a cold pile of ingredients became a steaming confection. Nothing was the same as it had been; everything changed, by adding energy, heat, creativity. With a trip to the supermarket and by following instructions, he, Todd Eldon—who could, in his own estimation, do almost nothing of value—was creating something wondrous and sweet.

One afternoon, Todd and Hannah stood at her kitchen counter, the day's baking in front of them. They had made a flourless chocolate cake decorated with dark chocolate shavings, a pecan pie, and a carrot cake. That would cover the order for the first part of the week.

"You're getting better and better," she said, examining his handiwork. "I'm impressed." Her apron—she was wiping her hands on it now—was splattered like a Pollock canvas with butter, flour, chocolate.

Todd shrugged. "It's not that big a deal."

"You're creating something. That's what's important." Hannah brushed a dusting of sugar from the counter into her hand. "Cooking is a fabulous skill to have if you want to impress someone you're interested in. I know I would just melt if a guy brought me something he had baked."

"I'm not interested in anyone right now." Todd went to the

cabinet to get a mug, anything to avoid this line of questioning. The first one he pulled out was white with a heart on it. Embarrassed, he quickly put it back in the cupboard and selected another.

"Really?" Hannah asked. "There must be someone."

Could he put it out of his mind long enough so that it would disappear? Why did it keep coming back like a bad memory?

"There's no one," he finally said, as he poured himself a cup of tea from the pot Hannah had brewed.

When he turned away from the sink a few moments later, he noticed Hannah looking at his book bag. The flap was open and the cover of Ethan's copy of the Capote novel was barely visible. Hannah pointed to it.

"That book. Where did you get it?"

"Ethan let me borrow it."

"I see." She pursed her lips, just slightly.

"Was I not supposed to have it? I can give it back to him if you want." Todd felt guilty, plagued with the suspicion that he shouldn't have asked Ethan for the book. It was his friend's private bond with Hannah; she hadn't given Todd anything for Christmas. After he finished it, he would give it back to Ethan. He would forget he had ever had it in his possession. That would set things right.

"It doesn't matter," Hannah said. "Enjoy it. It's a good story."

Ethan returned to Berkley after winter break feeling like he was entering a new chapter of his life; there was no invocation, no foreshadowing to tell him what might be waiting for him, and for the first time, he didn't mind. He worried about what Vivian Frasier had told him, but he didn't dare speak to anyone about it. It was unlikely that Hannah had harassed her colleagues, that she had made anyone leave the school. Whatever Vivian's motives were (and he wasn't even sure if she had motives, or if she was simply repeating gossip), Ethan decided to ignore what she had told him. Hannah was too good a person for any of it to be true. She had also become too much a part of his life for him to consider letting her go.

On his first night back, exhausted from his trip and in that half-light between wakefulness and sleep, he had a strange sensation: as he was drifting off, he sensed her on his sheets, the same aroma of lotion and perfume he had grown used to. It seemed improbable, yet he felt she had been there. It might have happened, could have happened. He dreamed of her throwing an old coat over her silk nightgown and running up the snowy golf course. She let herself into Slater. Mr. Sargent, the dorm head, gave her the master room key; she told him she needed to get a book to send to one of her students. Hannah padded down the hall, her boots soggy. The dorm was chilly; the heat had been turned off everywhere but the faculty apartments. She unlocked Ethan's room. It was exactly as he had left it. She ran her fingers over his books, opened his drawers, examined his closet. His bed was made neatly. She climbed in. She would rest there, just for a moment.

When Ethan woke the next morning, the smell was still there, but he thought nothing of it. He opened a window to air out the room.

One evening, about a week into the new semester, Hannah called Ethan at his dorm. "Come down to the house," she said. "There's something I want you to see."

He felt his stomach flip-flop, as he wondered what it could be. He quickly put on his boots and coat and rushed out of the dorm toward Hannah's house. Several days earlier, she had mentioned some more projects that she needed his help with—only, of course, if he had the time. Painting the ceiling in her study, wallpapering the downstairs bathroom. Ethan said he would be happy to help. She offered to pay him, but this time he refused. He didn't feel right accepting her money now, after they had become so friendly. He also didn't know where she was getting the cash—it bothered him that she might be scrimping to keep him around.

Shadows played on the tundra field of ice that blanketed the golf course. As he neared her porch, he saw that the living room was dark. He knocked on the front door, and Hannah opened it.

"Close your eyes," she said.

He did as he was told.

"Now step forward. That's it . . . one more step. Okay, now open them!"

Ethan opened his eyes. The dining table was laid out with a frosted cake, ablaze with candles, with the words *Happy Birthday, Ethan* written on it. The top of the cake was ringed with blueberries. Todd was standing next to the table, grinning.

"Surprise!" they both shouted.

Ethan was taken aback. "But—but my birthday was two weeks ago . . . how did you know?"

"Todd mentioned it to me, so we decided to bake you a cake," Hannah said. "Our own special recipe. I don't know why you didn't tell me earlier!"

"I'm not really into birthdays," Ethan said.

"Oh, come on!" Todd laughed.

"Your birthday is the most important day of the year!" Hannah said. "Now, make a wish and blow out your candles."

He couldn't believe it. Hannah and Todd had made this blueberry sponge layer cake—a real cake, not one from the supermarket—all for him, because they cared about him, because they loved him. Hannah was right. Birthdays should be special. Why had he essentially told his parents to ignore his? He knew his mother didn't want to, but it had always seemed silly, the years when she had decorated the kitchen with streamers and balloons just for the three of them. Ethan leaned over the cake, not certain what to wish for. Something hit him, a vague impression, like a stick-drawn imprint in the snow, of what it would be like to be happy. He decided he would wish for that.

Ethan had become engrossed that semester in a special painting project that would be advised by Susan Hedge. He wanted to do something narrative, so she asked him to pick a favorite fairy tale from his childhood. He had always loved the story of Hansel and Gretel, and he knew that the dark woods, the witch's candy house, and the two lost children would provide rich material. He decided to do a series of paintings that set the tale at Berkley, in locations familiar to every student: the nearby woods, the lake, the stream, the faculty houses. Ethan wanted to show in his paintings the darkness that surrounded people beyond their field of vision. He imagined the parents casting the children out of their house, the trail of crumbs they left behind, the witch being pushed into the oven. He had read this story as a child, but there was something about it now that appealed even more. His life was different from everyone else's; it was not the clean-cut, spit-polished jubilation of his fellow students. His mother was ill; he was friends, close friends, with one of his teachers. Sometimes he would think he knew nothing, that he wanted more to happen in his life, so he could own those feelings of darkness and rage, could feel he was a member of a different clan of people, people to whom *serious shit had really happened*, as if this were a marker that one had truly lived. And sometimes, when he thought about his mother, about the fact that she was dying (that—within a year—yes, it was true—she could be dead), he wished for every-thing to be peaceful, for nothing to happen at all, for the bland pleasantness of neutrality.

He told Hannah about his project one afternoon as they sat in her kitchen, and she approved wholeheartedly. "You'll have to do that painting you promised me."

"Of course," Ethan said. He looked over to her laptop sitting on the dining table, surrounded by what looked like pages from a manuscript. "What are you working on?"

Hannah sighed. "My novel. It's going slower than I expected. It will never be as good as what I have in my mind."

"I didn't know you were writing a novel."

She smiled, cradling her chin in her hand. "There's a lot you don't know about me."

"What's it about?"

"It's the story of Louisa Berkley." Hannah went over to the mantel and picked up the framed photograph of the older woman that Ethan had remembered examining in the fall. "Here she is."

Ethan looked at the photograph more closely, the severe haircut of the woman, her low-cut dress. "It's similar to her portrait in the dining hall."

"It was taken around the same time." She put back the frame. It was odd how Hannah had placed this photograph of a woman not related to her, a woman she was writing into her book, on her mantel along with photographs of people he assumed were her family. It made him wonder about the pictures of the lone boy, the only pictures that looked like they had been taken recently.

"What's the story about?"

"It's about her relationship with a young man who helped her when she was sick."

"What do you mean, 'relationship'?"

Hannah waved her hand nonchalantly. "They were sleeping together. I mean, the school archives all but state that as a fact."

"How old was he?"

"He was seventeen, and she was . . ." She paused for a moment. "In her thirties, I think."

"Do they end up together? In the book, I mean."

There was a sadness in Hannah's eyes. "No," she said, "unfortunately they don't. He marries a girl he meets at Yale."

"And what happens to Louisa Berkley?"

"In real life, she jumped from the penthouse of the Plaza

Hotel. But in my version, she goes to Paris and kills herself there."

"That's so depressing. Why do you want to write about a woman killing herself?" He felt himself frowning.

Hannah gave him a serious look. "I think that only those who have contemplated death can fully appreciate life."

He wondered if she could be right. He had never thought about this, even with his mother, even with everything.

"Why Paris?" Ethan had never been there, though he had read about it, heard stories about it. His parents had been there, while his mother was pregnant with him. During his childhood, he had been to London, Rome, and Vienna during a whirlwind summer trip through Europe. His parents had nothing against Paris, but they had enjoyed plenty of time there on their honeymoon, and weren't in a hurry to go back, at least not for a vacation. His mother had spent a few weeks there doing research for her book on Simone de Beauvoir when he was a child, but he had been in school during that time.

"It's more romantic, don't you think? Paris is a place where you can reinvent yourself, where you can be anyone you want to be."

It sounded wonderful, he had to admit. "What do you mean?"

Her eyes glazed over for a moment, as if she were transported to another place. She went over to the couch and flopped down on it, the mere thought of Paris exhausting her. "You arrive, and no one knows you—and that's a good thing. Every day, even when you're alone, feels like a perfect date. And then—when you're in love! It's even better when you're in love. The city is a shimmering confection. Everything becomes beautiful. The lights, of course, the architecture, but even things that are pedestrian—a half-smoked cigarette tossed on the street, the men on the garbage trucks, the fat woman who runs the local patisserie . . ." He loved the way it sounded; he thought he loved the way it sounded.

"But Louisa Berkley wasn't in love at that time. At least in your novel she's not, is she?"

"When she moves to Paris, she's heartbroken. But it's a city of travelers. It's a place you go to restore yourself, to meet a handsome stranger, to have a fling."

"So she goes to Paris, but then she kills herself? That sounds crazy." Perhaps it was crazy, or maybe it was brilliant. He didn't know which.

Hannah looked at him with a mad grin. "Well, of course it's crazy. That's what makes it perfect."

Several days later, Ethan met with Ms. Hedge about his special project. As he sat in her office, on the threadbare gray tweed sofa, she looked over his initial sketches, nodding with approval, occasionally punctuating the silence with a "hmmm" or an "oh yes." The room had that plaster smell that permeated the art wing, a fecund mixture of wax, clay, and pencil.

Ethan remembered something Hannah had told him. "Ms. McClellan said she might be able to arrange for me to show my paintings at the tearoom."

"Really?" Ms. Hedge looked at Ethan over her thick eyeglasses. "That sounds very nice," she said curtly.

Ethan started speaking more quickly. "I was talking with her the other day, and she was saying that if I did that, it might be a good bit of information for the people in college admissions to know about."

"I'm sure it would be helpful."

Ethan suddenly felt awkward under Ms. Hedge's gaze.

"You're not in one of Ms. McClellan's classes, are you?"

"Oh no," Ethan said. "We're just friends."

"Friends."

"Yeah, I help her with her projects every so often."

"I see."

"Is something wrong?" Ethan tried to read his adviser's expression.

"No, nothing's wrong, I just don't want you getting distracted from your work."

Ethan shifted on the little couch. Ms. Hedge turned back to the sketches, adjusting the glasses that had slid down on her nose. He thought of her buying them at the local drugstore after a pair were lost or broken, and it filled him with sadness, the idea of his teacher searching through a mirrored rotating rack for a pair that would frame her owlish eyes. He imagined accompanying her on this errand; perhaps he, too, would get new glasses, at the mall, or at the optometrist in a nearby town. But he didn't like the idea of hanging out with her. As his adviser, she had offered to drive him whenever he needed something, but he had never taken her up on it. It was as if she would be his mother, and he would be her son.

"Ethan, I was going to mention that I—well, Cass and I, we would love to have you over for dinner sometime. You name the date."

"Thanks—that's so nice of you—I, I guess I'll let you know. Things are kind of crazy right now and all—"

"Of course—there's no rush."

At that moment, Ms. Davis appeared at the door of the art department office. She was wearing hiking boots and a down parka with a mismatched purple wool scarf tied around her neck. She looked at Ms. Hedge. "Are you ready for our walk?"

"Yes, of course—we were just finishing up," Ms. Hedge said. Ethan detected a blush in her cheeks as she spoke to his English teacher. Ms. Hedge and Ms. Davis were an unlikely pair. Cass Davis was still young, in her late twenties. Students would snicker in the dining hall over the two of them, but Ethan thought it was sweet. They reminded him of his parents, bumbling along, two idiosyncratic loners who were able to enjoy each other's company despite the scrutiny of the rest of the world.

Ms. Davis looked at Ethan, then back at Ms. Hedge. "Maybe Ethan would like to come? We're walking over to the old quarry. It's supposed to be beautiful there at this time of year, everything dusted with snow."

"I should be going back to the dorm," he said quickly. "I have to get some studying done."

"You're too good, Ethan, too good," Ms. Davis said.

Ethan got up and left the office with his portfolio, shame creeping over him like mice. As much as he liked them, he was lying to these women. He didn't have to get back to the dorm. He was on his way to visit Hannah.

CHAPTER 11

On a Wednesday late in January, Todd skittered down the icy path that led across the golf course, late for his baking project. He and Izzy Jacobsen had just smoked a bowl in the fourth-floor bathroom of Slater. Todd had never shown up stoned at Hannah's before, but he figured it wouldn't matter. She was so loose about things; she let him smoke cigarettes on her back porch, though he was instructed to stub them out in a planter box if he saw anyone coming down the road near the lake.

When he entered Hannah's living room, he felt a rush of heat. The pot was some stuff he hadn't tried before, weed Izzy had bought during a recent trip to the city, and it was stronger than what Todd usually smoked. He could feel Hannah looking at him strangely from where she was sitting at her dining table grading student essays, stylish glasses perched on her nose. Maybe he was being paranoid.

He greeted her, took off his coat and scarf, and tied on a blue apron.

"Actually, I need you to make the delivery first," she said, pointing to three white cartons sitting on the kitchen counter. "I boxed up everything from last night. The list of supplies we're out of is on top."

Todd nodded. "Do you want me to take a cab?"

"Can you?" she asked. "I'm swamped with grading."

Todd called the taxi company, carefully dialing the number from memory. He had gone into town stoned before, but that was usually for fun, to grab a pizza with friends. This time, he had a job to do.

Twenty minutes later, Todd pulled up to the tearoom, the three boxes of desserts sitting on the seat next to him. In the small parking lot was a police cruiser, its engine idling. An older officer walked down the small path from the tearoom; then came Laura, who was being led by a patrolman. Behind them, Madame Beauchamp was in the doorway, screaming something Todd couldn't make out, her face blotchy and red.

Todd kept his head down in the cab, afraid Laura would see him. "You know," he said to the driver, "I don't think this is a good time to make my delivery. Can you drop me off at the supermarket? I'll bring these by later."

The cabdriver, a stout woman in a flannel coat who was missing two teeth, shrugged and turned the cab around in the parking lot. Todd looked out the back window.

"We can listen on the radio, hear what's going on if you want," said the driver, as she reached for the police scanner.

"That's okay," Todd said. "You can just drop me off at Perotta's."

He paid for the cab and went into the market. His legs were shaking. He was sure Laura was being arrested, or at least interrogated, for selling pot. Would she reveal the names of her customers? Perhaps if she turned some students in, they would treat her more leniently. Since his first purchase, Laura had begrudgingly sold to him, but she had never seemed particularly happy about it. He knew she resented students who could afford to spend their money on eating out and getting high. He took deep breaths, clutching the boxes tightly. Maybe it was his buzz that was making him nervous. If he were kicked out of Berkley, he didn't know what he would do.

He wandered around the supermarket for fifteen minutes, not buying anything, absentmindedly examining specials on cereal and soda. After realizing he must have looked very strange, a blond boy carrying three white boxes with a dazed look on his face, he decided to go back to the tearoom.

Madame Beauchamp wasn't on the first floor of the tearoom, and Todd didn't ask if she was upstairs. He handed the pies to Astrid, a Swedish girl who waited tables part-time. Astrid, whose English was poor, took the pies dutifully and went back to folding a pile of cloth napkins. He wanted to ask her what had happened, but he didn't think that was a good idea.

After Todd returned to the supermarket, this time purchasing the groceries from the list Hannah had given him (a task that took him three times longer than it should have; everything seemed to be at opposite ends of the store), he called the cab company and made his way back to school.

When Todd arrived with the groceries, Hannah was still grading papers.

"What do we have to look forward to?" she asked, referring to the latest order from Madame Beauchamp.

He had forgotten. "I wasn't able to ask. She wasn't there."

Hannah looked up, alarmed. "She's hardly ever not there."

Todd shrugged, hoping his story would hold. He knew Hannah would find out soon enough about Laura's arrest, but he didn't want to be the bearer of bad news, especially when he was indirectly involved.

"Let's just make her more of the usual then." She looked at him closely. "You're stoned, right?"

Todd nodded slowly. "I'm sorry. I didn't think you would be able to tell."

"Of course I can tell. Go to the bathroom and put in some eyedrops."

"I already did that at the dorm."

"Your eyes are bloodshot. I can't have anyone seeing you like this. I don't believe you went into town. Are you mad?"

"I thought you wouldn't mind."

"I don't want you to get in trouble." She paused. "You were getting it from Laura, right?"

Todd nodded guiltily. He went to the bathroom and put in the eyedrops that Hannah gave him. He knew he shouldn't have been doing this in the middle of the afternoon, on a school day. He felt like an idiot, as if Hannah could see right into him, how pathetic his life was.

He went back to the kitchen and started reading the recipe Hannah had marked for him in a cookbook. Nothing made sense. Scooping two-thirds of a cup of sugar with a half-cup measure— he couldn't find the correct one—was a concept that took nearly five minutes to master. He muddled through, fudging amounts, splashing milk on the floor, accidentally dropping bits of eggshell into the bowl and fishing them out again.

Hannah came over and grabbed the mixing bowl from him, starting to estimate the amounts from memory. "I'll do it," she said. "I can't bear to watch you fuck this up."

"I'm sorry," Todd said. "This was dumb of me."

"It's about self-control," Hannah said. "Screw around all you want, but don't ever let it affect the outcome of your day."

Todd went to sit on the couch, his face hot with shame. He wondered if he was capable of doing anything successfully, even the most menial of tasks, without messing something up. This never would have happened to Brian—and he knew that Brian had done his fair share of partying at Berkley. But somehow his brother had always been able to keep it all together. Brian had done all the things that guys were supposed to do, excelled in all the right ways, and still was popular. Meanwhile, Todd was left to sweep up the crumbs. He wanted to blame his mother for his shortcomings, for his penchant for self-destruction. He knew that wasn't fair, though, fucked up as her style of parenting could be. Whatever it was, as Todd sat there on the couch, watching Hannah across the room, cleaning up his botched work, he felt like a loser. One of the goals of the baking project had been to distinguish him from his peers. Instead, he was wasting his afternoon, messing around in a teacher's kitchen. His classmates were achieving, all around him, constantly, prizes and awards and adulation streaming toward them, and he couldn't even bake a goddamned cake.

That night, Ethan was studying for an AP Spanish test when Todd joined him in his room. His hair and clothes were mangy, as if he had gotten up from a nap and hadn't had time to shower or change. He flopped down on Ethan's bed and stared at the plaster ceiling, letting out a sigh. Ethan wondered what was going on; it was unusual for Todd to be so melancholy.

"Hannah was really pissed at me today," he finally said.

Ethan closed his textbook and looked at his friend. "What for?"

"I showed up stoned for our project."

"And she could tell?"

"Yeah. It was a stupid thing to do. But she'd never turn me in." Any other teacher would have taken Todd to health services or reported him for disciplinary action, which would have resulted in expulsion.

Ethan took a deep breath. He resented Todd's abuse of Hannah's friendship. Everything could come crumbling down: the school might find out that they were spending so much time at her house, and could decide they had broken some obscure, rarely exercised rule in the *Bluebook*. "It's not fair of you to put her in that position," he finally said.

"What, you're taking some kind of moral high ground?"

Ethan was surprised at Todd's prickliness. "No, it's just that we have a good thing going, being friends with her, and I don't want to mess it up."

"It's a slippery slope, Ethan. She lets us drink in New York and smoke cigarettes on her back porch, but we're not allowed to get high?"

"It's not 'we.' It's you." He felt self-righteous saying this, but it was true.

Todd scowled at Ethan. "Fuck you, man, you hang out there as much as I do."

"I don't show up stoned."

"I know it wasn't smart. You don't have to beat me up about it." Todd went across the room to Ethan's closet door and examined his face in the mirror, as if he might find something he had never noticed before.

"Something else happened," he said, after a moment. "Laura was arrested today at the tearoom."

Ethan sat upright in his chair. "What do you mean? For what?"

"For selling weed. At least, I'm pretty sure that's what it was."

Ethan felt his eyes widen. "Shit, what if she turns you in?"

"If she turned me in, she would have to turn Izzy in, too. And Izzy is a friend of her brother's."

It was just like Todd to be so relaxed about this. With the money his mother had, he didn't have to worry about the things that Ethan did. If Todd were kicked out of Berkley, he could always go to another school. It probably wouldn't take more than a few phone calls on Jackie's part.

Todd went back over to the bed, lying down on it again, his head hanging over the edge. Ethan watched him as he took a small lighter from his pocket and started flicking it over and over, creating a small flame in front of his face, then blowing it out again.

The next day, Ethan went to Hannah's house to show her a short story he had been working on. As she worked away in the kitchen, preparing a pot of tea for the two of them, he mentioned that Laura had been arrested at the tearoom.

"I know," she said, looking up casually. "I told the police about her. A guy I used to date works at the sheriff's office."

Ethan felt his voice quickening, a rush of nervous energy in his chest. "What? Why—why would you do that?"

"I didn't like what was going on with her and Todd. She shouldn't have been selling to you kids. If it continued, she could have gotten Madame Beauchamp in a lot of trouble. Not to mention Todd."

"I thought you and Laura were friends."

"We were friendly," Hannah said, as she poured out two cups. "I wouldn't say we were friends."

Ethan couldn't believe it. Turning someone in for selling pot was such a drastic thing to do. It seemed vicious, uncool, wrong. But maybe Hannah was only looking out for their best interests. Was she weighing Laura's future against their own? She was right; Todd had been in danger of getting caught. He would probably end up buying his weed somewhere else now, but at least it wouldn't be happening so close to campus. But Laura: Hannah had seen her several times a week for the past year or so, every time she had visited the tearoom. They had exchanged conversation, perhaps even confidences. And she had turned on her, just like that. Though he had never really known her, Ethan felt terrible for the girl, even if she had been breaking the law.

Maybe this was Hannah's version of love, of protection for Todd and the other students. Most faculty would have turned Todd in to the disciplinary committee. Instead, she had done the more difficult thing, had asserted herself so that he could stay in school.

Upon Ethan's hearing Hannah's side of the story, his first impulse was to mention it to Todd. But how would that help anything? He probably wouldn't understand, would think Hannah had been judging him—he already seemed to think Ethan was. By the time he left Hannah's that night, Ethan had decided against saying anything at all.

CHAPTER 12

When Todd received an invitation from Alex Roth to a weekend party at her parents' house in Greenwich, his first instinct had been to skip it. He knew it would be a noisy, raucous affair, with her parents away for the weekend and Alex's older brother, Kyle, buying alcohol for everyone. A year earlier, six months even, Todd would have jumped at the invitation, but now it had lost its appeal.

Ethan, upon hearing Todd was invited, insisted that they go. After some convincing, Todd finally agreed, though he didn't feel like hanging around Alex. He was certain she had only invited him so she could show him what a good time she was having without him by her side.

Todd and Ethan dutifully filled out the weekend permission slips that the school required for any overnight trip. About ten years ago, after a drunk girl had been raped by five members of the lacrosse team at an unsupervised party in Stamford, the school had started requiring all students to get permissions phoned in from the parents with whom they would be staying. The system wasn't foolproof: Kyle, a senior at Columbia who had attended Berkley himself, would be posing as Alex's father and calling in

146

the names of the twenty-three students who would be staying over on Saturday night. According to Alex, her parents were in Palm Beach for a long weekend; if all went according to plan, by the time they returned to Greenwich on Tuesday afternoon, they would have no idea that their daughter and twenty-three of her friends had ever set foot in the house.

On Saturday afternoon, Ethan and Todd took a taxi from the Greenwich train station to the neighborhood of Belle Haven. At the gated entrance, Todd had to tell a guard which house they were going to, and their names were checked off a list. The neighborhood was quiet, unnaturally so, as if the owners were all away.

Alex's house was a huge, white Colonial-style affair with a crescent-shaped driveway and a carriage house in the back for her parents' cars. Ethan knew there were only four people in the Roth family, and that Alex and her brother were both away at school. He wondered what their parents did with all that room.

Alex's brother, Kyle, answered the door. A tall, lanky guy with long hair gathered into a ponytail, he greeted Todd cautiously.

They were directed downstairs to the basement rec room, where the festivities were already in progress, even though it was only four in the afternoon. Alex's friends were playing pool, smoking, and drinking beer. There was a small bar in the corner stocked with liquor. The room was decorated with vintage athletic equipment on the walls, stacks of board games on the shelves, and tennis trophies behind the bar, all of which looked suspiciously like they had been assembled not by Mrs. Roth, but by a decorator.

"Hi, boys." Alex greeted them both with hugs. "Help yourself to the bar." Todd began fixing two gin and tonics.

From the time they had entered the house, Ethan sensed something in the air that was making him uncomfortable. Now his nose itched and his eyes were tearing. "Do you have a cat?" he asked Alex.

"Yeah," she said. "Two. Moxie and Kendall. Do you want to see them?"

"I'm allergic to the dander." He had a prescription for times like this, but he had left his medication sitting on the bureau in his room.

"Do you need anything for that?" she asked. "I may have some antihistamines upstairs."

"I'll be fine," he said. Though sometimes it would go away, the thought of having a dripping nose for the entire party was not appealing.

"Let me find you something," Todd said. He turned to Alex. "Is it okay if I go upstairs to your bathroom?"

"I'll go with you," Alex said. "Ethan, why don't you get some fresh air?"

Ethan stepped out the back door, which led to the flagstone-paved driveway in front of the carriage house. Outside, Kyle Roth was smoking a cigarette and talking on his cell phone.

Ethan took deep breaths of the chilly air and walked around the driveway, slowly sipping his drink. Several cars were parked there—a Range Rover, a late-model Mercedes, and a Volvo station wagon. He started to feel a bit better. He was sure the Roth house was kept clean, and yet it had felt like there was cat hair everywhere in that basement room. He cursed himself for having allergies.

Or maybe it was just a convenient excuse to avoid talking to anyone. He knew nearly everyone there, but he wasn't close with any of them. He didn't know much about their lives, and they didn't know anything about his. They probably saw him as a loser, a tool, an interloper who was trying to crash the party that was their Sixth Form year.

Kyle snapped his phone shut. "Taking a break from all the excitement?" he asked, as he walked toward Ethan, who was standing on the other side of the Range Rover.

"I'm allergic to the cats," Ethan mumbled. "Alex is getting something for me."

Kyle held up his pack of cigarettes. "Want one?"

Ethan took a cigarette, letting Kyle light it for him, though he knew smoking probably wasn't the best idea.

"You're a friend of my sister's?"

"Sort of," Ethan said. "More a friend of Todd's."

"Ah, Todd," Kyle said. "Troubled Todd."

"What do you mean?"

"I don't know. One minute he's all into my sister, and the next thing she knows, he's totally dropped her."

"I didn't know that was how it happened."

"And then he's hanging out with you all the time, and that woman, that teacher?"

"Hannah."

"Right. She's a trip."

"I like her."

"I guess I shouldn't judge. I never knew her."

"What's wrong with her?"

"Nothing, nothing at all. I've just heard she can get a little intense."

"How do you mean?"

"You know, you hear things." He took a drag on his cigarette. "She used to tell everybody about her divorce. Sounded like it was pretty brutal. People started saying her husband was still seeking damages from her, something like that. It was a while ago."

"People seem to talk about her a lot."

"Yeah, small town, small school. It's not like there's anything else to do."

Ethan nodded. He didn't want to hear anything more about Hannah's old life. As far as he could tell, she had left it behind her, back in Paris, and that was where it should stay. And yet nothing with her was ever simple; everything always involved story upon story, tales that would ebb and flow like the tide. Unlike with the rumors he had heard from Vivian, he was afraid to ask Hannah about it, afraid of being told it was none of his business.

Ethan tried to redirect the conversation. "Did you like it at Berkley?"

Kyle scoffed. "Probably was the best place for me to be at the time. But did I like it while I was there? Fuck, no. But it's all in the past. Can't say I think about it much anymore."

For Ethan, there was a sense of relief in hearing that he wasn't the only one, that not everyone had been as happy as Alex Roth and her friends seemed to be.

Kyle interrupted his thoughts. "I should get going. Alex wants me to pick up a keg, and then I've got to meet a friend at the train station. You coming back in?"

"I'll stay out here for a little longer," Ethan said, stubbing out his cigarette. "You know, my allergies."

"Right," Kyle said, smiling knowingly. "Your allergies."

Ethan looked at the older boy. Something about the cold, brisk air, the buzz of the gin and tonic, the cigarette, the fact that Kyle seemed a bit of a misfit himself, made Ethan want to open up to him.

"I'm not very good in these party situations," he said.

"Don't worry about it," Kyle said, giving him a pat on the shoulder. "No one ever is."

Todd followed Alex up to her bedroom. It was just as he had remembered it: little girl pink, with a canopy bed, strewn with stuffed animals from her childhood. Since she had gone away to school, she had never bothered to redecorate her room. The soft colors were a vivid contrast to her current wardrobe of vintage dresses and funky boots. Todd remembered all the times he had spent in this room, the times they had made love (and it was that, *making love*; Alex had said it was). He thought about how easy it would be to kiss her right now, what that would feel like. He hadn't kissed anyone since that afternoon with Ben. But he didn't want a girl's kiss, sweet like fruit. There was no mystery in her, no deep caverns to explore. He recalled his kisses with Ben, his kiss with Ethan. It was different, a guy's kiss, skin rough and scratchy like sandpaper, teeth harder, larger, tongue more firmly pressed against lips. The taste of cigarettes and beer.

"I think I've got something in here," she said. "I used to get allergic myself." She rummaged through her medicine cabinet, checking expiration dates on foil packages. "This is all a mess. I shoved everything in here. My mom says that before a party, you should put away all your personal stuff. God forbid anyone thinks you're human." She held up a small cardboard box. "Here's something."

"I'll take it to Ethan," Todd said, reaching for the package.

"Hold on," Alex said. "I want to ask you something."

Todd felt a shiver. "Yeah?"

"Is there something going on between you and Ethan? I mean, you hang out with each other all the time."

"No," Todd said. "I don't know what you mean."

"I was just wondering, that's all, don't get offended." Alex breezed by him into the hallway. "Let's go back downstairs."

After Todd gave him the medication, Ethan started to feel better. He drank beer after beer, trying to forget what he had just learned about Hannah. It scared him; he wanted to pretend he hadn't heard it at all. As he drank himself into a stupor, weaving his way from one conversation to the next, he became convinced that tonight he would have sex. It wasn't the first time he had been at a party and imagined this, but tonight it seemed likely: there were at least seven girls there, including Alex, who didn't have boyfriends.

Properly soused now, he was comfortable. He wasn't friends with these people, but at a party like this, intimacies were formed quickly. By being here, he was no longer Ethan, the transfer student from California. He was now one of Alex Roth's friends.

Kyle arrived with the keg and a friend in tow, and everyone started crowding around it and filling cups. Ethan didn't think he could drink more, but everyone else was, so he kept going. A stack of pizzas arrived around nine, and the group dove in.

By midnight, nearly everyone was wasted or passed out. Belle Haven's security patrol had already rung the doorbell three times to ask Alex to turn the music down. After making out with Julie Moore in one of the upstairs bedrooms, Kevin Bradshaw had been so drunk that he had tumbled down the back stairs, fortunately not hurting himself, but knocking several Roth family photographs off the wall. A few people had already thrown up, so many of the bathrooms were a mess.

Ethan steadied himself as he peed in the first-floor powder room. The floral wallpaper swam in front of his eyes. After washing his hands, he reached for a towel, but found they all had been knocked to the floor.

We try to be such adults, he thought, *and this is how we end up acting.*

He went back down to the rec room and sat on one of the plaid couches next to Alex and Cren, who was wearing a cowboy hat low over his eyes. Loud music was blasting, a deejay mix that Ethan couldn't identify, and several couples were dancing. Alex had changed into a black satin kimono and pajama bottoms. She and Cren were play-fighting, slapping each other's hands.

"I hate you, Cren!" she said in response to something Ethan couldn't hear. "I'm going to sit with Ethan!"

Alex moved over on the couch, landing herself right on Ethan's lap. She was clutching a reddish drink, and Ethan asked what it was.

"Bloody Mary," she said. "Staying ahead of my hangover."

"Can I try a sip?"

She handed it to him and he took a sip of the tart, spicy concoction. They started talking about school, and Alex asked Ethan about his college plans. The conversation was flowing, natural. It was never like this at school. He was making jokes, and Alex was laughing. It was exactly as he had imagined it. All he would have to do now, he thought, was kiss her.

"We have to hang out more," Alex said. "You're so much fun!"

No one had ever called Ethan *fun* before. *Thoughtful. Sensitive. Smart.* But never *fun.*

After they had been chatting for ten minutes, Todd slumped down next to them. He smelled of pot and cigarettes.

"What are you two up to?" he asked.

Alex was no longer on Ethan's lap, but even sitting next to each other on the couch, they looked like (he imagined, he dreamed) a couple. Ethan shrugged at Todd's question.

Todd leaned back on the sofa. "It's all downhill from here," he said to Ethan. "This semester, we can party all we want."

Ethan knew he wanted more than that, more than coasting by.

Alex laid her head down on Todd's lap. She mumbled something to him that Ethan couldn't make out.

"I'm going to go make some more drinks," she announced, sitting up briskly like someone risen from the dead. Todd followed her upstairs.

Was it all over so quickly? One minute he had Alex Roth sitting on his lap, and the next minute she was off with Todd again.

Now he felt tired. He shouldn't have mixed the allergy medication with so much alcohol. He was exhausted from the exertion of talking to people, of putting on a happy face for so many hours. He decided, with little surprise, that he wasn't cut out for parties.

Though he was still buzzed, it was only an illusion. He didn't have any connection with these people. He needed to find other friends, people he could talk to, people who understood him, people who wouldn't walk away when someone more exciting came along.

After Alex made fresh drinks, Todd followed her to her bedroom. He noticed with amusement that she had kept the door shut, with a DO NOT DISTURB sign from the Waldorf hung around the doorknob to keep out anyone who needed a place to fool around. Todd watched as she carefully closed the door behind them.

He sat down on her bed, leaning back and propping himself up on his elbows. He didn't know what he was doing here now, but he was too stoned to care. Part of it, he knew, was to keep her away from Ethan. Was that fair? *Fuck it*, he thought. *If I'm not having her, Ethan won't, either.*

Alex sat down next to him. She started chewing on a fingernail. Moonlight came in through the window, forming patterns on her pink coverlet.

"I've really missed you," she finally said, slurring her words so that it sounded like "mished you."

"Um, me, too." He felt like a jerk, but he didn't know what else to say.

Alex leaned toward Todd, steadying herself on his shoulder, and tried to kiss him. He gently pushed her away.

She looked at him with a mix of anger and confusion. "People are starting to wonder, Todd."

"Wonder about what?"

"You know what I'm talking about. You've had a girlfriend for most of your first two years at Berkley and suddenly all you want to do is hang out with Ethan."

"I've just been really busy, that's all." Todd felt like he was trying desperately to stay afloat. All he wanted now was sleep. Nothing else, just sleep.

"I don't know, Todd, it's sort of weird, that's all I'm saying."

"What's weird?"

"My brother came out to us."

Todd sat up. He felt his hands go icy, like the air outside. It had never occurred to him that Kyle Roth might be gay. How could a family like the Roths (rich, successful, conservative) produce a gay son? "Why didn't you tell me?"

"I didn't find out until recently myself. I mean, I had always suspected, but, you know, I hoped it wasn't the case. It's very sad. My parents are pretty upset about it." She took a sip of her drink. "Why are you so interested in this, anyway?"

"No reason, just curious."

"I should get back to the party," Alex said. "Have fun with Ethan."

Alex's bitterness didn't even register with Todd. As he left her room, only two thoughts occurred to him. First, that Kyle Roth was attractive, and second, that he was sleeping in a bedroom down the hall.

There were sounds coming from Kyle's room, low voices that Todd couldn't discern. He knocked on the door and the voices stopped. No one answered. He gently turned the knob, just to see if it was locked. It didn't move.

"We're sleeping," said a voice that sounded like Kyle's.

"Sorry," Todd said.

What was he thinking? He couldn't talk to the brother of his ex-girlfriend about this. Kyle would surely tell Alex, and Alex would tell everyone at school. But he wanted to talk to someone about it.

Todd stumbled up to the third floor to find an empty bedroom where he could sleep. Every guest room was occupied. Most of the floor space in the rec room would already be taken, so he tried the bedroom that Ethan was in. Maybe it had a couch where he could crash for the night.

Ethan hadn't locked his own door. Todd stepped into the room and let his eyes adjust to the dark. There was no couch, just a small bed with a wood headboard. Ethan's clothes were draped over a chair that sat in front of an antique writing desk.

"Mmmm?" Ethan groaned.

"Can I share the bed with you?" Todd whispered. "There's no free bedrooms."

"Sure," Ethan said. "Whatever." He rolled over on his side and fell back asleep.

Todd stripped down to a T-shirt and boxers. He climbed into the bed, being careful not to disturb Ethan or the comforter under which he was sleeping. He stayed awake for a little longer, listening to Ethan's breathing. After a few moments, he curled into Ethan's warm body, figuring his friend wouldn't notice, and even if he did, that he wouldn't care.

CHAPTER 13

The stretch of time between January and March was always the longest at Berkley. Ethan had heard about this period—the winter doldrums, the endemic seasonal affective disorder, the insomnia and depression that afflicted many students—but it wasn't until he had experienced it himself that he truly understood. Starting at the beginning of February, the entire campus was blanketed with five feet of snow for several weeks. It was the first time Ethan had ever been faced with this type of weather on a daily basis. While beautiful, the omnipresent whiteness made Berkley seem darker than ever.

Thankfully, his special project was consuming him. Because painting outside would be impossible in the cold, he had snapped photographs of the locations he wanted to include in the series. He decided to include a cemetery scene, and wondered how it could relate to the story. What about the other children the witch had killed, before her run-in with Hansel and Gretel? Maybe she had eaten them, but where had she buried their bones? He would call the image "The Boneyard of Forgotten Children."

One afternoon, he walked along the sloping edge of the cemetery, where the fence that enclosed the plots met a cluster of trees. Down at the opposite end from where Louisa Berkley's statue stood was a fresh headstone, positioned apart from an older grouping. The new marker was solid polished granite, inscribed simply with the name of a student who had been killed the previous year by a drunk driver. As Ethan took photographs from various angles, some including it in the frame, others leaving it out, he was faced with a feeling of profound uselessness. Art, he had always thought, was supposed to unlock mysteries: for the artist, for the viewer. Yet there was no answer here. There was no reason why a girl—a nice girl, a girl who had never hurt anyone, by all accounts he had heard—should be killed by a drunk driver.

Ethan had always fantasized that while he was working, there would be a brilliant moment when all mysteries would be revealed to him. But on days like this, he merely plodded along. He would reach the end: the painting would be finished, critiqued, analyzed. He and Ms. Hedge would examine what worked, what didn't. There might be some answers then. But now, nothing.

This painting, he feared, would be silly, melodramatic, macabre. What did he know about boneyards? What did he know about death? The two children might encounter this graveyard on their journey to the witch's house, as a foreshadowing of what was to come; they might rest for a moment, take stock of their weary limbs, their stash of bread crumbs. But it wouldn't help them; it would only whisper back to them with the quiet scratchings of underbrush against headstones, barren branches swaying against trunks, footfalls in the snow. The graveyard might be a warning for the viewer, but it would carry no significance for the children. It would beckon them farther along the path toward the house.

At the end of the day, when he was finished working, Ethan found himself intensely grateful for any activity that would take him away from his daily routine of classes and painting. He had continued helping Hannah with her multitude of projects, as they came up with new excuses to spend time together. He feared that some afternoon she might look up from her work and tell him he wasn't welcome, that she was busy, but that day hadn't come, not yet. There were, of course, the rumors he had heard about her past, but he put them out of his mind—it was all silly gossip from five years ago, and it didn't affect them now.

Whenever he crossed the snowy golf course and walked down the path to her house, he felt a twinge of guilt, as if he were transgressing, treading onto forbidden ground. It could have been the teasing he endured from Todd's friends, or the looks he got from Ms. Hedge whenever she suspected he would be spending an afternoon there. Secretly, he had started to crave the smell of her house—of pies baking, of fresh laundry, of the worn leather of the chairs in her living room.

He was happy, though, when an editorial meeting of *The Bones*, the school's so-called underground magazine, was held on a Monday evening. The magazine, like most things at Berkley, wasn't really underground at all; its publication was funded by the school, and the meetings were held in a conference room near the Dean's Wing. But in contrast to the official school newspaper, which was read not only by the student body but also by the alumni and parents, *The Bones* was distributed solely to the students and faculty. Short of hurting anyone, the magazine's staff was free to explore whatever issues they saw fit.

The publication was run by Tamara Schwartz, a Sixth Former from Greenwich Village, to whom Ethan had immediately taken a liking. She ran her meetings with expediency, taking suggestions, developing and dismissing ideas, and distributing assignments with the panache Ethan imagined of a tough New York magazine editor.

Among the articles assigned for the current issue were a report on tobacco use on campus, an exposé on how the admissions office recruited academically underqualified hockey players, and a humor piece on preppy abbreviations. Ethan sat next to Todd as they both took notes.

"Okay," Tamara said, scanning her list, "here's a big one. Linda Oates in the infirmary told me that every year there are three to four girls who get abortions at the hospital in Great Barrington."

There were gasps around the room.

"Who wants to do an investigation? I want someone to look at how Berkley is one of the last boarding schools in New England to have no formal sex education program. There are major contradictions here, guys. They give out condoms in the infirmary—if you ask for them, which people hardly ever do—yet they say officially that sex is not permitted at Berkley. And this thing about the abortions—it's a little scary."

Tamara adjusted her glasses defiantly. Ethan admired her ability to work the room.

"We all know that sex happens here," she said, pausing dramatically. "But this school doesn't want to talk about it. So who wants to do it?"

Ethan squirmed in his seat as he pretended to review his notes. It was a great story, a chance to practice his investigative skills, but there was no way he could do it. He understood the mechanics of sex—an early pubescence spent masturbating to the *S* volume of the encyclopedia had prepared him for that—but he didn't know if he could write an article about other students and their sex lives.

The room was silent.

"I could do a sidebar on the pro-choice movement," one girl said. "My sister is really involved with that."

"That's fine," Tamara said, "but that's not the issue here. The issue is lack of sex education. We're not saying abortion is right or wrong. We're saying that with more sex education and awareness among the student body, girls wouldn't be getting pregnant in the first place."

Tamara's beady eyes scanned the room. "Ethan—are you signed up for anything yet?"

Ethan shook his head. "I was hoping to—"

"How about this story? I know you would do a great job on it."

"I don't think—"

"You'd be perfect for it," Tamara said, as her coeditors offered murmurs of agreement. Ethan wasn't sure why there was such confidence in his writing abilities; he had only done a few short pieces for the fall issue.

His face grew warm as he considered the challenge. Maybe people saw him as the kind of person who had already had sex. In their eyes, he could be experienced. There was no reason to be afraid. He could write from what he knew; and what he didn't, well, he could get the information from books. No one would know that he, Ethan Whitley, was less experienced in carnal matters than the average Third Former.

Several nights before Valentine's Day, Todd and Hannah were making heart-shaped cakes for the tearoom. Todd had dumped a stack of papers on the kitchen counter, on the top of which was a form for sending carnations to students with little notes, a Valentine's fund-raiser that was run every year by the Fifth Formers. Flower-grams, they were called. People sent them to friends, boyfriends, girlfriends, both current and potential.

"Who are you sending carnations to?" Hannah asked.

"No one," Todd said. There was a time, his first year at Berkley, when he had received the most flowers in his class. Fourteen girls had sent him carnations. He had sent out eight. This year, he wouldn't send any. Maybe he would get a few, but they wouldn't mean anything.

"Come on, there must be someone you want to send one to."

"I don't know," Todd said.

"I know of one person."

Don't say it, he thought. *Just let it be.*

"Why don't we send him one together? You know, just for fun." She looked at him mischievously.

"Hannah! We can't do that. People would find out."

"We'll do it anonymously. Give me the form."

Todd handed it to her, and she began feverishly filling it in. Todd could always deny it, say they had sent it to be friendly, that it was a joke. Friends of his had played pranks like this in the past, though they were often mean-spirited. Several guys had conspired last year to send Jeremy Cohen a carnation with a message that read, *Die, Faggot.* Todd had tried to convince them not to, but no one listened. In the end, he pretended he didn't know about it when he saw a stunned Jeremy walking down the hall on Valentine's Day. Other students had played more creative pranks—sending carnations from former boyfriends or girlfriends, that sort of thing. It was all fictional and ridiculous. But this was different; in this, there was some truth.

"*Don't forget to include a message,*" Hannah said, reading from the form. "We may have to think about that one."

On Valentine's Day, Ethan was in his precalc class when two Fifth Formers arrived with the carnation delivery. Three carnations were delivered to Izzy Jacobsen, four to Katherine Stickley, a tall black girl who was the captain of the girls' swimming team, and eight to Tina Palmer, a girl who wore eye shadow and was rumored to be easy. Several other students got one each, including Ethan, who blushed when his name was called.

When the white carnation landed on his desk, he felt a quiver, a nervous feeling like he might vomit. It had to be from Alex Roth. Ever since the party, she had said hello to him when she saw him in the hall, though she had come nowhere near the level of enthusiasm reached that night at her house.

He opened the note slowly. *To Ethan,* it read, *in the hope that you find what you're looking for. From your secret admirer.*

Wasn't Alex the type of girl who would admit her interest openly? Ethan didn't know. But it did seem like Alex to write something so terse.

He clutched his carnation all day, holding the flower carefully so as not to disturb its petals. In the halls, he got knowing looks from people, as if he had been inducted into a secret fraternity of those who were liked, wanted, needed. His flower smelled fresh and sweet, like white linen. By the end of the day, Ethan had brought it to his nose so many times that it no longer had any scent to offer. He wondered how long it would live, how long it would be before Alex talked to him.

Todd joined Ethan in his room that night.

"I got a flower," Ethan said, motioning to the carnation sitting in a soda bottle on the windowsill. "But I don't know who it's from."

Todd looked at the floor, embarrassed. This had been a terrible idea. "It's from Hannah. Sort of from both of us, I guess, but mostly from Hannah. It was her idea."

Ethan's eyes darted over to the flower. "I wish you hadn't told me that."

"Why?" Todd started flipping through Ethan's CDs.

"I was hoping it was from someone else."

Todd turned toward Ethan. He noticed a smudge on his friend's glasses; he suppressed the urge to wipe it off with the sleeve of his turtleneck. "Who would it have been from?"

"I can't tell you. It's stupid. It never would have been from her."

"Who?"

"Alex. Your old girlfriend."

"Ethan, everyone knows that Alex is interested in Mike Blodgett." Mike Blodgett was the goalie on the hockey team, a burly Fifth Former from Minnesota.

Ethan was silent.

"I'm sorry," Todd said. "I'm just trying to be realistic. You should go for someone who likes you, who's interested in you."

Ethan looked like he was about to cry. "I have some studying to do," he said.

Todd went back up to his room. He was sorry about what he'd said, sorry about what he'd done. He should have let Ethan believe his little fantasy. He didn't want to harm his friend; he wanted him to be happy. Or maybe he did wish for Ethan to suffer, a little bit, to know how it felt.

Just as Ethan needed to recognize that Alex Roth was out of his league, Todd reluctantly had to accept that Ethan would never be interested in him, not in that way. What was most upsetting about it was that he sensed the two of them shared something unique, something that might never be physically consummated. He wanted so much for Ethan to be that person—not to have sex with, as he had, meaninglessly, with Ben Atwater, but to share something greater. For Ethan to be the one he could spoon late at night, as they had, ever so tentatively, and only because the bed was small, that night at Alex's party. For Ethan to be a person he could confide in without reservation at the end of the day. They were, Todd hoped, already connected in some inextricable way, simply by virtue of spending so much time with each other. But there was nothing permanent that could tie them together.

What they had was greater than simple friendship, of course: Ethan would save articles for Todd that he had clipped out, knowing they would interest him; Todd would show Ethan things he had written. When they ran into each other in the hall, Ethan would break out of his melancholy haze and give Todd a shy grin, the closest sign Todd would ever get from his friend that he was pleased to see him. He would think about Ethan—his delicate camel eyelashes, the hair on his arms, nearly black in intensity, the chest he knew his friend was puffing out to impress the girls, the thoughtful way Ethan would ask if he wanted anything when he was getting refills in the dining hall. Todd loved all these little things, and he knew Ethan liked him—and still, it would never go further than this. Todd, at seventeen, popular Todd, the center of attention, one who had rarely lacked for companionship: he had never been rejected by someone he cared for. He hated the feeling. It was cold and bitter and he couldn't shake it.

Ethan put his head down on his desk. He couldn't believe the flower had been from Hannah and Todd. He felt disgusted as he remembered the times he had smelled it during the day, pressed his nose against its folds. He looked at it again, sitting on his windowsill. It was wilting; its petals were turning brown at the edges. It would take no water. It was already dead when he got it. He wanted to toss it in the trash.

He thought back to Alex Roth. He had seen her earlier that day, laughing, gossiping with her friends in one of the seating areas along the school's main corridor. She had barely noticed him as he walked down the hall. It was silly of him to think she liked him. He knew little about her, but he doubted she was a person of substance. He might have to wait until college to meet someone who understood him. He could survive the seven months, if he had to.

He thought about that day's carnation ritual. People got flowers from their friends all the time. Maybe getting one from Todd and Hannah wasn't such a disaster. Todd said it had been mostly Hannah's idea. It was friendly, sweet, like something his mother would do.

Ethan turned off the fluorescent overhead lighting in his room, as it was giving him a headache. He looked back at the white carnation. In the softer glow of his desk lamp, it looked pretty again, shiny, effervescent. He was glad he hadn't thrown it away, not just yet.

CHAPTER 14

Ethan had spent whatever free time he had over the past several weeks working on his article for *The Bones*. He researched other boarding schools and the successes and failures of their sex education programs; he visited Fairview Hospital in Great Barrington, interviewing one of its administrators about what a seventeen-year-old girl would have to go through if she wanted to terminate a pregnancy. While Ethan had no moral problem with abortion, he hoped the article made it clear that providing a proper sexuality curriculum at the school would be a simple way to ensure that its female students would never have to make this choice.

As Ms. Oates told it, she had been a proponent of sex education from the moment she arrived at the school ten years ago, but had received strong opposition to it from the faculty and board of trustees, who believed in teaching abstinence. The provost, Mr. Downey, a heavyset man who had been at the school for twenty-two years, told Ethan that such a program at Berkley would only encourage sexual activity on campus. When Ethan caught the headmaster, Dr. Spencer, during his office hours, he told Ethan that "while any education is a wonderful thing, some experiences are best saved for one's college years." Ethan knew Tamara would love the fact that the Berkley administration was slowly hanging itself by its own bow ties. The school's blithe ignorance toward sex left Ethan nonplussed: couldn't they see that it was all around them, hormones and desire and hookups, friction virtually pulsating through the halls?

On the afternoon that the winter issue of *The Bones* was distributed to all five hundred students and nearly one hundred faculty and staff, everyone was riveted to it in the snack bar. While the magazine's editors were congratulated on the entire issue, Ethan's article provoked the most controversy. The next day, Dean Fowler stopped him in the hall. The dean of students was a towering, balding man with a penchant for wearing clothing not generally seen outside of prep schools: cloth belts with little anchors on them, blue and red rep ties, wide-wale cords.

"You've certainly rocked the boat, young man. A number of faculty members are quite upset about your article."

Ethan looked the dean in the eye. "I was just trying to effect some change."

"Change." The man looked out the window wistfully, as if he, too, had attempted change in his younger years. "It's a nice idea, but it won't happen. Nothing ever changes around here."

That evening, after a bland dinner of macaroni and cheese in the dining hall, Ethan went over to Hannah's house. He needed to get away from the constant scrutiny he had been under since his article had been published. In the past day, he had been approached by nearly two dozen students and faculty members, receiving responses ranging from congratulations to disapproval. The worst was a girl, a mean-looking Fifth Former who had stopped him in the hall and told him, "I think it's disgusting what you wrote. That kind of thing should be totally private," an encounter that had left him speechless. While he appreciated being noticed—

surely, it was better than invisibility—it was starting to wear him down.

When Ethan arrived, Todd was working late in Hannah's kitchen, frosting a batch of cakes. Spring break was less than a week away, which Ethan knew would bring Todd's project to a close. Verdi was playing on the stereo; Ethan recognized it as "La Donna è Mobile" from the third act of *Rigoletto*. It was a favorite recording of his father's.

Hannah had been in her study, typing away at her laptop, and now she came out to greet Ethan. She was wearing jeans and a white peasant blouse that was remarkably similar to the one Vivian Frasier had worn several months earlier on their ill-fated date.

"So," Hannah said, "how's our own Woodward and Bernstein?"

"Exhausted," Ethan said, sinking down onto the toile couch. "You have no idea how many comments I've gotten on the article. It's like I tried to open people's eyes a bit, to tell them the truth, and half of them are treating me like a leper for it."

"I have to admit," Hannah said, "that I was a bit taken aback when I saw the piece myself. Those poor girls. I wasn't sure if this was something that should be written about. There's got to be at least one girl who's already gotten pregnant this year. I worry about how she felt when this arrived in her mailbox."

"I didn't really think about that," Ethan said. Now he felt guilty, as if he had violated some sacred crypt of womanhood. As a male, did he have any right to be doing this story in the first place? But sex was something that happened between women and men; he had as much right to the story as a female student did.

Hannah sat down next to Ethan on the couch. "Honestly, though, this school makes far too much of a fuss over sex. You guys are teenagers. Sex is a reality. The school needs to open its eyes to it. You were right to do the story. Things like pregnancy wouldn't happen here if there was more education."

"Tamara said she's going to send the article to the trustees."

"That should raise a few eyebrows," she said with a wry grin. "I think we should have a toast. To shaking things up around here."

She pulled a bottle of champagne from the refrigerator. Todd turned from where he had been frosting the last cake. "No way!" he said, clearly delighted.

Hannah looked at him. "Now, you especially, don't tell anyone. This is strictly verboten."

She deftly popped the cork on the bottle so it made no more than a slight hiss, then took three glasses from the cupboard and began to pour. When she was finished, she handed a glass to Todd, and one to Ethan.

"To shaking things up—and to you," she said, looking Ethan in the eye as they all took a sip.

The first mouthful alone was intoxicating. Ethan looked around the room as he sat down again on the couch. So many things in this room, in this house, held his mark. He had sorted Hannah's books, organizing their colorful spines in a pleasing arrangement. He had helped her paint a table. He was almost finished with the trompe l'oeil ceiling—an original design of clouds and classical statuary—in her study (it was something she had started five years ago with another student, a painter, and it had never been finished). Next they were going to wallpaper the bathroom together. In the past six months, he had become part of this house, part of Hannah's life. He took another sip of champagne. The music whirled around them, enveloping them in their own private landscape. The more he drank, the more he could forget: that he didn't really belong here (wasn't, after all, his rightful place in the snack bar, sitting with Todd?), that Hannah had a past he might never understand.

"Have some more." Hannah topped off Ethan's glass. Todd held out his glass for more as well. "Fine," she said to him as she filled it halfway. "But you'd better behave yourself. No going into the snack bar and acting like you've got a buzz on."

"I promise," Todd said. He placed the last cake in a white cardboard box like the others, and took a long final swallow of champagne. "I should get going. I have to read a reserve book at the library." He hung his blue apron on its usual hook and packed up his things.

"Be good," Hannah said, smiling at him. "Be good always."

Todd left, giving both of them a shy wave.

Hannah sat down next to Ethan. "He's a sweet kid," she said. "I've grown quite fond of him."

Ethan nodded.

"That is," she said, "when he's not screwing around."

"What do you mean?"

"Todd is prone to getting into trouble. But I think he'll make it through the end of the year. After that, he can figure things out a bit."

"Figure things out?"

"I think he has a lot of growing to do. That's what this time is for in your life. There's so much you guys have to experience." She took another sip of champagne. "Look at me, babbling on like this. What do I know? I feel like a teenager myself half the time."

Ethan went to use the bathroom, feeling a bit tipsy as he shut the door behind him. The room felt cool, a refuge, sweetly scented. After finishing up, Ethan went back into the living room.

"I should go," he said. "I have a paper I need to finish."

"Stay a little longer," Hannah said. "Have another glass. You deserve it, after what you've been through."

She was right; he deserved to relax. He let her fill his glass and her own, finishing the bottle. His thinking was getting cloudy. Was it the champagne, or lack of sleep? It worried him to feel out of control, to let go.

Hannah curled her feet under her on the couch. The CD came to an end.

Ethan shifted. "Do you want me to put on some more music?"

"Let's just sit for a second. It's nice, quiet like this."

Ethan started getting restless. He hated silence between two people. Silence alone was fine, but silence in a pair implied the possibility of conversation, the burden of action. Whichever person acted first had lost the game. *Take deep breaths*, he thought. *Relax. There's no need to be nervous.*

"You seem bothered by something," Hannah said.

"It's nothing. I'm just tired."

Hannah put her hand on his knee. Ethan looked at it as if they were two disembodied things, as if the hand were not hers and the knee not his own.

He glanced over at her, giving her a worried look. He closed his eyes and tried to relax.

"Is this okay?" she asked.

He nodded, just a half nod.

She leaned forward and put her mouth to his. Her tongue rubbed against his lips, which stayed firmly shut. She held the back of his head with her hand. *Relax. Breathe.* His lips parted, and her tongue was in his mouth. He smelled her hair, its sweetness, and then felt guilty for doing so. He felt guilty for feeling anything at all.

He took off his glasses, folding them quickly and placing them on the coffee table. He didn't want to see.

As she kissed him, he felt himself stiffen in his pants. He tried to lean into it, to hide it within the folds of his jeans.

Ethan pulled away, and felt something slide down his cheek as he groped for his glasses. Water. Tears.

"I'm sorry, this was a mistake," Hannah said.

"No, it's my fault," Ethan said, the tears now flowing freely. "I just—" Perhaps sobbing would release the champagne from his bloodstream, get him to think clearly. Screw it. There would be no clear thinking tonight. He took another sip from the half-full glass on the table.

"I'm very fond of you, Ethan," Hannah said.

"I like you, too. I've just—I've never been with a . . . and I'm afraid—I just don't know, is this how it's supposed to be?"

"It can be any way you want." Hannah stroked his back. "Let's get you cleaned up." She went to the bathroom and got a wet washcloth for Ethan to wipe his face; she grabbed some breath mints from a drawer in the kitchen and tossed them to him. "These should help cover up the champagne."

After he was bundled up, and had checked his face in the mirror she kept near the door, he stood there, waiting for something to happen. The house was silent: no music, no chanting, no cars on the road outside. Just the two of them.

"I'm sorry, Hannah," he finally said.

Ethan didn't visit Todd in his room that night, and Todd never came down to the third floor. Ethan lay on his bed in the darkness, still dressed, only his shoes kicked off. On the ceiling, he could make out shapes formed by the dim lighting on the walkways outside. It was something he used to do when he was a child; he would lie on the floor of his parents' bedroom at night, after it was dark but before they had gone to bed, and stare at the ceiling. The particular melding of the streetlamps and headlights and the shutters on the windows made patterns on the wall and ceiling. Now that was all he wanted, those patterns, that quiet, but they seemed so far away.

What had happened with Hannah? When morning came, would he remember it correctly, or would it have faded away? Ethan could taste her on his lips, even through the crush of the mints, the champagne on her tongue, her freshly brushed teeth, a trace of her lip gloss. Something like strawberry. Something a teenage girl would wear.

What was he doing? A teacher had kissed him, and he had let it happen. Could he be expelled for this? Hannah could certainly be fired. She had made the first move. He had to get rid of the taste of her, to get rid of the evidence.

Ethan grabbed his toothbrush and shuffled down the hall. There was someone in the toilet stall—from the voice, he thought it was George Crenshaw—and Izzy Jacobsen was at one of the urinals. Ethan hoped he could get out of there without having to make conversation. He hated how his dorm mates talked to each other while using the toilet. Using the bathroom should be private. (Cren, whom Ethan secretly thought was beastly, had famously invited everyone on the floor last semester to examine a shit he had produced that was nearly as long as his forearm.)

Ethan turned the water on and started brushing. The steam pipes hissed near the window.

"Who is that out there?" said the voice from the stall. It was definitely Cren.

"It's me, Effum," said Ethan, through a foamy mouth of toothpaste.

"Cren, you didn't answer my question," Izzy said, in the general direction of the stall.

"What question?" There was the rattling sound of miles of toilet paper being pulled from the roll.

"The *only* question, you idiot. Did . . . you . . . fuck . . . her . . . tonight?"

"Naw, she wouldn't let me. Said we do it too much as it is, that it has to be special. I told her it was special, but she said she didn't want to do it on school nights. Only on weekends." His voice went higher in imitation of his girlfriend: "*So we have time to be romantic.*"

"Fuck that shit."

"I know. Eat and run, that's what you gotta do."

Cren flushed the toilet in a giant roar and opened the door of the stall.

"What's up, Ethan?" he said. "You messin' around with any-one?"

"No," Ethan said, spitting out a mouthful of foam and rins-ing. "Not currently."

Ethan went back to his room and sat down on his bed in the dark. Conversations like the one between Cren and Izzy made him sick. It was a horrible way to talk about women, as if they were animals, only good for one thing. It struck him once again that he was surrounded by sex at Berkley. Not sex in the abstract, the way he had written about it for his *Bones* article, but sex in the specific. Sex that was dirty and awkward and embarrassing. Sex that served people's needs. Even sex without love. What had happened between Hannah and him, that one kiss, had meant more than he imagined an entire night would of Cren or Izzy romping around with their girlfriends. Hannah cared for him, he knew she did. If they had sex—and he imagined that to be what would have happened, if things had gone any further tonight, for in his mind there was no spectrum of behavior, there was only having sex or not—it wouldn't be dirty. It would mean something.

Ethan decided his paper could wait until the morning. He stripped down to his boxers and crawled into bed, pulling the covers around him and hugging his pillow as if it were another person.

CHAPTER 15

After toasting Ethan's success, Todd had walked to the library, buzzed and happy, even as the sharp March wind on his face threatened to sober him up. The clumps of ice melting on the grass were treacherous, slippery. Around ten thirty, Brian called from Dartmouth, just to talk, and Todd sat slumped on the floor of the hallway, his back against the wall, phone in hand.

"You sound like you've been tying one on," Brian said.

"Is it that obvious? Just a little, I guess."

As Todd zoned out, Brian started going on about his fraternity, the girls he was dating, spring break. "Is your buddy coming to stay with you?" he asked.

"Um, who do you mean?" Of course, Todd knew exactly whom Brian meant.

"You know, Ethan—the kid from California."

"No—he can't make it."

Todd had asked Ethan if he'd like to come to New York to stay with him for a week during spring break, but Ethan had declined. He said he was trying to save money, that his parents expected him home in California. Todd wondered if that was the truth. He thought of the things he would like to do to win him back—CDs he would buy him, invitations to see bands, maybe even a trip to the Hamptons. Was Ethan sick of him? Had the carnation, a simple gesture of affection (Todd would twist it around in his mind to be nothing more than that), driven them apart?

Brian didn't pursue the topic, and Todd didn't encourage it. But he wanted to, badly. He wished he could tell his brother what was going on in his life, how he felt about Ethan, about guys in general. But not here, not in the hall, not while he was still at school. Instead, the two of them had a conversation filled with awkward pauses, as Todd felt his mouth drying up and he longed to get off the phone.

"I hear you're turning into the next Julia Child. Mom told me all about it. What's up with that?"

"It's nothing," Todd said. "It's just baking some desserts—it's not that important." He felt he had disappointed his brother by not swimming that semester.

"It's with McClellan, right?"

"It's ending soon."

"That's good."

"What do you mean?"

"Look, Todd, don't get pissed, but after I heard about your project, I called my friend, the one who supposedly messed around with her. It sounds like there's some bizarre stuff about her, things that happened when she lived in France. Something about a young boy. Someone she had an—I don't know, I guess, an . . . *affair*, with. She couldn't keep her mouth shut about it. The two of them had gotten stoned together, and she started babbling on. It sounded pretty sick."

"Okay . . ." Todd drew out the syllable, as he thought about this. It was preposterous, nothing more than a late-night drunken rumor. "And what am I supposed to do about that? I don't have

much contact with her anymore. Or at least, I don't have to."
Todd noticed a Fifth Former sauntering down the hall, and he
tried to keep his voice low.

"I just think you might want to steer clear."

"I am," Todd said. "I'm going home in a few days."

"And what about your friend?"

Todd knew Ethan and Hannah were getting close, but he
wasn't sure what it meant. "What can I really say to him? It's his
business if he's friends with her."

Brian was silent for a moment, apparently thinking about it.
"I don't know if there's anything you can say. You think they're
together?"

"They could be." Todd could barely stomach the possibility,
but sitting there in the hall, he viewed it distantly, as if it were
happening at another school, to someone he didn't know.

"Then let it run its course. He's old enough to make his own
decisions."

"Are you saying that—"

"I don't know what I'm saying. I just mean that when teachers
get close to students, things happen."

"Things?"

"It's the oldest story around. You can't stop human nature."

"Thanks for the advice," Todd said bitterly.

"It's not really your problem anymore. But if I were you, I'd
keep your distance."

As Todd got off the phone, his head was still swimming,
thanks only in part to Hannah's champagne. He thought about
the next quarter; he didn't have to see her. Their baking project
was nearly over, and they had raised five hundred dollars toward
the restoration of Louisa Berkley's statue. He knew he could
come over and help if he wanted to for fun, but a Fourth Form
girl had offered to take over his duties for the spring, and he didn't
want to get in the way. His own friendship with Hannah had
consisted mainly of going over to the house and preparing the

day's order of desserts. Ethan's relationship with her was something more.

He had loved that baking project; he knew he would miss it. It had allowed him to be completely focused, to think about nothing else. Not about Ethan, not about school, not about his family. The process became intuitive; like Hannah, he relied not on measurements, but on feelings, textures, wet and dry. It would stay on his hands, long after he left the house, those odors of butter and sugar and fruit, dough sticking under his fingernails, pungent aromas of ginger, nutmeg, cardamom, cloves. He started to think as he imagined a real baker would; when he closed his eyes each night, he saw flour and dough, smelled crust, dreamt of new blends of spices.

Now he fidgeted under the covers. It was nearly midnight, but he couldn't sleep. Perhaps he was jealous; perhaps he wanted Ethan all to himself. He sensed Hannah had a possessive streak, something he had noticed when she asked him about the Capote novel. And he knew that in the contest for Ethan's affections, Hannah would win.

One of Ethan's father's many aphorisms was that you should never make a decision until the last possible moment. The reasoning was that things changed over time; new information came to light. There would be no harm, Ethan thought, in waiting, letting things settle after their encounter. Hannah wasn't going anywhere. He would avoid her for a few days, and then he could see how he felt.

Two mornings later, he was in a fluster. He would see Hannah in the hall—she was ignoring him, too, it seemed—and he would feel the twitch in his stomach, the shiver in his groin that even masturbation (daily, nightly) hadn't been able to quell. He was turned on by a thirty-six-year-old woman. But she wasn't an average thirty-six-year-old woman. She had the body of a teenager, the hair of a model. He wanted her, and there was only one way, in his mind, to stop wanting something: to have it, to possess it fully. Instead, he waited, and attended classes, and painted, and read.

On the afternoon of the third day, Ethan shuffled down the hall near the English department, a route he had studiously avoided until now.

Hannah appeared at the doorway to the office.

"Hello," she said. She seemed dreamy, distracted.

"Hi," Ethan said, looking down at the floor.

"I'm cooking something tonight," she said. "Something I used to make in Paris."

Ethan nodded. He felt his ears go red.

"I think you might like it."

"What is it?"

"You'll see," she said. "Seven o'clock?"

Without waiting for a response, she drifted down the hallway, her battered leather book bag trailing behind her, heavy with novels and student papers, but seemingly weightless.

Ethan worked in the art studio that afternoon, preparing more pieces for his spring show. Everything should be normal. If he thought too much about his impending dinner with Hannah, he might ruin it. He went back to the dorm around six to take a shower; he wanted to look nice for her. He appraised his complexion in the bathroom mirror: he was freshly shaven, which made him feel like a little boy. He didn't know if Hannah would be attracted to that. Perhaps it was silly of him to worry. This was Hannah. She had known him for months. If she wasn't attracted to him now, she never would be.

In the shower, as the water ran over his naked body, he thought, *This is it, this is the last shower I will ever take as a virgin*. He stared straight ahead at the tiles and tried to put it out of his mind.

In an attempt to get as clean as possible, he had made the water hot, scalding his skin. As he toweled off near the frosted glass window, his flesh cooled to a bright pink, like a baby fresh from a bath.

Though he considered wearing something nicer, Ethan decided to put on the same clothes he always wore around Hannah: his favorite ragged jeans, untucked blue oxford shirt, Adidas sneakers.

The ice and snow were melting on the golf course, but there was still a chill in the air. Ethan held his duffel coat tightly around him as he walked down to Hannah's house.

When he arrived, she was wearing a man's white shirt, untucked with the sleeves rolled up, and blue jeans; a few shirt buttons were undone, revealing a tank top. She greeted him abruptly at the door with a pat on the shoulder. The lights had been dimmed, and the dining table was lit with two candles. Choral music was playing on the stereo.

The house smelled delicious. Hannah was making something called cassoulet that she explained was a stew of white beans, lamb, pork, and garlic sausage.

"I used to make this for my husband and his son in Paris," she said. "It's a special recipe from the little restaurant that was across the street from us."

"His son?" Ethan hated how Hannah spoke of her ex-husband as if they were still married, but still, he wanted to know more.

A slight blush started rising on Hannah's neck. "He had a son, from a previous marriage. A sweet boy."

"So you've sort of been . . . a mom before?"

"Oh no," she said quickly. "Nothing like that. Here, open this bottle of wine." She handed him a bottle of Cabernet and a corkscrew, which he held dumbly in his hands, wondering if he could figure out how to remove the cork without looking like a fool.

He tried to buy some time while he fiddled with the foil. "This all smells great," he said, as he surveyed the table: cloth napkins, a basket of freshly baked rolls, a salad tossed with Gorgonzola and sun-dried tomatoes. It was by far the most elaborate meal Hannah had ever prepared for him. He wondered if this was what Izzy and Cren had meant about girls wanting to make things special.

Hannah's phone rang, and she answered it. "Yes, hello, Cass." She rolled her eyes, as Ethan continued fussing with the bottle. "No, not a bad time at all, I'm just spending a night alone grading papers." She winked at Ethan, and he relaxed. Of course Hannah wouldn't mention that they were having dinner together.

Ethan heard Ms. Davis's voice through the receiver, buzzing like a little bee. Hannah motioned to him to hurry up and open the bottle. He frowned at her, wondering if they would be drinking all the time now.

"Dorm duty?" Hannah said to Ms. Davis. "Tomorrow night? I'd be happy to."

She hung up the phone. "Cass Davis has to go to a gallery opening in Great Barrington with Susan Hedge. God, these people, they can't make a simple request without telling you their life story."

"Ms. Hedge is my adviser."

"I know. She's a perfectly nice woman. She just suffers from the problem that most people have around here."

"What's that?"

"They've been here too long." She checked the simmering pot on the stove, ladling out a few beans with a wooden spoon and tasting them. She gave him a playful look. "So, are you going to open the wine or not?"

"Sure," Ethan said. "I just—I wasn't sure if we should be drinking."

Hannah smirked. "I think you could use a glass."

He paused at the bottle and corkscrew. He had gotten the foil off, but beyond that, he was stumped. He looked at Hannah. "I don't know how to open this."

She giggled. "You're so cute! Let me show you."

Hannah demonstrated how to open the bottle, carefully holding the instrument steady so as not to break the cork. "I can't believe your parents haven't shown you this."

"They don't really drink that much," Ethan said. "And they certainly don't let me drink."

"It's easy for me to forget you're so young." She poured out two glasses, handing one to Ethan.

He took a sip of his wine. "Most of the time, I feel younger than I really am. I feel like I don't know shit at eighteen."

"Well, you're far ahead of most of your classmates. The only ones who are in trouble are the kids who think they know everything."

Ethan thought of Todd. He seemed to know everything, though Ethan knew he didn't. Maybe Ethan was further ahead than he realized.

They sat down to eat, first starting on the salad and bread, then moving on to the cassoulet. It was rich, drenched in fat and butter. Ethan tasted each bite carefully, wanted to absorb the flavors individually, as if he were tasting Hannah herself. She asked him if he enjoyed it, and he assured her that he did.

After two helpings, Ethan was stuffed, but it was a pleasant feeling, the warm sensation of being well fed, of someone looking after him.

Ethan got up to use the bathroom, and Hannah cleared away the dishes. He didn't know what he was doing, but he wanted to carry things to their natural conclusion, whatever that might be. When he came back, she was standing at the kitchen counter. "Come here," she said, and he moved toward her.

She kissed him, lightly on the lips, holding on to him by his biceps. "Strong arms," she said, which embarrassed him. No one had ever admired his muscles before.

"Is this a good idea?" he asked.

"I don't really know."

Hannah grabbed her glass of wine from the counter and took a long gulp, then, after filling it again, handed it to Ethan for him to do the same.

He wanted it to be a good idea. He brought her body close to his, clutching her back, feeling her shirt and tank top over her skin, sensing how her body shifted under the fabric. She wasn't wearing a bra. Her body was tight and toned (from the yoga, he imagined, that she once told him she practiced alone), but holding her still felt like grabbing something fleshy and amorphous, something that couldn't be contained.

He pulled away and looked at her. Her skin was pale, shining in the candlelight, almost translucent. She was beautiful, even her imperfections: the fine lines around her eyes, the mole on the side of her neck. There was a sadness he hadn't noticed before, one that existed far beneath her daily life at school, even her life at home. It said, *I want more than I have been given.* Hannah wasn't the buoyant, energetic person he had met that day in the tearoom. He didn't know who she was, but he wanted to find out.

They sat down on the couch. Ethan began kissing her again, his tongue probing her mouth, feeling her teeth. He felt his hand move up her denim-encased thigh, toward the fold between her legs. She placed her hand on his.

"I think we should wait," she said.

He removed it. "Until when?"

"I don't know. When it feels right, I guess."

He had never imagined sex to be such a drawn-out process. Maybe Hannah wanted more from him. He didn't know if he could give it to her.

She stood up, running her fingers through her hair and letting it fall again at her shoulders. "I have an idea. When are you supposed to go home?"

"On Saturday, like everyone else."

"Stay with me for a week. It'll be wonderful, just the two of us."

Ethan squirmed on the couch. "I can't. It would cost too much to change my plane ticket."

"I'll take care of it," Hannah said.

"What if someone finds out?"

"No one will see you. I'll make sure of that. Besides, most of the faculty go away for spring break."

Ethan thought about his parents wanting to see him, and his desire to see them, to be with his mother. But spring break was three weeks long. One week less wouldn't make a difference.

"I guess I could do that," Ethan said. "I just—I don't know, I've never done anything like this before." He looked at the clock in her kitchen. It read 9:10 p.m., which was earlier than he thought it was. "That can't be right," he said, looking at his watch. It was five after ten. Hannah's kitchen clock had stopped.

"Hannah, I have to go—I'm late for check-in." Ethan grabbed his coat and ran to the door. "Can we decide tomorrow?"

"Go," she said. "Just go."

Ethan ran across the golf course. By the time he reached Slater, he was out of breath. Mr. Barnfield, a biology teacher who lived on the first floor with his wife and children, was locking the front door. He saw Ethan and opened it for him.

"Ethan, you're a bit late," he said. Barnfield the Stud: that was what the girls called him.

"I'm sorry . . . I was—I got stuck—I couldn't find a book I needed."

"Just try to be on time in the future," Barnfield said.

Ethan ran past him and bounded up three flights of stairs. Mr. Sargent, the corridor master and dorm head more casually known as "Sarge," was still doing check-in. The strange, squat little man proceeded leisurely down the hall, dispensing advice and joking with the boys in his thick Maine accent.

Izzy Jacobsen chortled as Ethan went running to his door. "Someone's been busy tonight!"

Ethan motioned to Izzy to keep quiet. Sarge had poor eyesight, and probably wouldn't notice his late arrival.

By the time the little man made it to his door, Ethan had caught his breath.

After Sarge checked him in, Ethan went into his room and collapsed on his bed. He had a headache from the wine, and the cassoulet was growling in his stomach. He stared at the ceiling. Nothing.

Ten minutes later, the door of his room opened. It was one of the Fifth Formers, Evan Douglas. "Whitley, phone," he barked.

Ethan trudged out to the house phone. "Yeah?"

"It's me. Do you want me to get your ticket changed tonight?"

"I don't know," Ethan said. "Can we talk about it tomorrow?"

"We need to take care of it now," she said. "Trust me, Ethan, it will be wonderful."

CHAPTER 16

When spring break arrived, Todd was grateful for the chance to escape to New York, for three weeks of uninterrupted autonomy. Upon his return at the beginning of April, his college acceptances or rejections would be waiting for him. If he didn't get in anywhere, he could take a year off, he supposed. He had applied to some safety schools, but his grades were less than stellar, and even those might be a stretch. He worried he had nothing to offer, at least when compared to people like Ethan or his brother.

When Todd stepped off the bus that dropped everyone in front of the Plaza, he was surprised to find his mother waiting for him, standing under the awning in a mink coat. He had forgotten that he had told her about his travel plans. In years past, he had usually caught a cab or hitched a ride with someone else's parents. But here, on the first day of his last Berkley spring break, his mother was waiting for him.

She was chatting with Izzy Jacobsen's parents. Seeing Izzy's mother and father together reminded him that he would most likely never have both of his parents greet him together. But today, one was enough.

* * *

On the first Saturday in March, while his classmates were boarding buses to take them to the airport or being picked up by their parents, Ethan stayed in his room. He had carefully packed his bag, though he wouldn't be going home, at least not immediately. He had told his parents that he would be staying with a teacher friend for a week, and they had been surprisingly easygoing, asking for little more than a phone number. Just after one in the afternoon, he grabbed his bag and made the trip down to Hannah's house. Overhead, there were dark clouds, signs of a storm coming. As he passed between the headmaster's house and the school cemetery, he ran into Ms. Hedge. She was carrying two cloth tote bags filled with books. As their eyes met, he halted, certain he had a guilty look on his face. He attempted a smile.

"Ethan! What are you doing on campus?"

"I'm leaving this afternoon," he said. He tried to think quickly, to say something believable. "Hannah—Ms. McClellan—is driving me to the airport."

"Why didn't you just take the bus?"

"She offered to give me a ride. My flight doesn't leave till much later."

Ms. Hedge looked confused. "Okay, well, have a nice break."

As she turned, Ethan noticed a look on her face, as if she was aware of what he was doing, but wasn't going to say anything.

He spent the afternoon with Hannah, working on the ceiling in her study, the two of them painting together, Ethan on the ladder, creating swirls of clouds bordered by gold statuary while she mixed paint below him. Ethan could feel the perspiration, brought on in part by Hannah's clanging radiators, dribbling down his neck, soaked up by his cotton T-shirt. He sniffed his armpit and found that he smelled like a construction worker, but he didn't care. He was happy to be creating.

When he arrived, he had been nervous, as if the entire situation might be a mirage, as if the past few evenings with Hannah had never happened. She had greeted him at the door with a perfunctory pat on the arm, and had directed him to grab a brush and start work on the ceiling. Perhaps it would be as it always had been, him coming over to help, nothing more than two friends hanging out. Was he really spending the week with her? He had glanced at the duffel bag hanging over his shoulder. She had asked him to stay; he remembered that. Now she was acting so normally that he wondered whether the other stuff had even happened at all.

Around six, Ethan took a shower in her upstairs bathroom. She had shown him the second floor once before, just briefly to let him admire the view, but this was the first time he had actually used Hannah's private bathroom. The shower was old-fashioned, a tub with clawed feet. As he rinsed off, his eyes wandered over the collections of objects on her shelves: pieces of sea glass, worn shells, fancy soaps from hotels, vintage French postcards. He felt comfortable in this inner sanctum, this place where no one could find him.

He sat on her bed after drying off, wrapped only in a blue bath towel. Her bedroom was in the house's attic; the walls extended to eye level before sloping up toward the roof. The ceiling and walls were painted a deep blood red, bordered by a black, white, and gold Beaux Arts frieze. A gabled window had a view of the woods surrounding the house. When he looked up at the ceiling, Ethan felt as if he were somewhere else: in Paris, in a jewel box, somewhere far away.

That evening, Hannah was noticeably more relaxed. The Police were on the stereo, and she was already well into a bottle of

Merlot by the time Ethan came downstairs. She handed him a glass, and they ate a meal, almost childlike in its simplicity, of hamburgers and homemade fries. The bottle of wine was nearly finished when she led him upstairs to her bedroom.

In the darkness, her duvet was a field of white, tempering the riot of color created by the room's decoration. Outside, the rain had started; tree branches moaned and swayed, scratching against the roof. She removed Ethan's clothes—shirt, jeans, socks, underwear (penis bobbing up expectantly)—and then her own, until they were naked together, side by side on the bed. He imagined the house cracking apart in the storm, plaster crumbling, pale skin, flesh, divots in the ceiling, round nipples, tight abdomen. Creaking and shifting on its foundation, light hairs brushing against skin, bedsheets, tongue licking ear, chest, stomach. Slowly, awkwardly, the holes in the ceiling widened into crevices, opened to the sky, took in the different sensations, hard, soft, round, flat, learned, through trial and error, what should be touched with fingers, nails, lips, teeth.

A tree branch clattered onto the rooftop as he came. She had slipped the condom on him; he had barely been inside her. He lay on the bed, Hannah next to him, as he wondered if it was over before it had even begun, about the fact that his body had burst open in ecstasy before he could enjoy the sensations for which he had waited so long.

Hannah didn't say anything, and Ethan was afraid to speak. He felt himself drift off in her arms.

When he woke (it could have been hours, or minutes—he wasn't sure), her eyes were open, watching him. He smiled.

"I can't sleep," she said.

"I'll stay up with you." He adjusted his head on the pillow, turning toward her.

"Ask me something."

Ethan paused. He reached out into the darkness, wanted to

grab at something important, something he might not otherwise ask her. "Tell me about your ex-husband. Alain, right?"

She sighed. "You really want to know the whole story?"

"Yes."

Ethan leaned up on his elbow and listened.

"We met several months after I moved to Paris. I was studying modern French literature—you know, Proust, Colette, Genet, Breton . . . you've seen the books."

Ethan nodded, not sure what to say. He was afraid if he appeared too eager to learn her story, she might reveal less.

"His name was Alain Reinard. Could you imagine anything more French?"

Ethan smiled, shaking his head.

"I couldn't—I used to tease him about it. He was a junior professor at the Sorbonne. I worked weekends at a bakery on the Rue Bourg Tibourg, a darling little street in the Marais. We actually met there."

She described her ex-husband as if he were sitting across the room: his shoulder-length hair, his leather jacket with the lamb's-wool collar, how he only smoked American cigarettes. Alain himself was nearly ten years older than Hannah, though according to her, he had kept his youthful good looks.

"He had a teenage son, which I didn't mind at all—I liked Bertrand, in fact. He and his wife had him when they were young. Bertrand's mother had died in a car accident eight years earlier. Alain had raised him, for the most part, alone." She sighed. "I admired him for it."

Ethan remembered the photos, the names in the children's books, but decided not to say anything for fear of seeming nosy. Hannah got up out of bed. "Would you like a glass of water?"

Ethan declined as she went to get herself one from the bathroom.

"We lived together in a small apartment for a year, and then he proposed," she said through the doorway. She paused as the tap ran. "I was happy. It wasn't easy, but we had a little bit of family money to get by. It wasn't going to last, though—I should have known that." She came back into the room and sat down on the edge of the bed, holding her glass. "I had seen it happen with my girlfriends. French men are somewhat resistant to the idea of fidelity. I would pick him up after work and I could see how all his female students would circle around him, like moths to a flame. I knew eventually we would have to move from Paris, perhaps get out of France entirely." She took a sip. "Does that sound crazy? I didn't want to control him. I just wanted him to myself. That's not too much to ask, is it?"

Ethan shook his head. "I don't think so."

"It was too late, though. Just as we were entering our second year of marriage, Alain slept with one of his students."

"Oh God," Ethan said. "That's awful." He was a bit perplexed at what else, if anything, was appropriate to say.

"Yes." She put down the water glass and lay back again on the bed, an arm behind her like an odalisque. "He only did it a few times, but I was devastated. I didn't think I could ever forgive him. I confronted him, and he was cruel to me."

"What do you mean?"

"He said things, the kind of things you can't take back. Hurtful things. It was absurd. I suppose he must have been unhappy."

She brushed her hair away from her forehead. "We separated, and then finally divorced. The hardest blow was that at the time we had been trying to get pregnant. All that had to be put on hold. I nearly had a breakdown—I could barely get out of bed, I was in such pain. I stopped working at the bakery, quit my job as a teaching assistant. I would try not to sleep—this is crazy, I know—but going to sleep meant waking up, facing the reality that he was really gone. It wasn't just that he was physically not there—the person I had married, the person I knew, wasn't the one who had slept with that girl. The Alain I knew never would have done that.

"A few months later, I decided to come back to Wilton. I had grown up nearby, and teaching high school seemed a logical thing to do. I took the job offer in the middle of the school year—an English teacher had died of a heart attack over winter break. That's how I got the house."

"No one else wanted it?"

"Ethan, death scares people. They think it will infect them, get under their skin. It didn't bother me. It's a lovely house. I'm lucky to have it." She paused, smiling just a bit. "And frankly, even though it was years ago, I don't think anyone has the guts to ask me to move."

That night, after she related the story of her marriage, Ethan himself had trouble falling asleep, knowing Hannah was lying next to him, living, breathing, human.

He wondered:

Was this a good idea?

What if they were caught?

Had she done this before?

What if his parents found out?

A small part of him craved the solitude of sleeping in his own bed, the marvelous freedom of stretching out and knowing he wouldn't disturb anyone else. This was a different sensation now, being close to another person. He decided to give in to it, to let it envelop him, to let his body curl around Hannah's, grateful for simple things, not worrying about past or present, right or wrong, happy for warmth, for softness, for security.

Ethan slept in the next morning, waking at ten. His eyes settled on the south-facing gabled window as he tried to remember where he was. His jeans were draped across a chair in the corner, his shoes kicked under the burlwood dresser. The air smelled of breakfast, of pancakes and sizzling bacon fat. He looked to the empty space next to him on the bed, to the indentation on the pillow, and he remembered. Hannah. Yes, Hannah.

Ethan laid his head down again. He was safe here, wanted. There were so few places where he felt this. In his bedroom at his parents' house, perhaps, but it was a different kind of want. Good parents were supposed to love their children. To be loved by someone else, someone who didn't owe him anything, was another feeling entirely. Staying at Hannah's house, in her bedroom, was to exist in a world apart, separate from Berkley, surrounded only by the wildness of the forest and the expanse of the lake.

He thought about their sleeping together the night before as if it had happened years ago. It was nothing, really, just latex against flesh, kissing, the feeling of rubbing one's skin against that of another human being, semen. (He had been naked—naked!—with a woman.) But it was exactly what he had desired, that connection, for so long. It was what people talked about, fussed over, wrote of, yearned for—and he had to admit, he had never understood it. Now here it was, so simple, as if he could reach out and possess it completely.

The door opened, and Hannah came in with breakfast on a tray. He realized he had never seen her in her house at this time of day; whenever he had been over, it was always afternoon or evening. Now, in this light, he could see the pale down on her arms, a scar on the front of her ankle, the way the individual blond and brown strands of her hair intermingled. "I thought you deserved to sleep in," she said, placing the tray at the foot of the bed. Ethan sat up and surveyed her offering: pancakes dusted with sugar, chopped apples and nuts, bacon, syrup, orange juice, milk, a cup of coffee.

He started to feel uncomfortable, as he touched the creamer

filled with syrup; it was warm. He shuddered, a quick shiver Hannah couldn't have noticed. "You didn't need to do this. I would have helped you make breakfast."

"I enjoyed it." She sat down on the edge of the bed, clad only in a silk dressing gown, and crossed her legs. Ethan imagined her getting up early, making breakfast, puttering around the kitchen, light streaming in through the front windows.

Hannah leaned forward and kissed him quickly on the lips. He closed his mouth, afraid of his morning breath. He wanted to know the rules, wanted to know how it all worked. Once you had slept with a girl, could you then kiss her whenever you felt like it? Could she kiss you? When did he stop being her lover and become a student again? When he left her house? When spring break was over? When he graduated?

She was sitting so close to him, he could see the minute pores on her nose, the puffiness of lips recently kissed.

After taking a sip of coffee, Ethan leaned back in bed and sighed.

"What's wrong?" Hannah asked.

"Nothing," he said. "I'm just happy about all of this, and I don't—I don't want it to end."

"Let's not worry about endings," she said. "We haven't even really started yet, have we?"

"What do you mean by 'started'?"

Hannah lay down on the bed, her head propped up on her elbows, her legs crossed at the ankles like a little girl. "I want to know everything about you."

"Everything?"

"Your dreams, what you want out of life. What your childhood was like. I want to know what makes Ethan tick. Tell me your secrets."

"There's not much to tell." That wasn't true; there was plenty to tell.

"So make something up."

"Do I get to know that about you? Besides what you told me last night?"

"In time," she said, turning over and lying on her back, her hair spilling onto the duvet. "You and I are like unfinished sketches to each other. Some of the color has been filled in, most of the lines. But I want to see everything, the details, the subtleties." She looked at him and laughed. "I'm ridiculous, waxing poetic like this so early in the day." She pushed the tray toward him. "Eat your breakfast before it gets cold."

Ethan poured syrup on his pancakes. "What are we going to do today? Can we go to the tearoom for lunch?"

"Ethan," she said sternly, "you know we can't do that. A lot of faculty haven't left yet."

"What will we do then? It's a clear day. We can't stay indoors."

"I have an idea," she said. "Finish up your breakfast and get dressed, and we'll go for a drive."

CHAPTER 17

A few hours after Ethan woke up in Hannah's bed, the two of them were driving seventy miles an hour in the direction of the Connecticut state line. When they exited the main gates of the school and passed through Wilton, they had left the top on Jean-Paul, Ethan crouched down in the passenger seat to avoid being seen. Now the top was down on the car and the wind was blowing through their hair. Hannah wore a beret, making her look like Faye Dunaway in *Bonnie and Clyde*.

"We're going topless!" she cried, as Ethan blushed. The air was brisk and damp; everywhere, there was wreckage from the storm: tree branches, piles of dirt and leaves. He and Hannah chain-smoked cigarettes as they passed bucolic horse and dairy farms, private driveways to weekend homes, dense thickets of forest.

Hannah pulled a scarf out of her glove compartment and wrapped it around her neck so that it fluttered behind her in the wind. "Isadora Duncan died this way, you know!" she laughed. "Her scarf got caught in the wheel."

Ethan cringed as Hannah kept driving.

After passing the town of Canaan, Hannah turned off Route

44 onto a small dirt road. At the top of a hill was a cream-colored clapboard farmhouse, a gray barn, and miles of rolling countryside. Hannah parked in the gravel driveway in front of the barn.

A white-haired older couple stepped out of the house onto the front porch, he grizzled and paunchy in a plaid shirt, she thin and gaunt, wearing chunky turquoise jewelry and a long, flowing dress. Hannah introduced them as Harris Longworth and his wife, Emma. He was a painter, an abstract expressionist, who had retired to the Connecticut countryside after living in New York for thirty years. Hannah knew the couple from when she had lived in Paris, where they had met at a dinner party.

Harris led Ethan and Hannah to the barn to show them his latest passion. Half of the hangarlike space held a nineteenth-century printing press, a giant black monster of a machine. He showed Ethan some of the books that used to be printed on it; Harris held them lovingly, as if they were his children.

"Do you know who invented printing?" he asked Ethan.

"Gutenberg?" Ethan said.

"No," Harris bellowed. "The Chinese! It was the Chinese who did the first printing! Unfortunately, they had so many characters—their system wasn't practical the way Gutenberg's was." He looked at his own machine sadly. "It's hardly ever the first person to do anything who gets all the credit.

"My dream," he continued, "is to print a full-length book—a novel—on the press." He pointed to Hannah. "I keep telling this one she has to finish her manuscript so I can produce a special edition of it."

"My novel wouldn't be good enough for your press," Hannah said. "You should do a classic. Something that's gone out of print." She paused for a moment, running a finger over the black metal of the machine. "Something romantic. Love poems."

Emma came in with a pitcher of iced tea and four glasses on a tray. "Harris, you know you could never print an entire novel on that old thing. It wouldn't hold up." She distributed the glasses. "How do you know each other?" she asked Ethan.

"I'm a student at—"

"Through mutual friends," Hannah interrupted, smiling brightly.

"You're really too much," Harris said, pinching Hannah playfully on the arm. Ethan didn't enjoy feeling like the punch line to a joke.

After a tour of the rest of the property and a viewing of Harris's latest paintings, Emma prepared an early supper for all of them: a roasted ham, freshly baked biscuits, green beans, all washed down with white wine. Harris entertained them with stories about the New York art world, and Hannah got a little tipsy, her cheeks flushed with the Pinot Grigio. Under the table, she put her hand on Ethan's right knee.

After the dishes had been cleared, Harris told a strange story about a wealthy man who had lived on Lake Wilton about fifteen years ago. He was rich beyond belief, had made his money in pharmaceuticals. One afternoon, he was out on his motorboat when his engine died. Unable to call for help, he was stranded. It was the middle of the week, so there was no other traffic on the water, and his radio wasn't working. He waved his orange hazard flag to no avail. He resigned himself to drifting until he reached the other side, which could take several days. Just before dusk, a local boy, a high school junior, having seen his flag, came to save him in his Boston Whaler, towing the man to shore. In a fit of generosity, the man offered the boy anything he wanted—a full ride at college, a trip to Europe, a new car. The boy chose the car. Two days later, a red Ferrari was delivered at the boy's house, and he happily drove it around for the next twelve days. On the twelfth day, while speeding down a country road at seventy miles an hour, he hit a telephone pole. Because he wasn't wearing his seat belt, he was killed instantly.

The table sat silently while Harris told the story.

"So, what's the moral of it?" Hannah asked.

Harris shrugged. "Be careful what you wish for, I guess."

Emma chimed in. "Good things aren't always good?"

"Oh, that's too depressing!" Hannah said. "Let's have some music. What a blue story!"

"I've always thought it was fascinating. The turns of fate. The rich man was so generous that he killed the boy."

"He didn't mean to," Ethan said. "The boy shouldn't have been driving so fast. He should have asked for the college education, not the car."

"Well, of course, he should have asked for the college education!" Harris said. "But that's exactly the point. It's not always safe to give people what they think they want."

"How about some dessert?" Emma asked, apparently eager to change the subject from her husband's dime-store philosophizing. "I have a peach pie."

Though it felt strange being the youngest there, Ethan enjoyed the company of these adults. He was struck, though, with the sensation that Hannah had this entire world, an adult world, of which he was not a part. She had histories with these people, stories she could tell and listen to and understand. Ethan longed to have his own stories; he didn't want to live in someone else's past. With Hannah, he was tilling over the life she had already lived. Sorting her books, eating her husband's favorite dishes, visiting her old friends. He needed to come back to the present, his present, but he didn't know how.

That evening, Ethan and Hannah returned to the house. It had been a long day, and he was exhausted from the pressure of acting like an adult in front of Hannah's friends. He was also starting to feel a slight scratch in his throat, probably from all the cigarette smoking; he hoped it wasn't the onset of a cold.

"I should get to bed," Ethan said.

"Sure," she said, distracted. "I'll meet you up there. I'm going to poke around for a bit. I might go for a walk."

He left Hannah in the living room and mounted the stairs to the bedroom. He longed for the respite of sleep. Everything felt like it was closing in on him: the fling with Hannah, the fact that he was on campus when he should have been at home.

Ethan woke up in the middle of the night, jarred by the sensation of Hannah nibbling his ear. They made love, wordlessly, and this time it seemed familiar. He lasted nearly five minutes, which seemed like progress—he thought of things that weren't sexy, things like schoolwork and roadkill and his mother's illness. He felt a tickle in his throat, a rawness, as he came, but he tried to ignore it, collapsing back into sleep.

The next morning, Ethan woke at quarter to eight with a sore throat. It was raining outside, and Hannah was already up. He trudged downstairs and fixed himself some hot tea.

The two of them spent the day reading and relaxing, but by that evening, Ethan's sore throat had developed into a full-blown fever. He lay on the couch while Hannah brought him tea, echinacea, zinc lozenges, vitamin C. He knew it was most likely exhaustion from school, from the excitement of everything that had happened. But he also wondered if this was a sign that something wasn't right. He wondered if he should have been home in California. He wondered if his own mother was the one who should be taking care of him.

CHAPTER 18

Though the skillfully airbrushed photographs on the backs of her novels would indicate otherwise, Jackie Eldon had just turned forty-eight, and she decided it was time to have some work done. She had scheduled her surgery to coincide with Todd's spring break so he would be around to keep her company.

Jackie was having a face and forehead lift, performed by Dr. Arnold Lieberman, a well-known East Side plastic surgeon. The procedure would take place on the second day of Todd's vacation; after that, Jackie had been prescribed ten days of rest. He spent the first several days in her peach-colored bedroom, bringing her ice packs to control the swelling. Dr. Lieberman had said that frozen packages of peas and corn were the best remedy, so Jackie spent the days watching old movies and talking on the telephone while holding packs of frozen vegetables to her face, all the while joking to Todd that when she was done, he should take the packages to the kitchen and tell Jorge to defrost them for dinner. She was loosely bandaged for the first day, and had been instructed to remove the dressings after that, revealing skin that was red and swollen. Todd imagined that after she had healed, she would come out perfectly, like the happy conclusion in one of her novels. Her few wrinkles would be gone, her flesh tightened, her frown lines and eye bags reduced. Reality would be transformed to fit an ideal. Todd wished it were as easy to change on the inside; he would change so many things about himself, if only he had the chance.

For Ethan, the next several days passed in a blur, as he descended into the blistering fog of his fever. He would lie bundled up on the couch, attempting to read, the only sound the *tap-tap-tap* of Hannah's keyboard in her study. Several days in, he wanted to see a doctor—a fever wasn't supposed to last this long, was it?— but she wouldn't allow it, reasoning that word would get back to the school. They continued their lovemaking at regular intervals (at odd times of the day, without clearing things off the bed, without taking their socks off), even at the height of his illness, as if they were the last two people on earth and procreation was their duty. Ethan didn't know the human body was capable of so many orgasms in one day, but Hannah kept pushing him, and he acquiesced. Each time, Ethan collapsed on the bed, exhausted, when they were finished, the sheets sweaty and rumpled. The hot sensation of guilt would wash over him as he stared at the red walls of the room, traced the details of the black and gold border with his eyes, glanced at the mirror over her dresser. While they were together, he never looked in that mirror—he didn't want to see what they were doing, didn't want to see how it was reflected from afar. He wondered if he was the first student to experience this. He knew he wasn't the first man—that inevitable fact didn't bother him—but there was something in her attitude, her determination about the whole business, that made him think it had happened before. He had examined the box of condoms in her bathroom, a box that was nearing expiration, a box that had certainly been opened long before he came into her life. Each little package represented to him one of her lovers, a long line of men streaming back into the past. He felt a twinge of nausea when his mind ventured to this place, to the idea that what they were doing wasn't right, that he, like all the others, would eventually leave Hannah's life.

She changed the sheets every day, washing and ironing them so each evening when they returned to bed, they were perfect: smooth, white, unsullied.

Over the course of the week, Hannah never got sick. It was as if she had a magical immunity, as if her hot white light was healing him, as if she were transmitting an elixir each time they were together.

When he woke in the mornings, he would feel, just for a moment, that he had lived there all along, that he had always called this place home.

One afternoon, Ethan woke from a nap to find Hannah standing over him. "The trip to Harris and Emma's may have been a mistake."

Ethan blinked his sleepy eyes at her, confused.

"Susan and Cass came by. Asked me to go on a walk. It didn't seem like them. They were so persistent. I said I wasn't feeling well. I didn't want them to stay, and I didn't want to leave you alone."

"Did they stay long?"

"Cass used the bathroom. It creeped me out. It was like they were doing everything they could to prolong the visit."

Ethan imagined what they might think of the house in its current state; was it obvious Hannah was housing an invalid? He wondered if they had seen the dirty dishes in the sink, if they knew she had been cooking for two. Could Ms. Davis have perceived the slightest male presence in the powder room, a hint of sweat, a splash of urine? Hannah was an immaculate housekeeper, but even with her attentions, the house felt to Ethan like it was crawling in sickness and decay.

"I can't stay here anymore," Ethan said. "They must know. This is crazy—"

"Susan wouldn't do anything," Hannah said. "She's your adviser. She likes you. Trust me, she won't say a word."

After the visit from her two colleagues, Hannah did tell Ethan that they shouldn't go outside, not even on the porch. She started locking the doors, even when she and Ethan were home together. His fever was still running high; his tongue was yellow, his skin pasty, and his head felt like it was closing in on itself. But being with Hannah made him whole, like two parts coming together. It gave him a reason to feel better. In the evenings, they played Scrabble together, making up words, joking and laughing, even through the confusion of his illness.

On Wednesday afternoon, Hannah pulled out a loaf of bread to make Ethan a sandwich and found its underside covered in mold. She went out to buy groceries, instructing him not to switch on any lights while she was gone. He sprawled out on the couch in her living room as the sun sank low behind the hills. Ethan wanted to feel a spring breeze, to clear the house of the stench of day-old garbage and that morning's breakfast, but he couldn't open any windows, for fear of being seen.

He was bored of reading, couldn't sleep anymore. He had perused her kitchen cupboards, had examined all of the photographs on the mantelpiece. The two of the boy were indeed of Bertrand, Alain's son, for whom Hannah apparently bore no ill will. Ethan's eye was drawn to the storage room in the back. He decided to take a look, just to see.

The door was unlocked. The room was filled with boxes, bric-a-brac from Hannah's past lives. Old tennis rackets, a rocking horse, skis. As he made his way past a stack of file boxes, he noticed a pile of paintings, partially hidden under a sheet. They varied in style and subject matter: landscapes, portraits, a still life. He was going to examine them more closely, to see if any had a signature (he suspected Hannah had done them when she was younger), when he stopped at one. It was of Hannah, a younger version of her. She sat in the corner of a room, looking out a window at a blurred cityscape, her blond hair free and unfettered. The style was loose, almost expressionistic, but it was unmistakably her, lovely and innocent. He looked at the back; on the wooden frame, it was signed in pencil: *Bertrand Reinard*, with the year. Ethan took the painting from the room and leaned the canvas against one of the chairs at the kitchen table. He wanted to ask her about it, to see if it would help answer some of his questions about her past. There was so little they could explore, locked in that house together; he hoped the portrait might get her talking about something beyond their lives at Berkley.

When Hannah returned half an hour later, she was in high spirits, as if the brisk trip into town had refreshed her. "They had the most wonderful bagels at that little bakery, so I picked up—" She put down her bag of groceries as her sentence was cut short. She was looking at the painting.

"Where did you find that?"

"It was in the spare room. It's beautiful. I thought you might—"

"What were you doing in there?"

"I'm sorry, I was bored, I was just poking around—"

"You're not supposed to go in there. Ethan, you may be staying here, but that area is private." It was a tone of voice he had never heard before, didn't even know she was capable of.

"I'm sorry, I just—the painting was so lovely, I thought you might want to display it." His voice quavered. What had he done? "I think you look so pretty in it."

"I wish you would put it away. Right now." She paused for a moment as Ethan remained frozen. "Oh, never mind, I'll do it myself." She snatched it up and rushed across the room, depositing it back where Ethan had discovered it and shutting the door behind her.

He sat on the couch, stunned. It was as if he had slapped her, as if he had just served her the most offensive insult.

"I'm so sorry, Hannah, I didn't know . . ." His voice trailed off. It must have had something to do with her ex-husband.

"God, there are plenty of books to read here, and you're bored!"

He had no idea what to say, so he went upstairs, anything to get out of her way. He washed his face with cold water, and then sat on the bed, nearly in tears, feeling the hot flashes at the corners of his eyes. What had he brought forth in her? What memory had he triggered by showing her that painting? The room wasn't locked. The stack hadn't even been completely covered. And yet something had caused this reaction, as if that painting in particular was off-limits. Was it the mere act of viewing her younger self? She didn't look terribly different from the woman in the painting. Perhaps it had to do with the time she had been with Alain, that a painting by his son reminded her of that. Ethan felt he should have known; he should have known not to delve into her past. He curled up on the bed, the deeply morose sensation hitting him that he would never get it right, that even when things appeared to be working, they weren't working at all.

On Thursday morning, he woke up from a wooden sleep, the type of slumber where he felt stiff and trapped within the armor of bedding. He had pulled the sheets completely around himself, so Hannah lay next to him, naked and exposed, her nightgown accidentally bunched up around her waist. He covered her quickly as she started to stir. Sitting up in the sunny bedroom, he realized he felt better. His fever had lifted; he had energy for the first time in days. Hannah opened her eyes and smiled at him, giving him a kiss. All had been forgiven from the previous afternoon; it had happened to two different people entirely. As long as he didn't tread on her past, he hoped he could enjoy the

Hannah he knew, the Hannah he had grown to love over the past six months.

"You're so delicious," she said, kissing him again. "I just want to eat you up."

As Ethan prepared to leave Hannah's house, he sensed a restlessness. He didn't know if it was in his head, or if it was all around him, the endless planning and moving about. Cooking a final meal for the two of them on Friday night, cleaning relentlessly—it was as if she had discovered that the house was filthy, and only a thorough bout of spring cleaning would remedy the situation. He felt his stay should be extended or shortened, but that it would not end happily if he left on his scheduled departure date.

The previous evening, the first day Ethan had felt better, Hannah came back from the bathroom, noting that they were out of protection. She asked him if he was comfortable not using anything.

A deep sense of exhaustion crept up Ethan's legs; though he was no longer sick, he wanted to go back to sleep. "I don't—are you sure that's a good idea?"

"It'll be fine," she said. "It will be wonderful." She had been tested, she said. She was on the pill. There would be no danger.

Todd had told Ethan about having sex without condoms. He had done it with one of his girlfriends after they had been together for four months. Ethan knew it was too early to be doing this. He trusted Hannah, but he didn't know if he was ready.

He told her again that he didn't want to do it, that they should wait until the morning, but Hannah convinced him, not letting go. They made love, twice that night, before falling asleep.

The next morning, Ethan was strong enough to tell Hannah he still didn't feel comfortable. She reluctantly made a trip into town to buy condoms.

While she was away, Ethan decided he really should shave, as he hadn't in four days. He had run out of fresh blades, so he went to search in the small cabinet in her bathroom to see if she had any disposable ones. He rifled around on the lower shelf, knocking over a few things: an extra tube of toothpaste, hand cream, cotton balls. He paused as he thought he saw the edge of a box of condoms—he would recognize that package anywhere, racy as it was, with all it represented—hidden from immediate view. He pulled it out; it was a brand-new, unopened box. She must have forgotten they were here. Or did she know and wasn't telling him? He found a razor, put everything back in its place, and set about shaving.

Soon after, she returned home from the drugstore, laughing about her awkward interaction with the pharmacist, joking that he must think of her as the town harlot, popping in on a Friday morning to buy prophylactics and nothing else. Ethan was about to point out the box she had forgotten, but he decided to let it be. He would avoid confrontation for the rest of his time there. They made love twice more that day; it was almost becoming automatic, and Ethan dared to imagine that he was skilled at it.

Despite her good humor about going into town, he could still see, as he put the condom on, how disappointed she was. She had offered him an invitation to intimacy and he had, after sampling a morsel, rejected it. He didn't want to hurt her, but after that moment of being inside her, of being as close to a person as one could be, he needed a break. He felt that morning that he had rescued himself, as if he had swum from the bottom of Lake Wilton and could breathe again. He was still in the lake, unquestionably, but he was treading water. He was no longer drowning. He would let himself feel the joy of being with her, the excitement, but he would know his boundaries.

On Saturday morning, Hannah drove Ethan to the airport. The conversation was awkward between them, and he found his attention wandering between surveying the country roads on the way to Hartford and looking at her. Something had hardened in

Hannah; perhaps it was simply that they were out in public, and she couldn't show her affection.

As they rode together in Jean-Paul, he thought about how he loved feeling close to her, but also sensed the relief of saying good-bye. He felt a pressure lifting as he realized he belonged at home. He belonged with his family.

"I wish you could stay longer," she said, as they pulled up at the terminal.

He knew he couldn't, that it was time to go back to California.

CHAPTER 19

Todd continued to mope around the apartment, taking care of his mother when she needed help, but mostly watching television and smoking pot. He couldn't tell if Jackie, in her Vicodin haze, could see he was stoned half the time. Spending so much time with her, he suspected they might run out of things to talk about; Todd wanted to turn her attention away from him, so they chatted about other people. He mentioned to her that Ethan's mother was ill. He knew that Jackie, perversely, liked to hear about tragedies. Cancer, especially. It gave her a sense of balance. She didn't want it to happen to anyone close to her; she didn't want it to happen to anyone at all. But if it had to, a person once removed was the perfect distance. It was her system of spiritual penance, an explanation for all the good things in her life. She was blessed, and so others must suffer.

Midway through the break, Todd decided to go downtown to pick up some more pot. There was a dealer he usually called, a connection through his friend Brooks, but there was something about the adventure of heading to the East Village that Todd liked.

He took the subway to Astor Place, and walked east down St.

Mark's; he knew that was the place to go, near Tompkins Square Park. He stopped in front of a bookshop to light a cigarette. As he cupped his flame away from the breeze, he noticed something familiar in the window. It was Ben Atwater's short story collection, his name suspended above an illustration of a man's shoe. The thought of Ben sent off a pang in Todd's stomach, but he kept walking. He wouldn't buy a copy; he had other things to think about. Several days earlier, he had called Ethan's house in California. His father had picked up the phone, and said Ethan wasn't home. "Didn't he tell you?" Mr. Whitley said. "He's spending the week helping one of your teachers." Todd had hung up slowly after thanking Ethan's dad. He wondered if he should call Hannah. He didn't want to, not for fear of what he might find out, but because he was afraid she might not let on that Ethan was there. He couldn't stand the idea of them lying to him. Perhaps it was better not to know.

He and Ethan and Hannah had been a virtual threesome for much of the winter, and now, in his most horrifying of nightmares, he had been shut out. The idea of Ethan sleeping with Hannah—and that, he thought, must be what they were doing, for why else would they be spending so much time together?—sickened him. There had been the warnings from Brian, but what could Todd possibly do? Ethan had lied about his vacation. Not only had he rejected Todd—multiple times, really, in the most subtle of ways, though Todd had never made more of an advance than he had that night in the cemetery—but he had denied him knowledge of the most intimate of moments. His friend could be losing his virginity this very instant, and Todd might never know. All because it was with a teacher, someone Todd could have directed Ethan away from. By paying more attention to him. By introducing him to more girls. But no, Todd had wanted Ethan all to himself. And because of that, he had lost him.

* * *

After buying two dime bags in the park, Todd headed back uptown to the apartment. He opened the giant window in his bathroom, shoved the buds into his one-hitter, fired it up, and inhaled the sharp, sweet smoke. Todd went over to his bed and sat up against its headboard with the burning pipe still hot in his hand.

A few moments later, his mother appeared at the door. She wasn't wearing any bandages, just a light layer of foundation to cover some of the redness. He had to admit she looked better. Tighter. More like she used to in pictures with his father.

"I just wanted to see if you were home," she said.

"Of course I'm home."

His mother sniffed the air. "Are you smoking again?"

"I had a cigarette." He knew she didn't care, but he still didn't want her to know how much pot he was smoking.

"It doesn't smell like a cigarette."

Jackie walked over to the bed and picked up the one-hitter. She grabbed the lighter, raised the pipe to her mouth, and took a long inhale.

Todd jumped up off the bed. "Mom! What are you doing?"

"Fair's fair. It's my money you used to buy the stuff."

"Right, but—" Todd sat down again. His mother was so strange.

"Tatiana went home for the day, I finished two chapters, and I think I deserve to relax."

Todd sighed. "I guess so."

She put the pipe down on the table. "Try not to burn the place down," she said. "I'm going to see what's happening with dinner." She walked to the door, and then turned around, stifling a cough. "Oh, and, honey?"

"Yeah?"

"Next time, use a real dealer. I haven't smoked stuff this bad since I was in high school."

* * *

That evening, after his buzz had worn off, Todd went drinking with Brooks Stewart, who was on spring break from Dalton. He had just returned from skiing in Aspen, where his family owned a cabin, *cabin* being the operative word for a three-story, five-bedroom house in the mountains, complete with chef's kitchen, home theater, and sauna.

After seeing an action movie at the nearby multiplex, they stopped at a Korean deli and bought two six-packs of beer. The boys sat drinking on the steps of the Met, looking down Eighty-second Street. The waxing moon cast shadows across the stonework, illuminating the columns of the museum.

Brooks's family had a patrician lineage that went back to the seventeenth century. He had always accepted Todd, though Jackie's money fell squarely under the category of "new." It was something most people ignored; in New York, one could rise through the ranks with astonishing speed. Jackie, for all her stature, her glamour, her position in New York society, had, just twelve years ago, been little more than a secretary. Their family, the three-person Eldon clan, was nothing compared to the Stewarts, generations of whom had attended Ivy League schools, belonged to the city's most prestigious clubs, had their daughters debut at cotillions and marry into other wealthy families. Todd and Jackie and Brian had everything money could buy, but they didn't have lineage. Jackie always said that it didn't matter, that if you behaved in a decent way, you would be accepted by anyone.

Brooks told Todd about his application to Harvard. He had gotten a recommendation from his uncle, who was a trustee; he hoped that would guarantee his acceptance.

He took another swig of his beer and looked at Todd. "What's been going on with you?"

"Nothing. The usual." Todd picked at a hangnail, hoping Brooks wouldn't interrogate him too much.

"How's school? Are you dating anyone?"

"No. It's fine. I don't know."

"That bad, huh?" Brooks gave him a lopsided grin as he started peeling the label off his beer bottle.

"I guess so."

"Well, I'm fucking bored as hell in the city. I can't wait to leave. It's supposed to be so great, your senior year and everything. Do whatever you want, you know?"

Todd nodded.

"But it's not. School gets too small. I can't imagine how it must be for you, being stuck up there in the sticks all the time."

Todd wanted to tell Brooks how he was feeling. It was all too fantastic, somehow, to explain his concerns about Ethan. Sure, what his friend did was his own business; Todd had no firm responsibility to him. Through the daze of his beer buzz, Todd yearned to shake off his connection to Ethan Whitley, his ridiculous obsession with this guy from California who had chosen to spend his holiday with a teacher instead of with him.

Todd realized, though, as he chugged down another beer, that he was angry: Ethan could do what he wished, and he could take the consequences with it. If he wasn't going to let Todd in on his secret—and how long had this been going on for? Weeks? Months?—then Todd felt no compunction to help him. He wouldn't tell him what Brian had said. The information would be meaningless anyway.

Still, Todd felt that after all they had shared, after all his attempts to introduce Ethan to his friends, to integrate him into a normal life at Berkley, he had, in the most elemental way, failed.

During his flight to California, Ethan dreamt that Hannah was sitting next to him, that she was coming home to meet his parents. She was going to tell them Ethan would be living with her from now on. His parents hadn't said anything about it; they had been mute. Ethan and Hannah drove back to Wilton in Jean-Paul and began their new life together. As he woke, he felt himself lurching in his seat, his head lolling forward, aching from the weight.

He inhaled the cold, stale plane air. They were to land in thirty minutes. He was sitting near the front of the cabin, and the stewardess was handing out little cups of champagne, just a few sips in each. "Left over from first class," she explained, handing one to Ethan. "You're old enough, right?"

He nodded, as the flight attendant winked at him. (Had she sensed he was a young man on the verge of adulthood? Was that what he was?) The champagne tasted a little bit like Hannah's, not so rich, rather like he imagined airplane champagne to taste, not that he knew anything about the finer points of wine or champagne. He smiled at the process of accumulated knowledge. It wasn't so much about learning; it was more about faking it until you were proficient. He thought of the last time they had kissed, and he felt pinpricks of excitement in his thighs, a giddy elation as he collected his belongings and exited the plane.

When they met at baggage claim, his father offering an awkward embrace, Ethan wondered if he sensed a change in him. Since everything had happened with his mother, his dad had become much freer with expressing affection. Lawrence Whitley still didn't really know how to reach out to his son. But he would grasp hold of that nebulous mass known as emotions; he would try.

They walked together to the parking garage, passing families, young children, couples with strollers. He wanted to say something to his dad about what was happening with Hannah, about his confusion, but he didn't know how he would phrase it. Lawrence dealt with circuits and diagrams, systems that were logical and rational. There was nothing rational about what was happening to Ethan: his odd, clandestine relationship with Hannah, her frosty reaction to the painting, the accidentally misplaced condoms. The fact that despite feeling the relief of coming home, he already missed her.

"Where's Mom?" Ethan asked.

"Your mother isn't feeling well," Lawrence said. "She's been in bed for a few days."

Ethan looked at him, searching for a story in his father's face. All these months, his parents had assured him that his being away would be best, but now he wasn't certain. "Why didn't you tell me?"

"She didn't want you to worry. We knew you were coming home today."

They drove back to Palo Alto in silence, listening only to the muted strings of the local classical music station. When they arrived at the house, Ethan ran in to see his mother. He imagined she would be fine, sitting at her computer, happily typing away, her gray hair tied up in a ponytail.

"Mom!" he called. He heard the muffled sound of the television from the bedroom.

"I'm in here," she said.

He bounded in. She was lying on the bed, her head propped up on a stack of pillows. Her hair was still short; it had recently been cut. The windows were open, letting in the night air, and there was a fresh bouquet of tulips, the kind from the grocery store, on the bedside table. His father had done everything to make the room pleasant. She reached for the remote control to pause an episode of *Mystery!*, a longtime guilty pleasure of hers.

"What happened?"

She smiled sadly. "Those little cells of mine won't stop working. They just keep multiplying like crazy."

"Did you go back for more chemo?"

She nodded. Ethan looked down at her hands. Her palms were wrapped in bandages.

"What are those?" he asked.

"It's nothing. It's just . . . it's just a reaction to the drugs."

"Let me see."

His mother slowly unwrapped the bandage on her left hand.

Her fingernails were darkened. The palm of her exposed hand, slick with ointment, was red, swollen, and peeling.

"The bandages keep me from scratching them."

"Does it hurt?"

"It itches," she sighed. "I'm starting to think that's worse than regular pain." She bit her cheek. "On the inside of my mouth, too. At least I get all the morphine I want." She reached for a cup at her bedside table, and sipped some liquid through a straw.

Ethan looked down. "I feel terrible. I should have been here."

"Honey, I don't want you worrying about this. It's nothing."

"It's not nothing. Your hand looks—it looks bad, and you didn't tell me."

"Ethan, the most important thing is your education. And this teacher, this friend you have . . . we weren't going to stop you from staying with her."

"What if something else had happened?"

"It's not as bad as it looks." She started wrapping up her hand. "They say the swelling should go down in a few weeks."

Ethan stared at his mother. With her hands wrapped up like that—those hands that allowed her to write, to communicate with the world—she didn't look human. He wished she could peel off the bandages, making the swelling go away as one would tear off a glove. "I can't go back to school. Not if you're like this."

She looked at him sternly. "You will finish at Berkley, whether you like it or not. I don't care if they have to send me in a wheelchair. I'm going to see my son graduate from high school."

Lawrence appeared at the door. Now, under his eyes, Ethan noticed the dark circles of worry.

"Come on, kiddo," he said. "Let your mother rest."

As he carried his duffel bag to his room, guilt hammered away at him. He had caused this by not paying attention, by not asking after his mother's condition. If he had come home a week earlier, this might not have happened. His mother would be healthy, energetic, working on her latest book, spending time outdoors.

Part of him, though, wanted to go back to Hannah's house. This couldn't touch him there. He didn't know, of course, once he returned, if things would be the same. Surely they couldn't carry on in the same way while school was in session. There was that, a simple reality, and then there was the greater possibility, a hazard he pushed to the far reaches of his mind.

The greater, more terrifying risk was that nothing stayed a secret at Berkley Academy for very long. While so much was unspoken in those halls, while rumors flared up and then died over the course of an afternoon, it was a place where everyone eventually learned everything. Ethan wasn't naïve enough to believe he and Hannah might be an exception. There had been the visit from Ms. Hedge to Hannah's house; there was the school security patrol that could surely see their silhouettes in the evenings. There was the pharmacist in town who would chatter about the schoolteacher buying contraceptives. And there was Todd, who Ethan thought surely suspected something, and whom he had, in turn, cruelly pushed away, for fear of recrimination.

She called him every night he was home. Speaking long-distance—Ethan in his own room, Hannah less an actual person than an idea, a voice coming through the receiver—strengthened their curious bond. It was the purest form a relationship could take; there were no distractions, none of the mirage of emotions that physical intimacy created. Ethan wondered if he would remember these times when he would carry the cordless phone from the kitchen, taking her calls in the privacy of his bedroom, lying on that rocket ship bedspread, these times when they were together but also far apart, as the best ones they had enjoyed. It was uncomplicated, freed as they were from the constraints of school and age and appearance. He told her things he might not have told her in person. He said something, finally, about his mother. She chided him for not mentioning it earlier; she felt terrible, she said, about keeping him away from his parents. He would look out his window into the darkness of the yard as they spoke, thinking of her, several thousand miles away, alone in her house by the lake.

A few days later, he was hanging out at a café on Waverley Street in Palo Alto. Ethan had escaped from the house to do some reading, and was sitting outside with an iced coffee, the warm California weather a relief after New England's winter. He was still feeling awful about his mother's situation, but he did his best to focus on the few things that were good in his life: that he would be hearing soon from the colleges to which he had applied, that the school year was almost over. And that he had finally had sex, was having (he was almost certain) a relationship, confusing as it was.

"Ethan?"

He looked up. It was Vivian Frasier, in a flowery skirt and white tank top.

"It's so good to see you. What are you doing here?" She leaned against the empty chair at his table. He motioned for her to sit down.

"I'm on spring break."

"Of course. How's school going?"

"It's good," he said, stirring the ice around in his cup with a straw. "I'm, uh, dating someone." It was the first time the phrase had occurred to him, though it sounded utterly ridiculous. *Dating someone.* No one had ever asked him if he was seeing anyone in the past; it was as if he were diseased, as if asking it might implicate the questioner into his horrible chasm of despair.

"That's terrific! Who is she?"

Ethan paused. There was no way he could tell her; in the harsh sunlight, he hardly knew himself if it qualified as real. "Just a girl at school," he finally said. That much was true.

"I'm so happy for you."

"Thanks."

Her face clouded for a moment. "You didn't happen to share

any of our conversation from last December with Hannah McClellan, did you?"

Ethan got a queasy feeling. He took a sip of his coffee. "Why's that?"

Vivian continued. "Several days after we spoke, she called me. I don't know how she got my number, I guess maybe through the school. She said she had heard I had been talking about her. She basically implied that I shouldn't see you."

"Oh God," Ethan said. "I mentioned that I had met you, and I asked about that crazy story about the couple who left the school. She said it wasn't true. I'm sorry. I never should have brought it up." He hated this. Vivian was crashing in on his reality, the reality he had helped create.

"I told you, Ethan, she's crazy. But don't quote me on it this time."

"I won't." Ethan pulled out his pack of cigarettes and lit one, taking a sharp drag. He had been smoking more and more since leaving Hannah's. His parents had been so preoccupied that they hadn't said anything about the smell that had started to permeate his clothes, hair, skin.

"Since when do you smoke?"

"Bad Berkley habit, I guess."

Vivian reached forward, took his cigarette, and put it to her lips, exhaling a long drag herself. "The school can do that to you," she said, giving him a wry look.

There was something in her tone that was nearing self-righteousness, which Ethan resented. Would things have been better for him if he had stayed in California? Should he have resisted his parents' desire a year ago to send him to the East Coast? He would never know.

"It's not like I have a choice. I only have a few more months there."

"They're always the strangest ones," she said. "Inevitably, a few kids get kicked out. Some coast through, assuming they got into good schools. And others just fuck around, though no one really seems to notice."

"How was it for you?"

She paused, remembering. "I was sad, mostly. Sad to leave, but also sad about everything I'd missed. I had a steady boyfriend through most of the spring, and I spent so much time with him, I forgot about a lot of my friends."

"I think that may have happened with me as well," Ethan said. "This girl I'm seeing . . . it's gotten kind of intense."

"That can happen," Vivian said. "I just wish someone had told me that you only get your senior spring once."

The mere phrase *senior spring* seemed yet another promise made by Berkley, a fantasy constructed, a parade of photos in the yearbook, a spread in the school paper. Ethan had the grim premonition that it would not be like that for him, that there would be no lounging on beach towels on senior grass, enjoying volleyball games, donning a backward baseball cap and cycling into town. He realized, unexpectedly, how much, how desperately, he longed to turn everything around.

On his last full day at home, Ethan sat with his mother in her bedroom. It was darkened but for a reading lamp, as she was fading in and out of sleep. She was surrounded by books, as she had been her entire life, which comforted Ethan, as if she might not feel so removed from the world. He was never sure what to discuss with his mother, how much to tell her (Should he tell her anything at all? If so, what?). He had been vague about the details of life at Berkley, and she hadn't pressed him.

On her bedside table was a worn hardcover copy of the Woolf essay "On Being Ill." Ethan picked up the slim gray volume and flipped through its pages. After he had read for a bit, his mother woke, and smiled at him.

"It's a bit dark," she said, motioning to the book.

Ethan shrugged. "I like it. She describes things so beautifully." He put it down on the side of the bed. "I'm not sure I want to go back."

He knew his mother would assume her expected role. "You have to," she said. "You don't have a choice. Come on, you don't want to hang out here with me. I've got time. And you'll never get those months back again. You belong at school."

"I guess so. I, just—things haven't exactly gone the way I expected them to."

"How so?"

"I thought I would have made more friends. You know, stuff like that." It was embarrassing to admit this to his mother, though he imagined she suspected it.

"Everything will change for you when you're in college," she said. "I know it will. It did for me, it did for your father. You may not find what you're looking for at Berkley. You may not find it at college, either. But, Ethan, you can't let these circumstances take hold of you. I know things have been hard, but this doesn't give you a free pass to be miserable. We sent you to Berkley so you could be happy. So you could have a better experience than you would here. Please don't tell me it wasn't worth it."

"No, it was," he admitted. "I guess it just wasn't what I thought it would be."

She smiled. "Nothing ever is. But you've got to take control of things. You could end up in New England or five miles down the road. You must promise me you're not going to let all this"— she motioned around her—"get you down."

"Okay." He realized that she thought her sickness was responsible for his malaise. It wasn't, but he didn't know how to tell her.

She smoothed over the blanket, rearranged some of the pillows behind her head. "Honey, you're not angry that you left, are you?"

"No, I'm not. I think it was the best thing for me."

"Good. I couldn't stand it if you were." She turned to her cup of water. "Do you think you'd be up for a trip to the kitchen?"

He nodded, and went to refill her cup. When he returned, she was reading a book, so he picked up the Woolf again, not wanting to disturb her. He turned the page, and a sentence stood out, as it was underlined in light pencil: *We do not know our own souls, let alone the souls of others*. The section was about being alone, how sometimes that was better than attempting to understand the mind of another person. He knew this, far too well. His eyes rested on the words until they became jumbled and blurred, and he was forced to take off his glasses, to stare at the nothingness at the foot of his mother's bed, anything to avoid the fact that even with Hannah in his life, he was still, at heart, alone.

CHAPTER 20

Todd's memories of his father were separate and distinct, like dioramas in a museum, wholly cut off from a larger narrative: crouching on the toilet lid in his parents' bathroom and watching his father shave, the roughness of his face before, the smoothness afterward. Don taking him and Brian to the park, before they had moved right across the street from it, playing in the bushes with his brother while their father watched nearby. The four of them eating brunch at a restaurant (something on Columbus Avenue; Jackie had not been pleased with the service), his mother insisting that they wash their hands before eating, their father saying it didn't matter, that a little New York City dirt never hurt anyone. The way his father smelled after he drank his scotch at night, slightly antiseptic, sugary, a hint of rotting wood. The night he had let Todd, age four, take a few sips and then watched as his son wobbled his way back to the boys' shared bedroom.

Don Eldon had been striking, a man who could have stepped out of a Jockey underwear ad, an NYU graduate, a business major from an upper-middle-class family in Rye. Jackie loved him even though he had never really succeeded at anything. He had his real estate license; his parents had been supplementing his modest broker's income for years. As Jackie's career started to explode—it was her fourth completed manuscript that finally sold, making all those long nights worth it—it became clear that she and the boys could get along without his money, if they ever had to.

At the same time, Don's family threatened to cut him off after an incident one Thanksgiving when he drank too much during dinner, yelled at his father, and passed out in a guest room for three hours. By then, Jackie had sold the proposals to her second and third novels, garnering six-figure advances, and they had used the money to rent a better apartment on the East Side. Todd could never recall the day his father disappeared; it had not been prefaced by shouting or doors slamming or meals ruined. He only remembered the days after, his mother emerging from the bedroom and dragging herself to the makeshift office in the corner of the den to ensure that she would meet her latest deadline. An au pair cared for the boys, five and nine, while their mother worked, taking them to the park, making them dinner. It wasn't until several months later, when the papers were signed, that Jackie said their father wasn't coming back. She told them, that afternoon in their kitchen on East Seventy-fourth Street, the one that smelled faintly of Merit Ultra Lights, that while they might not have their father anymore, she would make sure they got everything else they wanted, even if did not involve having a man in the house.

Todd's cell phone started chirping while he was lying on his bed, laptop in front of him, simultaneously instant-messaging with friends, reading his favorite blogs, and surfing for porn. His father hardly ever called, and when he did, Todd usually got the call as a voice mail; it was as if they were incapable of connecting, even over the phone.

Don was in town unexpectedly, and wondered if they could meet at a diner near Washington Square. He was there now, killing time. Could he buy his son lunch?

Todd had no plans, so he agreed to come downtown, throwing on a navy peacoat over the jeans and sweater he had been wearing. Todd wondered why he hadn't called earlier. Maybe he was worried that Todd would tell Jackie, and she would advise against it.

Todd didn't care. He would have gone anyway.

This was the first visit he could remember that hadn't been initiated by his mother, though she had sworn in recent years that she was giving up, that the rewards her boys were getting out of the relationship far outweighed the trauma their father put them through. Don would be forty-five minutes late in picking them up at the airport in Fort Lauderdale, would make them sit through dinners at steak-and-lobster restaurants with his latest girlfriend, a woman who no doubt would be gone the next time they saw him. He would get drunk on chardonnay served from a carafe and go on rants against Jackie, how awful she was, how she used people and spat them out. The women his father dated were nearly always the same, cheap imitations of his mother: a Jackie with enlarged breasts, a Jackie with a tan, a Jackie who wore tank tops to restaurants.

Todd's mother used to insist that the boys visit him at least every few years, that they needed to have some kind of relationship with their father, as much as she no longer loved him, as much as getting him to connect with his sons was a chore. It was important, she had always said, that her boys had him in their lives. He had never fought particularly hard to see them; lately it seemed that if his ex-wife didn't want them to visit, he wasn't going to object.

But now, Todd thought, as he rode the train downtown, this was different. He felt like a schoolgirl invited out by her crush. He wanted it so desperately, that intangible sense of an older man caring for him, though he had no idea what it would be like—having his father in his life, seeing him sober (his mother had mentioned recently that he had stopped drinking, but that didn't always change people, she warned). Maybe he would visit more often. Maybe he would come for holidays.

His father had chosen a sad little diner near the park, a place where an overweight woman with dyed-red hair wearing a rhinestone-studded top sat at the cash register, a giant bowl of mints in front of her. Love songs hummed in the background. Todd glanced around: people eating alone. Perhaps this was the hour, two or three o'clock, when people did that. Locating his father wasn't simply a matter of finding the one single person sitting in a booth. There were half a dozen people eating alone, virtually an entire restaurant of them—old ladies, skate punks, misfits—all of them watching, looking.

His father glanced up from his copy of *USA Today*. He was different from the man Todd remembered, the man he had seen more than a year ago, the man he imagined when they spoke on the phone on holidays, or when Todd needed something—though needing something and getting it were two different things where his father was concerned. He was cleaned up, though he still looked like an out-of-towner in his Dockers khakis and linen button-down shirt. Todd was momentarily embarrassed to be meeting him, to be related to him.

Don got up from the booth. He reached out a hand to Todd, and Todd (foolishly, he would later think) grappled his dad like a monkey, attempting a hug. His father halfheartedly patted his back, segueing the embrace into one of those uncomfortable man-hugs, the type when neither party knows exactly when to let go. To hang on too long would chip away at the rugged veneer that a man like Don Eldon had so carefully built up over the years. Thankfully, they both pulled away at the same time.

In front of his father was a half-full glass of what looked like ginger ale. Todd slid into the booth, placing his messenger bag down on the flower-patterned vinyl.

"I'm glad you could make it," Don said. There was an awkward pause, as Todd wasn't sure what to say. He picked up the menu that had been placed in front of him, a heavy tome he knew would contain five hundred different choices, all of them potentially mediocre. He examined his father's face. A few more lines than last time, around his eyes: too much time spent in the Florida sun. He had put on a few more pounds. But there was something within him, Todd decided, that was good, something in him that wanted to reach out. He had to believe that. Todd had held up his end of things. He didn't smell like cigarette smoke; he had brushed his teeth, fixed his hair. He looked nice, the way a son should look when meeting his father. He had not worn anything that was too fancy, or too preppy, anything of which his father wouldn't approve.

"What are you doing in New York?" Todd asked. He would get a burger, he decided. A burger was safe; a burger was always the same.

"I wanted to see my sons. Brian hasn't called me back yet. I don't know where he is. I don't like this, not knowing where my kids are."

You caused this. You were away for all those years. You can't expect us to be waiting for you when you come back.

"I guess he's just busy," Todd said. It was his duty, he felt, to protect his brother's privacy. He knew exactly where Brian was—at home now, recovering from a hangover, easily reachable. If Brian hadn't called their father back, there was probably a reason.

"I want to see my sons. Is that too much to ask?" His father didn't seem angry as much as he was sad. But Todd didn't feel sorry for him.

Todd took a deep breath. "No, not at all."

"Then why won't he call me back?"

"I don't know. Maybe he doesn't always want it to be on your terms. There were times when we wanted to see you, too, and you weren't around." Todd couldn't believe he was saying this. He shifted in the booth, felt himself checking his bag, his coat, as if they might have slid onto the floor.

"Come on, kid, I've had a lot on my plate. You know how that is."

Todd started tapping his feet. He wished the waitress would come and take their order so he could eat, so he could stop looking at his father, stop examining the broken capillaries that spread outward from the peak of his nose, stop staring at his bushy, blond, ungroomed eyebrows. He wished he had something to do with his hands. He sat on them, slowly rocking back and forth, hoping it would calm him.

And the other thing. His father could never know about that. He would never accept it. Probably wouldn't even understand it, wouldn't know what it really was. Maybe he had seen it on television or in a newspaper article. There were so many barriers in their relationship already, so many topics that had never been broached: *He doesn't even know where I've applied to college. Who I've dated. Who my friends are. What I like to do in my free time.* He thought about explaining the baking project, his friendships with Ethan and Hannah. His father would think it was all odd, unmanly, queer.

Don took a sip of his ginger ale. "I'm not going to beat around the bush. I need you to ask your mother something for me."

Todd looked at his father skeptically. "Yeah?"

"I'm putting together a deal up here. It needs financing. It's to get a project going, a development down near Boca. Just a few hundred grand. It's pocket change for her. I thought she might be able to help me out. You know, it would be good for all of us. I could give you guys shares in it."

Todd looked at his father in disbelief. "You invited me here to ask me for money?"

"I'm not asking you for money, kid. I just need some help in convincing your mother. She barely even takes my phone calls. I thought that if you said something to her—"

"Dad, you left." Todd felt his throat swelling. He took a sip of the water that had been delivered to the table. "We didn't have anyone. You're lucky—you're lucky that Mom was so successful, because if she hadn't been—well, our lives would have been a lot different."

"I know, I know. Your mother's a big star. I can't get on a god-damned plane without seeing someone reading one of her books."

"So that's why you came to New York. For this project."

"I came to see you guys. And for some meetings."

"Meetings." Todd sat back in the booth. "Meetings with developers."

His father was asking him for help. Todd had asked him for help, to visit him, for advice, so many times. This wasn't how it was supposed to be. Would this bring them closer together? Would it make his father love him? He thought about asking his mother for the money—she would never give it to him, he was sure of that—and what that would say about him. Even considering it made him feel like a chump (he thought of the sad little diner, of the lonely people, of the woman at the cash register; this was not his world). He didn't want it to go on like this.

Todd slid out of the booth.

"Where are you going, son?"

"Dad." Todd stepped away, momentarily fearful his father might hit him. He still remembered being spanked as a child. The punishments came quickly, often for the smallest infraction: for speaking out of turn, for breaking something accidentally, for expressing a negative opinion. He didn't put it past his father now to reach out with one flick of his arm, to punch him in the gut. "It's too late, Dad."

"What?"

"I'm—I'm sorry. It's too late."

"What the hell does that mean?"

Todd took one more step away from his father. "You're going to have to figure that out for yourself. I'm sorry."

"Stay with me. Have a meal with your dad."

"I can't. I have to go."

Don leaned over and grabbed Todd by the arm, clenching hard and looking at him directly. "Do not walk away from your father! Do you understand that? You do not walk away from your father. What kind of little shit do you think you are?"

Todd felt his hands shaking. "Maybe you should have thought about all this twelve years ago. When you left us. I—I can't." He felt the tears wanting to come, but he held back. He pulled his arm away, grabbed his coat and bag, and rushed to the door, past the other patrons, past the woman with the red hair and the mints. He was sure everyone was watching, all the people with their lonely lives. He had made a scene. Once again, he had screwed up.

He rushed out toward Sixth Avenue and was immediately grateful for the chilly air on his burning face and neck. He crossed the street when the light turned and continued walking west, deeper into the Village, his peacoat wrapped around him for protection. Would his father follow him? He wouldn't care enough. Todd heard his cell phone ring, but he didn't answer. He stopped to take a cigarette from his pack, lit it, felt the smoke mingle with his freshly brushed teeth. He needed to be outside. He kept walking, past clusters of tourists, up West Fourth Street, toward Seventh Avenue, past rows of town houses, people, none of whom had this chaos in their lives, paper wrappers on the street, trash cans filled to capacity. He passed sex shops, with their horrible, beastly window displays of porn and dildos.

A homeless man lying slouched against a lovely prewar building, a constructed fort of boxes and plastic grocery bags surrounding him. He detected the smell of urine, saw a sole latex glove discarded on the sidewalk. He passed tacky restaurants and bars where college students and his friends, if they ever ventured down here, would go. He thought he had been on these streets before, but he wasn't sure. There were shops offering sunglasses and studded leather belts and T-shirts that read *New York Fucking City*. He passed a gay bar called the Monster; he knew it was gay by its gaudy displays in the windows. He crossed a crowded intersection near a little park and continued walking west. He finished his cigarette, stubbed it out on the ground. He didn't know where to go. Somewhere anonymous, a place where no one would know him. He would walk to the Hudson River, to see the wide expanse of water that reached across the channel to the industrialized shore of New Jersey. He would feel the wind on his face, feel far away from his life, from his father in the sad diner, from his mother and her scars and her peach-colored womb of a bedroom. He would not cry; he would hold it all in. This wasn't his fault. Someday, he would be grateful for this moment.

West of Seventh Avenue, it was quieter. He walked past brownstones, plaques announcing their landmark status, with their red and black and hunter-green doors. He turned corners, went left, went right. He passed a combination tailor and dry cleaner, a half-finished jacket hanging on a mannequin in the window, the seams exposed. A used-book shop, first editions sheathed in plastic. Little cafés, brunch places East Siders would go on weekends. A Ralph Lauren store, even. He found himself on this quiet block, a little street with trees growing not out of bare patches of dirt, but from little plantings of daffodils and tulips, just starting to emerge from their bulbs. Bakeries. Antique stores. He slowed down, started to breathe again. He saw a name he recognized, a shop. Eduardo Design. Nick's boyfriend had a shop by that name. He looked into the window. Knickknacks and objects, little ceramic dogs and bookends and vases and a pair of lamps with burnt umber shades. He saw a pair of dark Italian eyes staring back at him, a gesture of a wave. He would have to go in; he would have to say hello to Eduardo. He hadn't seen him since that Christmas dinner; he didn't really know him at all. Nick's boyfriend opened the door for him. Was this what having a boyfriend was like, someone who had a life during the day when you were not with him, not the clinging sensation he had always associated with his girlfriends? A little bell on the door jangled to signal Todd's arrival, making him jump.

Eduardo stepped back to let him enter, standing next to a tiger maple chest covered in silver picture frames, frames filled with black-and-white photos clipped from magazines. He looked smart in his navy blue slacks and white tailored shirt, sleeves rolled up to reveal tan forearms. "Todd, what are you doing down here? Is everything all right? You look like you've been running around."

Todd grunted a hello as his eyes pinballed around the little shop, from object to object: andirons, rugs, tables, chairs. "I was just, you know, in the neighborhood."

"How are you doing? Do you want something to drink?"

Todd shook his head, steadying himself, his coat, his bag, as if he might lose his footing and topple over. "I'm fine." He held on to the side of a mahogany table.

Eduardo looked embarrassed for a moment, as if he weren't sure what to do with this teenage boy, this alien life-form in his private space. "So this is my shop. Your mom's been here before. Bought some picture frames. I gave her a discount, of course." After a moment, he hurried behind the wood counter, through a doorway leading somewhere, and brought Todd back a bottle of spring water, even though he hadn't asked for it.

Todd dropped his bag at his feet and took off his coat, holding the bulky wool form in his arms. He sipped the water gratefully, as Eduardo relieved him of his coat, hanging it on a rack. Todd breathed in the musty aroma of the shop, the smell of worn antiques and the sandalwood candle that Eduardo was burning. It was only then that he felt himself begin to cry.

"Oh my God, you poor thing, what's wrong? What happened?" Eduardo went over to where Todd was standing and pulled from his pocket a folded white handkerchief, which Todd took. It was the simplest, most graceful of gestures, Todd would later think, for who carried a handkerchief anymore?

Todd wiped his cheeks as Eduardo removed an elaborate display of kilim pillows from a leather club chair, and motioned for Todd to sit. He sank into the chair, felt the springs against his bottom. Eduardo stood behind him for a moment and patted Todd's shoulder. He appreciated his touch, the soft, warm human contact. Eduardo went to sit on a Morris chair across from him, crossing his legs (at the ankle, Todd noted: not so gay) and holding his hands together over one of his loafers. Todd kept sobbing, just a quiet whimpering.

"Do you want to talk about it?" Eduardo asked. "If you don't, it's okay."

"No, I don't care," Todd finally sputtered. "I just met with my dad. We had lunch. We didn't eat lunch. I ran away. I couldn't. He wanted to . . ." His voice trailed off momentarily. "He wanted to borrow some money. That's why he wanted to see me, because he needed money. That fucking prick! He doesn't deserve us."

Eduardo nodded. "You're right. He doesn't deserve you." He looked thoughtfully up at a point above Todd's head. "Does Jackie know he's in town?"

Todd shook his head.

It was clear Eduardo didn't know what to say, so Todd kept talking. "I don't think I should tell her. It's better if she doesn't know. It'll just upset her, especially after the, you know—she had some surgery."

"It's okay, Nick told me."

"Anyway, he's disgusting. I can't believe he came all the way to New York."

He expected Eduardo to say something to the contrary, but he was silent. Todd started crying again. "Eduardo, it's all so fucked up. My best friend at school is sleeping with this teacher, and I think I was in love with him—I don't know—we kissed, and no one knows. No one knows."

Eduardo nodded again, suddenly sage in his new role as Todd's confidant. "I had a feeling it was something like that. These things happen. They're supposed to happen. You're young. You're a baby."

"Please don't tell my mother." Todd looked at him through his hot tears. Jackie couldn't know about any of this. Not now. Not yet.

He couldn't remember the last time he had cried. His tears set free something that might allow his confused, battered heart to heal. He had never felt so concretely how it was an organ, not simply an idea, but how its pulsing of blood created chemical reactions, how he could feel its warmth in his chest when he was happy and a rawness when he was alone, when he thought about Ethan, when he woke in the morning, fearing something—that was how he knew, painful as it was, that he had a heart, an organ that had everything to do with the experience of love.

School was only four days away, the end of spring break. He wondered if he could go back now, now that he had told another person his secret.

"You're going to be fine," Eduardo said. "Your mother is an amazing woman. She'll always take care of you."

"She's too busy," Todd said. "She thinks of me like one of her employees."

"That's not true." Eduardo paused. "I don't know. I hope it's not true. You can always come here. Nick's your godfather, right?"

Todd nodded. It was true, a fact he tried to forget. Nick was his fairy godfather. His mother had asked Nick to swear, after the two of them had become close, that were anything ever to happen to her, he would take care of her boys.

Eduardo continued. "You can always come here. You don't have to, but if you need to, you can."

There was something about the shop, with its andirons and orchids, its silver collection of paperweights, that made Todd feel safe. No one he knew would ever come here.

"Let me close up and take you home." Eduardo handed Todd a tissue from a box behind the counter, for Todd had now completely dampened the handkerchief he had given him.

"You don't need to do that. I can make it home okay."

"Todd, right now it all seems like it matters so much. At your age, everything does. Every little thing. But five years from now, you won't even remember this."

Five years seemed like a long time to wait. He allowed Eduardo to bring him his coat, and he bundled up. He would get a cab, a cab that would take him safely back to the Upper East Side. He would return home; everything would go back to the way it had been before.

Eduardo saw him to the front of the shop. Todd turned around as he stood on the threshold. In a moment of abandon, not caring if anyone was watching, Todd wrapped his arms around him and gave him a hug, muttering thanks into his ear, and this gay man who lived in the West Village, the boyfriend of his mother's agent, this man whom Todd didn't know very well, hugged him back.

CHAPTER 21

Ethan spent all day Sunday traveling back to school. He was unsettled by a message Ms. Hedge had left at his house on Saturday afternoon. He had returned her call that evening, but hadn't heard back from her before boarding his plane the following morning. He was certain it had to do with Hannah; Ms. Hedge was too sharp not to notice that something had been amiss.

Upon his return to campus, before even unpacking, he called both of them, but found that neither was home. Being back at school was an entirely new sensation. When Ethan went to the snack bar—familiar raunchy smell of sizzling beef patties on the grill, classic rock, cups of soda, alliances formed, renewed, confidences exchanged—paranoia struck him, as if everyone knew about him and Hannah. The next day, he saw Dr. Spencer, the headmaster, talking to Dean Fowler in the hallway near their offices, both of them glancing at him momentarily, then returning to their conversation. Ethan tried, with little success, to assure himself that no one knew, that everything had happened during spring break, in a world far away from the everyday life of the school.

But he couldn't: he knew gossip traveled quickly, and all it would take was a mere suspicion to reveal what had been going on.

He was worried, too, about what Vivian had told him. He wanted to believe Hannah hadn't meant anything by the phone call. She was probably trying to make sure Vivian wasn't spreading nasty rumors about her. At Berkley, the only currency people had were the stories they could tell about each other. Now that he was in a similar position, he understood.

He ran into Ms. Hedge later that day in the hallway of the art wing. He approached her cautiously.

"Just the guy I've been looking for!" she said.

He nodded, attempting a smile.

"I had to call you at your parents' house—I just couldn't wait to talk to you—"

"Yes?" He was becoming impatient.

She was breathless. "Ethan—I had a chance to really look at your paintings over the break—they're absolutely wonderful! I'd like to do something, with your permission. May I enter them in the state art competition? We can send them slides of the entire series. I think they'll be impressed by your work."

Ethan found himself both relieved and flustered. "Of course— I mean, that would be great. Thank you."

She smiled at him. "They were just such a treat. Just exquisite." Her voice grew quiet for a moment. "It's rare, I have to admit, that these projects work out—not many students are capable of working on their own. I can't tell you what a joy it is to have a student who can handle that kind of responsibility."

Ethan blushed. He tried to look for hidden meaning in her statement, but wasn't sure if he should.

The next day, there was a commotion at the school mailboxes when Ethan walked by. He went to check his, and found it was filled with four thick envelopes. His hands shook as he pulled them out. The first was from Stanford.

Congratulations! it read on the back flap. He turned to the next two: Columbia and Brown. He opened them carefully, feeling their thickness, the weight of the paper. *We are pleased to accept your application.* . . . He stopped there. He looked at the last one. Yale. It was also a heavy one. He opened it.

He had been accepted. He stared at the letter with incredulity. He checked again, to make sure it was really addressed to him.

Carrying his envelopes, Ethan walked down the hall toward the snack bar. He felt people looking at him differently. More than a few glanced at him with what looked like resentment. He ran into Todd.

"I got in," Ethan said. "I got in to Yale. What about you? Did you hear from Brown?"

Todd pulled a crumpled letter out of his pocket. "I was wait-listed."

"You'll get in," Ethan said. "I know you will."

"I don't know," Todd said, momentarily distracted by a group of students walking by. "I doubt it."

Ethan telephoned his parents that night. His mother was excited, calling his father over to pick up the extension.

"We want you to go wherever you'll be happiest," she said, which disturbed Ethan. They had always been adamant that Stanford would be the best place for him, and now they didn't seem to care.

That evening, he went to see Hannah. He had run into her earlier that day, though she had been deep in conversation with another student, and he hadn't wanted to interrupt.

She was in a celebratory mood when he arrived. "I heard about your college success! It's wonderful." She gave him a hug before he had a chance to take off his jacket. "I missed you so much. It was torture not having you here."

Ethan nodded. He looked around the room, appraising its

contents. It looked the same as it had two weeks ago, familiar, like home. But he wasn't sure he wanted to be there.

Hannah put on a CD and then sat down with Ethan on the couch, rubbing his thighs through his jeans. The music came on, a Philip Glass album, sharp atonal chimes that pulsed in the air.

"I think we should take a trip together. After you graduate. Just the two of us."

"To where?"

"I want to show you Paris. My Paris. It would be amazing. If you've never been—oh, I can't wait! It's such a magical place."

Ethan shifted on the couch. "I don't know, Hannah. I'm probably going to get a job at home, something at the university, you know, make some extra cash before school starts."

"Don't be silly—we can go to Paris, and then you can find a job here in town. After a trip there, you'll be a new person. You can live with me. Like spring break, but longer." She took a sip of her tea.

"Hannah, I don't have the money to go to Paris."

"Don't worry, I can pay."

"You shouldn't have to do that."

"Ethan, I want to take you. I want to make things right again. Apart from this school, from what we have here."

Ethan wasn't sure what she meant, and he didn't want to ask. He felt her fingers running through his hair, stroking the locks behind his ear. He shivered as he edged away from her, just slightly.

"Are you okay?" she asked.

"I'm fine. Maybe some different music."

"Of course." She switched off the stereo with the remote control. "Do you want to go up to the bedroom?"

Ethan nodded.

They mounted the stairs together, Hannah ahead of him. Ethan looked at her white dress, the way her body moved under it, her bare ankles, her sandaled feet.

He sat down on the edge of the bed. It wasn't made; the sheets were rumpled, heavy with sleep. He sensed something in the disarray he had never noticed before: the room had the aura of promises made, then broken.

"I've never seen the bed like this," Ethan said.

"See what happens when you go away?" she said.

As they made love, Ethan stared at her face. She looked beautiful, the moonlight shining against her hair. When he closed his eyes, her face began to transform. It became the mask of a witch, a gnarled, ashy creature, something out of a picture book from his childhood.

He opened his eyes again, and the vision left him. He looked at her, and she was the same—lush, angelic, full of mystery.

That evening, Sarge pulled Ethan aside in the hall after check-in, and Ethan followed him to his book-filled study. He didn't know Sarge well, but the history teacher had always been friendly. Though he had a reputation as a taskmaster, sometimes Ethan felt sorry for him; last month, several of the boys had decided to show up for check-in naked, proud as peacocks, their dicks flopping, making the little man turn red as a beet at the sight of so much young male flesh.

"Come have a seat," Sarge said, motioning toward a chair. He smelled like a strange combination of mothballs and aftershave.

Ethan tried to relax. As usual, Sarge had an old movie playing on his television; Ethan recognized it as *A Streetcar Named Desire*. He looked up at the collection of stuffed birds on the shelf behind the couch (a barn owl, an eastern bluebird, a red-tailed hawk), at their crooked beaks and beady glass eyes. It felt as if they were watching him, judging him.

"You're quite the success story, aren't you?" Sarge winked at Ethan.

"I guess so," Ethan said shyly, as he stared at the green shag carpet. "I don't know."

"I wanted to congratulate you. We're all very proud of you. I knew you would do well."

"Thank you," Ethan said, as he felt his throat tightening.

"I'm concerned about you, though, in these final weeks. I don't want you to let your, your . . ." Sarge stumbled over his words. "Your *social life* overshadow what's important. You're in the final stretch now. You need to focus on graduating."

Ethan didn't dare ask him what he was talking about. "I understand," he said. "Thank you for—thank you for looking out for me."

"Ethan, temptation is a funny thing. We've all faced it. You can't let it get the better of you." Sarge paused for a moment as Ethan got up, before motioning to Ethan's waist. "You might want to zip up there."

Ethan looked down in horror at the flap of blue boxer shorts peeking through his fly. In the hurry to get out of Hannah's house that evening, he had forgotten to zip his pants. He rushed to correct the error.

"Don't worry about it, Ethan. Happens to everyone." Sarge smiled and patted him on the shoulder. "Go get some sleep."

He didn't want to go to Paris, not right now. This summer he belonged at home, taking care of his mother. He spent the following afternoon with Ms. Hedge, making final preparations for the exhibit of his paintings in the small gallery off the vestibule of the school's main entrance. That evening, he didn't visit Hannah. He couldn't explain it; he just knew he needed some time away. When he returned home from the library, there was a phone message taped onto his door.

Hannah called.

He didn't call her back. When he checked his mailbox the next day, there was a note, printed on cream stationery with blue ink. His hand shook slightly as he read it.

Where are you? Call me. H.

Ethan didn't know much (didn't know anything, really) about relationships, but he was nearly certain that they weren't supposed to work this way. He quickly shoved the note in his backpack.

That evening, after check-in, Izzy Jacobsen stopped Ethan in the hall.

"Hey—Ms. McClellan came looking for you. She looked kind of, I don't know, confused or something." There was a seriousness in his voice, no hint of his usual jocularity.

Ethan heard the phone ring down the hall. "When did she come by?"

"Just before check-in. I told her I would give you the message."

George Crenshaw leaned out of the utility closet that doubled as a phone booth. "Whitley, you got a call!"

Ethan went to pick up the phone without thanking Izzy.

"What's going on?" she said. "Why haven't you called me?"

"I'm sorry. I've been busy."

He closed the door to the closet, carefully cupping his hand over his mouth so no one could hear. He took shallow breaths of the dusty air.

"I need . . . I need some room," he said.

"What do you mean?" Her voice sounded so distant from where he was, in a closet that smelled of industrial-strength cleaning fluids, a closet with a dirty mop leaning up against the wall.

"I don't know, Hannah. Something doesn't feel right. I don't know what it is." He couldn't say it. *You're too old for me. You're a teacher. You're too needy. I can't give you what you want.* He was realizing, slowly, the culmination of all his doubts from the past few weeks.

"Ethan, we haven't really been together in two weeks!"

"I know. I'm sorry." He didn't know why he was apologizing. What did he owe her? In the hallway, he heard some of the younger boys roughhousing, their bodies slamming against the door as they wrestled with each other. Joking, laughing.

"Why don't you come by tonight?"

"It's past check-in."

"No one will see you. I'll make sure of it."

"You know I can't do that."

Someone knocked on the door. "Hurry up!" a voice said. "I need to use the phone!"

"I have to go."

"I made blueberry cobbler."

"Hannah, I can't," Ethan said, before hanging up.

CHAPTER 22

Several afternoons later, Todd went to the infirmary to get a sports red card, the pass that would allow him to skip club volleyball and catch up on his sleep. He had been feeling down for several days after being wait-listed at Brown, and all he wanted now was to feign illness and be left alone. When the nurse stepped out of the room, he managed to take a handful of pills from the infirmary's supply of prescription drugs. He knew his mother swore by the sleeping pills, and it couldn't hurt to try a few of the sedatives. Last summer, several times, he had stolen his mother's Xanax—nothing she would notice, just a pill or two, its scripted *X* making him imagine he was doing something illicit, like a raver deep in a cocktail of Ecstasy and ketamine—to dull his feelings, to sand off the sharp edges, the indecision, until he was doing nothing but floating. Now he tapped out a few pills from each bottle, knowing the senile nurse would never notice they were gone.

As Todd walked back to the dorm, he chewed slowly on a pale yellow sedative. Things began to feel okay. He might not be going to Brown. He had gotten into some other schools. Not great schools, like Yale, where Ethan would be going, or Dartmouth, where his brother was, but good schools. He needed to be content with that.

He wandered into the library. Everything was bright, empty. The library had never been a place he had lingered; it was always somewhere he went just before class, before study hall, to finish an assignment. He wandered over to a shelf of books, one near the back.

He knew it was there, but he had always been afraid to look. It was known as the fag shelf, the collection of gay nonfiction. Coming-out stories. Biographies. Gay studies. Books about HIV and safe sex. He had passed it hundreds of times.

Todd took a book from the shelf, an anthology of teenage coming-out stories. He slipped it into his bag and walked out of the library.

The next day, he went back. He had devoured the volume he had snatched the day before, locking his door and staying up until one in the morning to finish it.

Jeremy Cohen was sitting in a worn leather armchair, reading. Todd had never spoken to him; he was exactly the type of kid who terrified Todd about the prospect of exploring his sexuality. He was a thin, pale boy, with curly light brown hair that hung over his eyes. Not a bad-looking kid—actually, Todd mused, he was rather attractive. Still, he wasn't a guy's guy. What irony: Jeremy's problem wasn't that he was gay, but that he was the wrong sort of gay.

"Hi," Todd said.

Jeremy looked up. Todd wondered if he should be near these books with someone watching. But Jeremy wouldn't care.

"Hi," he said. "What are you doing here?"

"I'm looking for a book." He glanced at the shelf. He noticed several of them were in a different order than they had been the day before. Someone else had been looking at them. He took the book of coming-out stories out of his bag and placed it on an empty spot on the shelf. He picked another one that looked good—it was a memoir with a photo of a cute, preppy boy on the cover—and slipped it into his bag.

"You're not supposed to do that," Jeremy said. "You're supposed to check them out."

"Oh yeah?" Todd said. "Fuck off."

When Ethan was walking alone in the hallways, when he was sitting in class, when he was taking a shower, he would think about her. Not only about how to get away from her, but how much he cared for her. How could he desire someone while also knowing she wasn't right for him? He wanted to be with her, but he was also afraid of her, afraid of what she might do. She had turned Laura in for selling pot. He wondered what she could do to him.

And still, there were the unanswered questions about her past, the strangeness he had started to sense around her, the condoms she claimed to have run out of. He was still afraid to ask her about any of it, for fear of what he might find out.

Everywhere he went, she was there, with some new reason for him to come over, some opportunity he couldn't turn down. He wanted to make more friends in his own class, but whenever he tried, it became clear that those bonds had been forged long ago, that with less than two months left in the school year, it was best for him to stick with what he had. He tried to busy himself with his own work, but each evening, he was pulled back into her world.

Ethan was sitting at Hannah's kitchen counter one night eating a bowl of soup when there was a knock on her door. It was Dean Fowler. He was out with his dog, but it was clear he wasn't there for a social visit. Hannah greeted him warmly and let him in. (How, Ethan wondered, could she remain so calm?)

"Hello, Ethan," he said.

Ethan mumbled a hello as he felt prickles of heat running up his neck.

"You'd probably best be going," Hannah said brightly to Ethan.

He put his bowl in the sink. Did the school know about them? His eyes darted over Dean Fowler's plaid shirt, his khakis, his muddy duck boots. No, this couldn't be happening. *No.*

Ethan's legs wobbled as he grabbed his backpack. Had he left anything personal in Hannah's living room, anything the dean might seize upon? A piece of clothing, a T-shirt that couldn't possibly belong to her? If he had, he knew Hannah would come up with an excuse. She was good at that, making excuses.

As he crossed the golf course, his feet felt heavy. Ahead of him, Slater glowed like a beacon calling him back to his former life. He wondered how he had allowed this to happen. If they were caught, surely he would be expelled. He would lose his offer of admission to Yale. He would have thrown everything away.

He stumbled on the muddy grass in front of the dorm. He felt a hand on his shoulder as he righted himself.

"Careful there, Ethan." It was Mr. Barnfield. "Watch where you're going."

Ethan looked at him, his perfect blue eyes, his wavy blond hair. He was the Berkley ideal, had a family, a golden Labrador. He followed the rules.

Ethan knew something was wrong. Something had gone terribly wrong.

CHAPTER 23

That night, Ethan couldn't sleep. He had tried calling her several times, but she wasn't answering. Alone in his room, the pale moonlight seeping in between the cracks of his window shades, he stared at the ceiling for hours. He finally drifted off at four in the morning, waking up with a jolt at six. After getting out of bed, he looked at himself in the mirror, at his drawn, pale skin. He often felt this way upon waking, before showering, as if his features hadn't properly arranged themselves on his face, though this morning the effect was exacerbated.

He would go to breakfast early. Most of the campus was still asleep as he headed toward the main building.

Once inside, he chose a table in the corner. He scrutinized each person—faculty, administration, students with their books and newspapers under their arms. No one noticed him. Just before eight, Dean Fowler entered the dining hall and quickly located Ethan. As if out of a bad dream (and yet also so simply, an everyday request), he asked Ethan to see him in his office after second period. Though he pretended this was not something to get excited about, Ethan fidgeted through his first two classes of the day, Spanish and AP English. Had Ms. Hedge said some-thing? (Here he was, sitting in Ms. Davis's class, trying to act like everything was normal, when his teacher's girlfriend, his own adviser, could have reported him!) He had never been called into the Dean's Wing before, and aside from the minor reproach he had received for his *Bones* article, he had not had any significant contact with the dean. Would he be informed that he was on some kind of probation? That he would face the disciplinary committee? That he might not be allowed to finish the year? After second period, he dodged his way among the sea of stu-dents traveling between classes. Ethan entered the Dean's Wing, walking down a hallway that smelled so adult, like a pocket of the outside world. Dean Fowler beckoned him in when he arrived at his office door.

Ethan stood dumbly inside the entrance, not sure if he should sit or stand.

"Why don't you close the door behind you?"

Ethan did as he was told, and decided to sit down. He noticed that the dean was wearing a tie with little lobsters on it, a detail that would have, under any other circumstances, amused him.

"You've been doing well here, Ethan, haven't you?"

Ethan nodded.

"Enjoying your second semester classes?"

He nodded again.

"That's what I understand—your adviser, particularly, speaks very highly of you. That's why I'm concerned. You've got less than two months left in the year. We—the school, that is—have heard you have a friendship of sorts with Ms. McClellan."

Ethan made a weak gesture of admission, horrified that the school was aware of what had been going on between them. How much they knew, he couldn't be sure.

"We don't like to discourage friendships, if you will, with fac-ulty members, but I can't say that we encourage them, either.

There are limits." The dean momentarily became flustered, as if he had worked himself into an argumentative quagmire. He quickly composed himself.

"What I'm saying is that you should be out with your peers, enjoying the beautiful weather, in these last weeks. Fulfilling your last set of academic commitments. Making summer plans. Do you understand what I mean?"

"Um, I guess so—are you saying—"

The dean interrupted him. "Son, I'm saying that you can't spend time at Ms. McClellan's place any longer. Her cottage is technically out of school bounds after sundown, and let's just say that for you, it's off-limits altogether. Are we clear about this?"

"Yes." Ethan chuckled inwardly at the dean's use of the word *cottage* to describe Hannah's well-appointed household—how easily people could fool themselves through simple semantics.

"You have college to look forward to next year—you know, we haven't seen that kind of success in years! I hear you got in at all your top choices?" This was clearly a topic the dean felt more adept at discussing.

"That's right."

"Let's not ruin that then. The last thing that we as a school want is for you to throw that all away over some silly . . ." He suddenly seemed at a loss for words. "*Mistake*. Ethan, enjoy this time, but keep your eye on the prize."

"Thank you." Ethan didn't know what else to say, as he made his way out of the Dean's Wing, his legs shaking at the encounter. Nearly everything in the dean's argument had been unsaid—the school seemed to know about them, and was going to turn a blind eye. Had he made it out unscathed? It would solve the problem that had been gnawing at him, that he didn't belong with her. He would simply have to tell Hannah what Dean Fowler had said—surely, in fact, she had been given a similar speech. How narrowly he had escaped! Other students, as Vivian had mentioned, would be kicked out over the next several weeks for indiscretions of drinking, drugs, spending time out of bounds. But he had made it—less than two months, and he would be free: free of the school, free of Hannah. He had had a taste of a relationship, of (dare he say it?) an affair—but now he wanted to skip back to being eighteen again. And he wasn't a virgin anymore! He had flirted with this idea over the past few weeks, the realization that he now knew what he was doing. Maybe other girls would be attracted to him—perhaps he would give off some sort of signal that he was experienced, that he could give and receive pleasure openly, not as a novice, but as someone who had been through, at the very least, a crash course.

More than anything, he was grateful he wouldn't have to break up with her; they could acknowledge, the next time they ran into each other, the unfortunate nature of the dean's news, how closely they had eluded being caught. Perhaps they would write letters to each other over the summer, talk on the phone every once in a while. But Ethan would be free of his obligation to continue seeing her, to live with her, to go to Paris.

Had he loved her? Were there ever real feelings if they could be so quickly discarded? He had no idea—all he knew was that the school had declared it forbidden for them to meet, and that this had validated his own misgivings. He was freed of having to make any decision.

Later that afternoon, when classes were letting out, Ethan sat under the birch trees on senior grass, finishing his reading for the following day's history seminar. His mind was at ease; he didn't hear Hannah behind him until she was about ten paces away.

He glanced up from his book, giving her an uneasy smile. "Hey."

She seemed nervous, as if someone might spot them. "I need to speak with you," she said quickly. He had never seen her agitated in this way before.

"Hannah, we're not supposed to see each other. The dean told me this morning I could be kicked out."

"You're not going to be kicked out," she said. "Look, we should talk."

"What about?"

Her eyes darted up behind him, and he turned as well, though there was no one. "I can't discuss it now."

"Can you tell me the nature of it?" He felt so formal with her, as if—it seemed, almost—they had broken up. There was a wall between them, a shift in their relationship.

She sighed. "Ethan, I can't—just come meet me tonight. Nine o'clock?"

She didn't give him a chance to respond. Before he could say anything, she turned around and walked back across the expanse of senior grass, her dress fluttering slightly in the breeze, her footsteps heavier than he had ever known them before. He realized that for things to end properly, they would have to meet again at the house.

When he arrived that evening, she was sitting at her kitchen table with a glass of wine in front of her. He looked to the counter and saw a bottle of red that was nearly finished. Ethan wondered for a moment if he had done the right thing by showing up.

"I'm glad you came," she said. There was something pathetic in her tone, as if he were speaking to a different person than the one he had known.

On a chair opposite her, in exactly the same position he had placed it several weeks ago, was the portrait of her, the one by Alain's son. Ethan looked back at Hannah and saw that her eyes were red and teary. She took a gulp of wine.

"Of course. I mean, it's not like they're watching your house or something." It was a pitiful attempt at a joke, but it brought back Ethan's anxieties of what might happen. "So what's up?"

She looked at him intently. "We need to keep seeing each other."

"Hannah, you know we can't. The school says we can't. We're lucky to have gotten this far. I think it's best if we leave this in the past. We can still be friends."

A strange look of recognition crossed her face. "Oh my God— *you told them!* You told the school we were seeing each other and that you wanted it to stop. You told the dean to come to my house. I knew it—how else could you be so cavalier about this!"

"Don't be ridiculous. Why on earth would I tell them? Do you think I want to get in trouble?" He paused, suddenly insulted. "I'm not being cavalier about this. I feel terrible about it. But, Hannah, there's nothing I can do."

He stood up and got himself a glass of water. He had become so comfortable here, had felt he could help himself to whatever he wanted. Hannah took a pack of cigarettes out of a wicker box on the table and lit one. She motioned to Ethan to take one, but he declined. She tapped her ash into a saucer after taking a long drag.

"I'm sorry—you're right—I'm being absurd. It's just all been too much. The dean coming here, you not wanting to spend as much time with me." She looked at the bottle of wine. "I shouldn't have started drinking. That was silly of me. And then, of course—" She motioned to the portrait.

"Why did you bring that out again?"

"I don't know. Because I'm a glutton for punishment, I guess."

"What do you mean?"

She sighed. "I can't let what happened back there happen again. I can't lose someone else."

"You mean Alain?"

"Not just Alain."

"Who else then?"

Hannah took a deep inhale on her cigarette. "It was years ago. I've tried to forget it, but I can't."

"What happened?"

She looked at him sternly. "Ethan, you can't tell a soul."

"Of course not." He felt so duplicitous, promising this, but he had to know what happened to her, about this strangeness. He hoped it would help him figure out how to confront her now.

"When I lived in Paris, I made a horrible mistake."

Ethan nodded, motioning for her to continue. He felt a sharp pain run through his belly, the feeling that he was about to learn something he didn't want to know.

She continued, her thumb and forefinger carefully tracing the stem of the wineglass, as if it might hold some answers. "Bertrand, Alain's son, was very precocious. Flirtatious, even. He was fifteen, good-looking, and very . . . developed. Told me he preferred me to the girls at school, that I was the most beautiful woman he had ever seen. After I found out Alain had been cheating, I allowed him to seduce me. Or I seduced him. I suppose it depends on how you look at it."

Ethan sat at the table, his mouth agape. "Hannah, fifteen years old—were you insane? And the son of your husband? Your stepson?"

"I never should have let it happen. I was just so angry—I had so much rage toward Alain that I wanted to hurt him however I could."

"But what about the boy? Didn't you think of him?"

"I know, I know," she said. "I guess in a way I was fulfilling some kind of fantasy of his. It was my self-destructive streak. Every time we did it, I knew it was wrong."

"'Every time'? How many times were there?"

"It went on for a few weeks. Just while Alain and Bertrand were staying with friends. He used to sneak back to see me. And then Alain found out."

"What happened then?"

"He was furious. He kicked me out of the apartment, and

Bertrand as well. I got a place of my own. I never saw Bertrand again."

Ethan looked at the portrait, the care with which it had been created. This would explain her reaction to it. He remembered the photos. "You keep pictures of him. On the mantel."

"Yes. I don't hold anything against him. He was a good kid."

"Hannah, he was *fifteen*."

"It wasn't illegal, at least not in France. Hormones are raging, you know how it goes. I never would have done it if he hadn't seemed so experienced."

Her argument was so flawed, he didn't even know where to start. Ethan found himself sputtering. "But still—come on! It's not—it's just not right."

"I don't even know what's right or wrong anymore. It's only three years younger than you are. Those French kids certainly put up a swagger."

Ethan felt a shiver. "Hannah, this is really weird."

"It's in the past. It doesn't affect us."

"We still can't see each other."

"We'll make it work somehow," she said, stubbing out her cigarette.

"Hannah, you know we can't." He looked at the clock. It was nearing check-in. "I have to go."

"Come see me tomorrow?"

"Hannah—" There was nothing left to discuss, not tonight. He stepped out onto her front porch without saying good-bye, made his way down the stairs and through her small garden. A brick had come loose on her walkway, and he nearly stumbled over it. Righting himself, Ethan kicked it out of the way. There was a time, he thought, when he would have replaced it, when he would have set it back in its cavity. Now he was struck with the same sensation he had when he had irreparably ruined a drawing or watercolor—scratched the paper down to its fibers, let the colors muddy together until they were nothing but brown—the feeling that it was past saving, that it had no home beyond the dustbin.

Had all this really happened to her, with Alain, with his son? Hannah's past had seemed so distant before, like pages in a scrapbook, only real to her. She was tangible to him in the present, and yet there was this history, these stories that were presenting themselves—he couldn't escape the idea that somehow they were being told for his benefit, these scenes from the often gruesome film of her life, that he was supposed to feel sorrow or pity or compassion. He only felt disgust.

Yes, what had happened to her was in the past, and no, it might not have been illegal, but quite simply, by any logical reasoning, it wasn't right. If the school knew about it, she would surely be fired. It didn't seem possible that he could tell them, or that he should. He might jeopardize his own future. But if he didn't do something, there would be more messages, more phone calls, more visits. And that, even if only for six more weeks, he couldn't stand.

Ethan continued walking up the golf course, each mass of darkness giving way to another, hoping he wouldn't run into any couples out for a moonlight tryst. That was where he should have been, lying on the green with a girl from his class, brushing her hair away from her face, comparing notes on classes, on their upcoming summers, on the senior parties people had already started to plan. He didn't belong with a thirty-six-year-old teacher. He was enraged that he had gotten himself into this situation, that he had allowed this to happen. Not only had he been denied the pleasure of experiencing his own life; he had been drawn into the turmoil of hers.

The next evening, Todd was reading the memoir—it was about a guy very much like himself, a guy who came from a good family, a guy who was just trying to figure it all out—when he heard a knock on his door.

"Yeah?"

Jeremy Cohen popped his head in. Todd looked at him warily as he slid the book under his pillow and sat up on his bed.

"Can I come in?"

Todd gave him a half nod.

Jeremy shut the door behind him. Now that he was in the light, Todd could see that his right eye was bruised, nearly closed shut.

"Jeremy, what happened to your eye?"

"It's nothing . . . I fell off my bike."

"Come on, what really happened?"

Jeremy looked down, and Todd could see his ears turning red. "I got hit."

"By who?"

"George Crenshaw."

"Why?"

"He said I was looking at his dick in the shower. I wasn't. Why would I want to look at him? He's disgusting!"

"Jeremy, that's terrible. Can't you tell someone about it?"

"His friends said they would kill me if I said anything. I'm not, you know, such a strong guy." He paused, as if what he was about to reveal would be a surprise. "I'd never actually been in a fight before."

Todd gave him what he hoped was a sympathetic smile. He felt sorry for him. There was no way Jeremy could take on Cren.

A breeze outside rattled Todd's window shade. "Did you need something?"

"I, um, I saw the book you took out the other day. I've read that book."

Todd felt a wave of shame, as if he were hoarding pornography under his pillow. "Oh, that, it's nothing. It's for a paper."

"I thought maybe you were, you know—"

Todd looked down. "No, I'm not."

Jeremy stood there, clearly confused about whether to stay or to leave.

"Anyway, I've got some more reading to do," Todd said. "English paper. Haven't read the book yet."

"Sure. I guess I'll, uh, see you around."

"Right," Todd said.

When Jeremy left, Todd felt short of breath. He hated that Jeremy knew. He needed to make it to the end of the year. If he wasn't careful, he could end up with a black eye himself.

Hannah left Ethan alone for several days; it surprised him, though he sensed she might merely be waiting, like a snake, for the right time to strike. How had their relationship, once fun, turned into this? What had started as forbidden, as desirable, as a treat, had turned into a burden. Now the business about her past in Paris had made her repellent to him. Ethan didn't know what to do, if anything, but he wanted to be prepared for the next time he ran into her. On such a small campus, it would only be a matter of time before they crossed paths.

He decided he would speak to Ms. Hedge and ask her advice. He was taking a risk, but it was a calculated one. There was an unspoken code of honor among the Berkley faculty, particularly among advisers and their advisees. The school rules, as outlined in the *Bluebook*, were unyielding: if a teacher knew about a transgression, he or she was under obligation to report it. The reality was more malleable: acting, as the faculty was, in loco parentis (a phrase thrown about so often in boarding school life, and yet rarely examined), they wanted the best for their students. They wanted them to be happy. They wanted them to graduate. And so minor transgressions were overlooked. Sarge knew about the Fifth Formers who smoked in the showers; he most likely knew about Todd and his pot habit. Teachers, over the years, had concealed and helped to rectify, without the administration ever knowing, everything from being caught out of bounds to unplanned pregnancies. Ms. Hedge, Ethan reasoned, most likely already knew about Hannah and him. He had behaved dishonorably toward his adviser, not heeding her casual warnings, but she wouldn't hold this against him. He believed he could confide in her.

Ethan stopped by her office after classes, but she wasn't there. Ms. Jordan, the plump ceramics teacher who always smelled of clove cigarettes, said her colleague had gone out to the woods, near the creek, to do some sketching. Ethan thanked her and made his way out of the main building, down the campus drive, out the school gates, and across the road into the woods. He had only been to the woods a few times, when Todd had shown him the cabins. People did all sorts of stuff in those broken-down shacks—smoked cigarettes and pot, drank, had sex. It would be just like his art teacher to be oblivious of the fact that she might encounter one of her students breaking a school rule as she blithely sketched away.

He found her several hundred feet down the dirt path leading to the creek. She wore a nylon knapsack and was carrying an oversized sketch pad under her arm. He called out to her, and she stopped and turned around.

"Ethan! What are you doing here?"

He moved closer, so they were only twenty yards apart. "Can I talk to you?"

"Of course." She motioned for him to join her. "Let's go to the spot where I'll be sketching. It's near the creek." They continued walking down the path, as Ethan tried to calm his racing heartbeat; he was suddenly nervous about the potential failure of his plan. "I only have an hour or so," she said. "I'm meeting Cass over at Edwards Field for today's meet."

"What are you working on?"

"A series of studies. Wildflowers."

Along the path, as they moved deeper and deeper into the forest, the air was thick with dirt and sunlight and quiet. It felt like a safe place for him to ask his teacher about Hannah.

"You wanted to talk to me about something?"

"Yeah. I—um, I've really screwed up. I've gotten sort of involved with—"

She paused on the path and looked at him. "Ethan, I know."

"I'm so sorry—it never should have happened, and I should have told you—I should have asked your advice."

"Ethan, these things happen. You could have gotten in much worse trouble than this. Believe me, you have no idea the kinds of shenanigans some students get themselves into."

He exhaled. "You have no idea what it means to hear that. I thought you might turn me in."

She looked chagrined. "Oh dear. I'm not sure I was much help on that front. I did something rash a few days ago, and I'm sorry. I was the one who told Dean Fowler about your friendship with Hannah. He assured me that you wouldn't get in any trouble. I didn't say to what extent the relationship had developed, of course—that's between you and Hannah, and as far as I'm concerned, that should stay between you. I just said I knew you were friends, and that I feared it might distract you from your studies."

Ethan might have been upset, but the revelation didn't bother him; he was relieved that it had been her and not someone else. "He seemed to know more than that."

"That would have been his own conjecture. Ethan, I'm so sorry. I should have talked to you first."

"It's okay—the whole thing has to end. That's the problem. She won't let it go. I've told her I can't see her anymore, but she won't listen. I don't know what to do."

They reached the creek, and she put down her things, motioning to Ethan to sit next to her on an old log. She pulled out her sketch pad, but then turned to him, realizing that he needed her more. "Can't you just avoid her?"

"I guess so. But she keeps wanting to see me."

She took a deep breath as she looked out over the creek, the water flowing lazily over the rocks. "Would you like me to say something to her?"

"No—that wouldn't feel right. And I'm not sure it would help."

"I could talk to the dean again," she said with a sigh. "But of course we'd then be taking things to a whole new level. Hannah could be fired, but your name would certainly be dragged into it. They might put you on probation if she confirmed their suspicions. They would have to tell the colleges where you've been accepted, and we certainly don't want that."

The conversation started to feel strange, as if they were co-conspirators in a secret plot. Ethan realized he had always felt kinship with this misfit of a woman, eclectic in her tastes and harboring a lover of her own, thirty years her junior.

"I could keep trying to avoid her," he said. "I just don't know how well that will work. It hasn't so far."

She opened her sketch pad to a blank page and started surveying the landscape of flowers. It was as if she didn't want to look him in the eye while she answered, as if her words would be less damning if their gazes didn't meet.

"Hannah has a destructive impulse," she said slowly. "When she first arrived, we were friends. It didn't last long. We're civil now, but that's about it. She's not an easy person to get close to." She looked at Ethan sternly, as if she had said too much. "Ethan, I need to trust that all this will stay between us."

"Of course."

There was a pause, and he couldn't tell if she was trying to signal with her silence that she didn't want to talk about it anymore, but he pressed on. "I know this may sound odd, but do you know anything about what happened to her before she got to Berkley? She told me some crazy stuff about her life in France."

Ms. Hedge looked unnerved. "I don't know, but I think there was . . . an ugly incident. Something happened with her ex-husband, though I don't know exactly what. She's never wanted to talk about it."

Strangely, Ethan felt privileged, an odd sense of pride, that Hannah had chosen to confide in him and no one else about the specifics of her past. "That's all you know?"

She nodded.

"So what do you think I should do?"

"Ethan, you need to stay away from her. If she harasses you again, I can try to get involved, but it could be very awkward. You've worked too hard this year just to throw it all away. With your situation, starting new this year—"

It didn't escape Ethan that there was the unspoken in what she said, that simple euphemism of *your situation*, meaning *your mother*.

She gave him a pat on the back. "I just want you to enjoy yourself next year. You can start fresh, put all this behind you." She dismissed the first sketch she had made and turned her pad to a fresh page. "Ethan, please be careful around Hannah. You don't know what could happen. I don't want you to get hurt."

The two sat in silence for a few moments longer, the only sound between them the gentle back and forth of her pencil as she sketched the spidery blooms in front of her.

That evening, Ethan was studying in his dorm room when he received a phone call from Hannah. He was reminded of the very first call he had ever gotten from her, when he was nervous and excited about the possibilities that lay ahead.

"Thank God you're there!" she said brightly. "I'm booking

our tickets to Paris. Does the week after graduation work for you? Of course, you'll want to spend some time with your parents, so maybe two weeks after? What do you think?"

"Hannah, are you crazy? I told you I wasn't going."

"I think I can get an upgrade to first if I do it on Air France. Let's see here . . . seats are available—"

"Stop it!" Ethan said. He tried to keep his voice down, but he couldn't.

"I'm not going to," she said. "I'm going to call your parents right now to tell them. I mean, they should know about our little trip, don't you think? They'll be so pleased. I know they will."

Ethan gripped the receiver with a trembling hand. "If you call them, I will kill you."

"I wouldn't throw around words like that, Ethan," she said coolly.

"I'm sorry. I just—"

"I know—you got a bit worked up. Why don't you come down to the house and we'll talk about it?"

Ten minutes later, despite his better judgment, he was on his way down to her house, careful not to let any faculty spot him. Ms. Hedge wouldn't approve, but this time he was going to cut it off. He would make clear to her that there would be no trip, that they were not to see each other.

When he arrived, she was sitting quietly in her darkened living room, lit only by a few candles. There was something missing: no music, no cake baking in the oven. Only silence and darkness. She was sitting at the table; in front of her, there was a deck of tarot cards, some of them arranged in a reading. The one closest to him was the Empress, a queen sitting on a throne. Her mood seemed different; he had expected her to be on her laptop booking a ticket.

"What are you doing?"

"Sitting. Thinking." She quickly swept up the cards and put them into the stack.

He stood behind one of the chairs, leaning on it with his hands. "Hannah, we can't do this."

She looked up, idly shuffling the cards, her nimble fingers adept at handling them. He hadn't even known that she did tarot readings. "Do what?"

"What we're doing is not right. We need to take a break from seeing each other. Not because the school said so, but because that's how I feel."

"Seeing each other?" Hannah put down the deck.

"You know, what we've been doing."

"You don't really want that, do you?" Her hair hung lazily over her forehead, and she brushed it out of her eyes, tucking it behind one ear. There was an edge to her voice, a gravelly hardness, the feeling of broken glass.

"Hannah, I don't know. All this talk about the summer . . . I'm not even sure I want to stay in Wilton, let alone go to Paris."

"Don't be silly," she said, leaning toward him, reaching out to grab his hands—too far to grasp, but a gesture, still. "It'll be wonderful. Just you and me. I have money saved up. We can book tickets tonight."

"Hannah, I can't do this anymore. It's getting too weird. I'm only eighteen."

She paused. "I can't believe you're saying this. You're saying you want out?" Even in the candlelight, he could sense her eyes boring into him.

"Yes," he said quietly. "I want out."

Maybe this was it. This was where she would set him free.

"I can't grant you that," she said. Something glimmered in her eyes, a fierce defiant spark that wouldn't loosen its grasp.

"Why not?"

She leaned back in her chair. "I got some news today. I went to the doctor. I'm pregnant."

Ethan seized up. There was no way. He didn't know what to say, how he was supposed to feel. He managed a few words. "I thought—I thought you were on birth control."

"I went off it."

He felt a headache coming on, a dull throbbing at his temples. "You went off the pill without telling me?"

Hannah sighed. "Ethan, I've wanted a baby for as long as I can remember. This may be my last chance to have one. And you—well, you're just perfect. Handsome, smart, someday an Ivy League grad, I'm sure. Don't worry, you wouldn't have to pay for it or anything. I can raise the child on my own. But I'd like you to do it with me."

Ethan started sputtering. "You can't do that—you can't just have a baby without asking the guy first. That's—that's not how it works."

"I'm sorry, Ethan. I need to do this. And I want you to do it with me."

He went over to her couch and sat down, placing his head between his knees, rocking back and forth slightly. He heard himself groaning faintly. She didn't come over to comfort him. She stayed in her chair.

He felt so stupid—insane, deserving of punishment—to have trusted her. When had it been? When they had been together over spring break. When they had stopped using protection. She had trapped him into this, trapped him into owing her something.

During the day, in the early, bright spring light, Ethan shuffled to his classes in a haze. People were starting to wear shorts in the afternoons; there were volleyball games on the courts near Cabot Dormitory. Students were lying out in the sun, throwing Frisbees, tossing tennis balls to faculty dogs. He ignored them, staying on the concrete paths between the dorm and the main building and the library, never veering, never participating. In the dining hall—dark now, a cave—he could barely keep food down. In the evenings, he thought it might be better, but it wasn't. He could only sleep for a few hours each night. He lay on his side in his bed in that liminal state of sleeplessness, wishing for anything to take him away, as his eyes wandered over the white shades on his windows, his stereo system, his stack of CDs, textbooks, a pair of jeans on his desk chair, the mirror on his closet door. Why had this happened to him? Weren't students like Todd the ones who got themselves in trouble? Weren't they the ones who sat before the disciplinary committee, sent their girlfriends to get secret abortions, had their parents called in to set things right?

As the days went by, Hannah kept demanding that he come back to the house, to talk to her, to make arrangements. But he couldn't. He also knew he couldn't walk away from a child, one he had helped create. He couldn't imagine it—a sprawling, living creature, growing inside Hannah. He had no experience with babies, no comprehension of what they involved, what it really meant for someone to be pregnant.

Around midnight on Monday evening, Ethan went up to Todd's room. He was lying on his bed, the sheets messy, reading a book. Todd closed it quickly when Ethan came in, shoving it under some papers.

Ethan asked him to come have a cigarette, and they slid out the window at the end of the hallway onto the rusty fire escape that was shielded from the ground by a large oak tree. Ethan nearly tripped over the ledge in his woozy, tired state, a good night's sleep still elusive. The leaves rustled in the breeze as they lit up. Ethan felt the relief of the smoke.

He had decided, earlier that day, that he would confide in Todd. Now he slowly explained the situation with Hannah, the pregnancy, her strange history in Paris. Todd looked surprised, though it quickly gave way to concern.

"I don't know what to do," Ethan said, his voice choking up. "I'm sorry I didn't tell you about it. It was stupid." He thought he might break down. He steadied himself by holding on to the railing.

"Ethan," Todd said. "It's not like I didn't think it might be happening. I mean, I didn't know for certain." He patted Ethan's forearm. Ethan shivered as he felt his friend's fingers graze the dark hairs near his wrist.

"Does anyone else know?"

The two of them paused as they heard security drive by several stories below, the whirr of the engine, the wheels on pavement. They were undetected, safe in their tree palace.

Todd exhaled a stream of smoke. "No. I mean, people might suspect. But people suspect a lot of things. I'm not sure . . ." His voice trailed off. "I'm not sure you were the first person this has ever happened to."

"What do you mean?" Ethan felt a horrible sinking in his gut.

"That's the problem. I don't really know. I've been hearing things about Hannah, that she gets mixed up in things. My brother told me some stuff before spring break. I didn't want to mention it to you. I figured it was none of my business." Todd paused. "I guess I should have said something."

"I'm so messed up about it. I've been thinking about it constantly. I can't even sleep."

"You want some sleeping pills? My mom takes them all the time. They'll knock you right out." Todd the pusher. The solution to every problem. So typical.

Ethan shrugged. "Sure, I guess. I would kill for six hours." He took a deep breath, the wet, sharp smell of leaves and smoke. "But can you help me with this? I mean, beyond the sleep thing? The bigger problem?" Ethan suddenly feared Todd might have nothing more to offer than a pilfered set of prescriptions. He was grateful when his friend spoke.

"I guess I could give Brian a call tomorrow and see if he

269

knows anything else. Just come to my room now and get the pills. It's getting late."

The security car made another pass, its lights illuminating the road ahead of it, but never reaching into the trees above.

That night, Ethan slept dreamlessly, his worries sedated by the hypnotic effect of the pills. The next day, as he woke up to the cool morning fog and trundled his way down the hall to take a shower, he felt clearheaded. He thought about his situation: if he had gotten Hannah pregnant, he would have to stay in her life, and he would have to remain on good terms with her, which would mean keeping up the facade of their relationship, at least until graduation. His parents would be furious when they found out. He imagined the look on his mother's face, one of complete surprise; his father, he thought perversely, might be pleased his son had finally scored. Even if the school never found out, Ethan wasn't certain he could make it to graduation. He didn't know if he could keep pretending with Hannah after she had lied to him like this.

Todd had asked Ethan to cut his athletic requirement that afternoon and meet him at Colonial Pizza, a small dive in town known for its cheap, greasy slices. His friend was already there when Ethan slid into a vinyl booth near the front of the restaurant. Todd had ordered a Coke, and he motioned to the waitress to bring Ethan one as well.

"I called my brother, but he didn't know much," Todd said. "He gave me the number of his friend at Williams, Tyler Bartlett. I left him a message earlier today, but I haven't heard back yet." Todd motioned to his cell phone, sitting next to his paper napkin on the table. While its use was forbidden on campus, it had never stopped Todd while he was in town.

Ethan had always found it obnoxious and unnecessary—as if making a restaurant reservation or calling his mother to check on something were ever that urgent—but now he was grateful for it. "What are we going to ask him?"

"My brother said he thought the situation might be sort of similar. She wanted to keep it going, he didn't want to. Maybe he knows something that will help you."

"Did you tell your brother about this? Todd, I don't want people talking about it." The idea of anyone else knowing was ghastly.

"Don't worry, I didn't tell him much."

Ethan looked at him skeptically. "Would this Tyler Bartlett guy really tell you about this sort of thing over the phone? Why would he talk to you?"

Todd took a sip of his Coke. "He'll talk to me. I've met him a few times, when Brian still went here. But you're right—over the phone might be weird." He fiddled with the straw wrapper, making it into a little ball. "You know, Williamstown isn't really that far away. Maybe forty-five minutes, something like that."

"You're joking—we're going to go look for him?"

Todd shrugged, the hint of a smile at the corners of his mouth.

Ethan looked at him sharply. "Todd—this isn't some kind of game."

"I know that. I'm sorry." Todd picked up the phone. "Let me call him again." He left another message. Ethan noticed several of the pizzeria's patrons giving Todd nasty looks. It was always clear when Berkley students had ventured into town; they looked and acted differently from the local high school kids. The message received was usually that they weren't welcome.

"You seem a bit too happy about this," Ethan said. "Or at least, happier than I've seen you in a while."

"You haven't seen much of me lately."

He looked down, embarrassed at being called out as a poor friend. "I guess now you know why."

"Let's just say this gives me something to think about besides which colleges I'm not getting into." Todd offered a goofy grin. "Like, for example, Williams. Fat chance of ever getting in there."

Ethan surprised himself. "I think we should go. You're right— we have nothing to lose. No one will ever find out. It's not like I could get in any more trouble than I'm already in."

Todd dialed the local cab company, but was told no cars would be available for half an hour.

"Come on," he said to Ethan, slapping down a five for the two Cokes.

"What are you doing?"

Todd waited until they were outside the restaurant. "Might as well break several school rules, if we're going to break one." He started walking, turning onto Main Street in the direction of the road leading out of town. "Let's wait for a car that looks like it's not from Berkley—we'll try to hitch."

It took them twenty-five minutes and three different queries, but finally a landscaper's truck stopped whose driver was delivering some shrubs to an inn in North Adams, just five miles away from Williamstown. The two of them admitted that they were students nearby when the driver asked, but other than a few scraps of perfunctory conversation and the sounds of a conservative talk radio show, the trip went by silently. As Ethan breathed in the airy soil smell of the truck's cab, he wondered if they were doing the right thing. To meet someone who had slept with Hannah felt like facing up with an opponent. Even though he wanted to get away from her, nearly wished he had never met her, the idea that she had felt as strongly about someone else, someone whom he was about to meet, was horrifying.

The two were dropped off in the center of the Williams campus, amidst its Colonial edifices and rolling green lawns. Ethan marveled for a moment at how no one paid them any attention, at how they, standing there in their khaki shorts and Polo shirts in the late afternoon, book bags slung over their shoulders, looked like any college freshmen. They started up the street in search of a campus map.

An hour and a half later, they stood in the art center's sculpture studio with Tyler Bartlett. It hadn't been easy locating him; Todd had a crumpled sheet of paper with his dorm name on it, but no one in his suite had known where he was. After waiting around for half an hour, a friend stopping by had ventured that Tyler was most likely in the studio, finishing up his senior thesis.

As they headed over to the arts building, Ethan had noticed how relaxed the campus seemed. By comparison, life at Berkley existed on a sped-up clock, all imposed by a ludicrous, artificial schedule. Their urgent little mission suddenly felt trivial. Music came from a dorm entryway, students enjoyed the warm weather, homemade banners were flung over windowsills announcing dances and protests and rallies. All this would be waiting for them in just a few months at their respective colleges. Ethan briefly allowed his mind to wander over next year's possibilities before focusing back on Hannah and her demands. Yes, he would be leaving the school in about four weeks, but if what she had said were true, if she were really pregnant, there would still be matters unresolved.

Todd said he remembered Tyler from the times Brian had brought home friends from Berkley. Todd recalled his brother's friends as exotic to him at the time, wild animals viewed on a safari. Tyler had apparently been an athlete, lean and fit, the type of guy to wear some form of sports apparel at all times, whether a letter jacket or a well-worn pair of track shoes and yet, also—though this seemed implausible to Ethan, limited as his experience was—an artist. When they had entered the studio, Ethan examined what he eerily viewed as his competition, coupled with the uncanny sensation that he could be looking at an older version of himself. Tyler was still wiry, with floppy blond hair, though his skin looked slack; it had the grayish hue Todd had once said was the sign of a true pothead.

The studios smelled of plaster and solder, clay and wood shavings. It was an environment that normally would have fascinated Ethan: student work displayed, far more sophisticated than that at Berkley; bulletin boards announcing gallery shows; the odd bit of student graffiti on the walls.

Tyler was lost in thought as he appraised a piece of conceptual metalwork, abstract forms on a stand, interlocking shapes. Ethan had to admit that it was good.

He looked up, noticing the two boys.

"Todd Eldon!" he said, as a slow smile broke out over his face. "What the hell are you doing here? Aren't you supposed to be at school? Back at the old prison?"

"We're on a little road trip," Todd said, in a voice that Ethan noticed as different from his Berkley demeanor: more serious, more direct. "I tried calling you on your cell phone—my brother gave me your number." He motioned to Ethan. "This is my friend Ethan."

He and Ethan nodded at each other.

"Sorry about that—I've been crazed finishing this up." He pointed to the sculpture.

"It looks great," Ethan said.

"Needs some work, but it's getting there. Come on in, you guys. What's going on?"

He pulled two metal stools from under a counter and motioned for the boys to sit. As they got closer to Tyler, the distinct smell of marijuana and nicotine wafted their way. Tyler may or may not have been stoned, but he did have the telltale bloodshot eyes and slightly slowed down speech. A pack of Marlboro Lights hung in his shirt pocket.

"This is so weird—I talked to your brother last month. Still owe him twenty bucks. Seriously, he doing okay?"

Todd nodded. "Yeah—it's sort of about that. We wanted to ask you about Ms. McClellan? You know, the English teacher at Berkley? I know it's personal and all—"

Tyler got up to open a window to air out the room. As he turned around, Ethan was afraid he might be angry at the intrusion.

"Yeah," he said simply, sitting down again. "Seems so long ago. I guess it's pretty much public knowledge now."

"Brian told us about, you know—"

Tyler smiled. "Todd, it's okay. I know what Brian told you."

"A friend of mine—a friend of ours—has gotten involved with her."

Tyler groaned. "Not a good idea."

"How so?" Todd asked.

He shrugged. "You know her, you know what she's like. Your brother told me about your special project."

Ethan cringed, though he found himself removed from the conversation. Todd's sudden creation of "a friend" had made it all seem so distant.

"So who's your friend, what's going on?"

Ethan broke in before Todd had a chance to speak. "It's me. I've been seeing her. Todd, it's fine. We're not at school anymore."

"Let me guess," Tyler said. "Painter? Writer?"

"Both." Ethan nodded.

Todd pressed on; Ethan was grateful he didn't have to. "Okay, so I know this is kind of odd, but Brian said there was a relationship with a kid? Something back in France?" Ethan wondered if Todd was getting some kind of perverse pleasure out of this interrogation.

Tyler paused, and then nodded. "It was messed up. One night, she and I got stoned together. It was a Saturday, late check-in, so we decided to have some fun. She could be wild. We both got baked, and we were in bed, and she just started talking about it."

"It was with Bertrand, right?" Ethan asked, feeling like he had to be sure. "Her husband's son?"

"I can't remember what the kid's name was, but yeah, it was

her ex's son. Freaked me out a little bit, I have to admit. She kept saying it wasn't illegal. Still sounded wrong to me."

"Whatever happened to the boy?" Ethan asked.

Tyler spoke slowly. "I thought you guys knew. The kid died. He killed himself."

Todd scowled. "What?"

"After his father found out, he threw him out of the house. The next week, he was dead."

Ethan was stunned as the three of them sat there in silence.

"How did he do it?" he asked quietly.

"She never told me. We ended things pretty soon after. It was all too intense—I was about to graduate, and for her, it was a total rebound. She had dated some guy in town for six months, and then she was dumped. She started flirting with me at a gallery opening on campus. I had never had something like that happen to me before."

"Was it difficult breaking up with her?" Todd asked.

"Yeah—she didn't want to end it. But it wasn't like she really had a choice. I was on my way out."

"Were you ever in touch with her again?" Ethan asked.

"No. I never quite figured her out. Regular girls are—compared to Hannah McClellan, they are utterly uncomplicated."

"How's that?" Ethan asked.

"There's a sadness in her. It's like you can't really make sense of her, no matter how much you try. I always thought it had something to do with her not being able to have children."

Ethan thought he hadn't heard correctly. "What do you mean?" he asked.

"There was something with her—can't remember what it was. But she can't have kids. Like getting her tubes tied. But a disorder. She was pretty messed up about it."

"Are you completely sure about this?" Todd asked. Ethan had no idea how Todd could respond so coolly.

"As much as I can be—I don't mean to get graphic here, but

after the first couple of times, we didn't use protection. There wasn't any need. Hell, I was only eighteen years old."

Ethan wasn't used to such personal information being tossed about so casually, as if they were in a locker room. Tyler's experience plainly appeared to mimic his own. Had there also been the long meals, the stay at her house? The projects done together? The sense of infinite possibility?

The rest of the conversation passed in a blur as Todd made small talk with Tyler and then said they had to be getting back to Wilton. The sun had started setting, and Todd motioned to Ethan that he would call them a taxi.

Ethan followed along in a stupor. Tyler Bartlett wasn't a bad guy; Ethan was grateful for that. Someday, he could be in the same position as Tyler, evaluating his work for a senior thesis. Still, he wanted to be different from Tyler Bartlett, different from all the others, however many there had been.

He chided himself for focusing on the most trivial of matters. The idea that Hannah's stepson had died—worse, had killed himself—was beyond comprehension. Maybe it wasn't true. Maybe it was a crazy story she had made up to shock people.

Tyler's story flashed, scene by scene, in Ethan's mind: the two of them getting high together, having Saturday evening assignations, sex without protection, Hannah wanting it from him just as she had wanted it from Ethan. That Tyler had been a rebound for her, that she had still pursued him. That she had never gotten in touch with him after he left. That this was a pattern for her, that Ethan was possibly one of many, and at the same time, he wanted to believe, special.

Above everything, though, was the potential reality that Hannah could not have children. It had never occurred to him that she could be lying. She had, after all, presented no proof, no directive from her doctor. Like Hansel and Gretel, enticed by the witch with good food, warm beds, and the promise of happiness, he had merely taken her word for it.

* * *

As the taxi turned on the country roads from town to town, Ethan tried looking out the window. He didn't feel comfortable talking to Todd with the driver sitting two feet away from them. The sun had finished setting, and it was that hour before it turns dark, the hour of blue-gray light when objects morph into one another, things are not as they seem.

Ethan finally spoke. "What do you think we—I mean, I—should do?"

"I don't know," Todd said. "Should we confront her?"

"Do you really want to do that? I mean, to do it with me?"

"Ethan, I'm angry about this. She's messing with you. She tricked you into trusting her, and now it turns out she lied about it. You need to get her to face reality, to stop intimidating you."

Ethan motioned with his eyes toward the cabdriver, wishing Todd would be more discreet. "She left me a note today," he said quietly. "She wants me to come for dinner tonight. I suppose you could come with me."

Twenty minutes later, the cab let the two of them off outside Berkley's main gates. They walked back to the dorm, heads low, their sneakers padding softly against the damp grass. Ethan was in no mood to speak to anyone, but this dinner was unavoidable. They would visit her one last time.

CHAPTER 24

When the two of them showed up at Hannah's house, she had been roasting a chicken; the smell drifted out the open windows and onto the porch. In his room, Todd had shared with Ethan several shots of vodka to help calm their nerves. Hannah opened the door, and Todd noticed that her fair skin looked puffy, as if she had been crying and had tried to cover it with makeup. She wore jeans and a white cotton tank.

"Boys," Hannah said, "it's been so long since I've seen you together." After giving them both hugs (Todd tried not to cringe), she made her way to the kitchen counter and started opening a bottle of red wine. "How's everything going? Would you like a drink? Why not, right? You're almost out of here."

Todd nodded. "Four more weeks."

"Ethan?"

"Sure." He nodded. "That's fine."

"Come relax, have something to eat." She had laid out some cheese and crackers on the kitchen counter. "We'll have a nice little meal, just the three of us." Hannah started putting out a third place setting at the table. "I'm going to go freshen up," she said. "Why don't you put on some music? Something happy."

Todd flipped through her CDs as she went upstairs. Ethan took a bite of a cracker smeared with Brie. They had agreed they wouldn't confront her immediately; they would make sure she was relaxed first, that she wasn't on the defensive, and then would explain what they knew, that quite simply, she couldn't hold Ethan to any sort of commitment.

Todd picked out one of Chopin's nocturnes, feeling like the gravity of the situation, as much as Hannah might try to ignore it, demanded something serious. The piece had barely started when Ethan announced he wasn't feeling well. Todd asked him what was wrong.

"I think it's the vodka—empty stomach and all," he said. "I might be sick."

He headed for the bathroom as Todd gave him a pat on the shoulder.

A few moments later, Hannah came down the stairs. Todd sensed that something had changed in her mood; she was like brittle candy, cold and sweet at the same time. She stood near the kitchen table and appraised the music Todd had picked, nodding approvingly. She was wearing a white dress, the same dress she had worn the day Todd and Ethan had first met her at the tearoom.

Todd took a gulp of his wine, not sure what to say.

"It's terribly exciting, isn't it?"

"What?"

"Ethan hasn't told you?"

Todd looked at her, confused, not even willing to guess what excited her.

She patted her stomach. "You know!"

Todd felt a beating in his thighs, the feeling of blood flowing through him at a faster than normal rate. He had no idea she would start launching into this charade so quickly. He took another sip of wine, hoping it might steady him. "Hannah, come on. That's not really fair. Ethan told me about what happened—"

He stopped himself. This wasn't his business, but he was having a hard time pretending.

"It's not a matter of fair, Todd," she said. "Ethan and I are having a child. He's going to marry me."

Todd was stunned. Ethan had been right; she was crazier than they realized. Todd had never seen this side of her; she had always been relatively rational. A bit eccentric, perhaps, but not like this. "Hannah, he's eighteen. I don't think he's ready to marry anyone."

She looked at him with a smirk. "Now, that's not for you to decide, is it?"

Todd resolved not to say anything about what they had learned that afternoon. He tried a different tack. "Can't you see what you're doing to him? He's depressed all the time. You've destroyed him."

Her voice grew sharp. "I haven't destroyed anyone. Keep talking this way, and I'll start telling people about the two of you."

"What about us?" Now Todd felt a hot prickly sensation rushing to his face.

"You're not the only one who likes to go to the cemetery at night, Todd."

He remembered the kiss he and Ethan had shared, the kiss they had both tried to forget. "So what?" he said. "We kissed each other. We were drunk." He cringed at the admission, though there was a sense of relief in telling the truth. He took another gulp of wine.

"I know about you, Todd. I don't imagine you'd like other people to find out, would you?"

Todd thought about what had happened to Jeremy Cohen.

"Not to mention your smoking and drinking. I could get you kicked out for what you're doing right now."

"Okay, cool it, Hannah, you've made your point." He put down his glass.

"Good," she said, taking another sip of her wine. "I'm glad we understand each other."

He needed to let Ethan handle this, and handle it delicately, if he wanted to keep his sexuality private, if he didn't want his life to shatter before he left Berkley.

"Why don't you go and see how Ethan is doing?" Hannah said. "He's been in there quite a while."

Ethan had gone into the bathroom to splash some water on his face, to stifle his nausea. He heard bits of conversation and real-ized that Hannah and Todd were snapping at each other. All over him, most likely. He wanted this to be over, to get out safely. His nausea retreated, and the warmth of the vodka returned to his stomach. He took a quick slurp of water from the tap.

There was a knock on the door, and Todd's voice.

When he stepped back into the main room, the smell of food overpowered him in a way that made him feel, for a moment, like he might be sick again. He held it in.

Hannah and Todd were sitting at the dining table, the un-touched roasted chicken between them. The lights had been turned down and the room was glowing with candles. Todd was smoking a cigarette, a burning ember that floated up to his lips and then down again, thin curls of smoke spiraling toward the ceiling.

Ethan sat down at the table's empty chair. Hannah took a gulp from her wineglass and then started to carve the chicken. "I'm so glad we can all have dinner like this."

The three of them ate in silence, the only noise the light touch of the piano coming from the stereo. As Ethan ate the meal she had prepared (chicken, asparagus, potatoes), it all started to taste the same, as if Hannah had been using the same recipe for all the months they had known her, as if the impression that things were different each time had been an illusion.

After a few bites, Hannah looked up. "Come on, now! This isn't a funeral. What's going on with you two?" She poured more wine in her glass and took another sip.

Ethan shrugged.

"We're just tired," Todd said.

She clapped her hands. "Let's talk about—let's talk about our trip to Paris." She turned to Todd. "Ethan and I are going to Paris this summer."

"I don't know about that," Ethan said. He looked down at his plate, wondering how long her pretense would continue.

Hannah nudged him. "When we come back, we'll set up house here, for the rest of the summer. It will be wonderful. Just think—you and me, together. We can do whatever we want, go wherever we want to go."

Ethan tensed up. "Hannah, you know that's not possible. I'm going to school in the fall."

Her voice quickened. "So I'll move to New Haven. They have schools there where I can teach."

Hannah put her hand over Todd's. "The four of us. The four of us can do it together."

Ethan snorted. "The four of us?"

"Yes, you, me, our child, and Todd."

Ethan gave Todd a sideways glance. This was too strange.

"Oh, and what am I supposed to be?" Todd said. "The funny uncle?"

"Our child's uncle. Or—I know—you can be our son."

Ethan looked at the two of them. He had to stop this, but he didn't know how.

"That's right," Hannah continued. "You can be our other son."

Todd looked at her skeptically. Ethan realized that he was playing along. "How do you know you're going to have a boy?"

"I just know it." She patted her belly. "Three boys."

She got up and started to clear the table. "It will be wonder-ful . . . Wonderful . . ." her voice started to sing. "Wonderful . . ."

"Stop it!" Ethan snapped. "Just stop it!"

"You can't stop it," Hannah said. "In fact, I'm going to book another ticket tonight. I've already got ours reserved. Do you like first class, Todd? Come with us—I mean, I'll have to be careful, but it's safe to travel abroad in the first trimester, don't you think? Particularly with my two chaperones—"

Ethan banged the table with his palm. "Goddammit, Hannah! Look—there is no baby. You can't have children. I found that out today. There's no way you're pregnant. I don't care how many times we were together. It's not possible." Ethan noticed Todd flinching.

Hannah looked as if she had been struck. "Who told you that?"

"Tyler Bartlett. Do you remember him? He certainly remem-bers you. We went to go see him. He told us all about you." Ethan was shaking. He couldn't believe he was screaming at her like this. He wanted to control himself, but he couldn't. "About everything. That you can't get pregnant. And what happened to Bertrand. He'd be alive if it weren't for you." Ethan knew he was going over the edge as Todd gave him a peculiar look.

The last accusation stung Hannah the most.

"None of that is true," she said, her eyes frantically searching the room. "You can't believe what people say."

Ethan pushed his chair away from the table. "Then tell us what happened."

"Yes, there was the affair. I've told you that. It was horrible. It never should have happened. Alain discovered what was going on, and he kicked us both out."

"And?"

"Bertrand was homeless. I never knew. When he found out about us, Alain treated him like an adult. He just let him loose. Bertrand lived on the streets. Apparently he tried to contact me, but he didn't know where I was. And then he killed himself. He jumped off a bridge, drowned himself in the river. You have to understand—he was very unstable. Really, he was not a normal young man."

Ethan noticed, as she told her story, how she twisted it around to relieve herself of the burden.

Hannah continued speaking. "Alain and I were divorced, and I moved away soon after. What happened with Bertrand was never revealed. It would have been too shameful for Alain."

"That boy would still be alive if it weren't for you," Ethan said. "He would be twenty now."

"You don't know that. It's not my fault Alain kicked him out. I can't help it that his father was heartless."

"You're a monster." Ethan felt his voice grow cold. "You should be fired. You shouldn't even be teaching here. Todd and I should tell the school."

"Don't say that, Ethan, please. I know it was a hideous, rash thing that I did, the affair. I've regretted it ever since."

"This is absurd," Ethan said.

"I have done everything in my life since then to make up for that mistake."

"Oh, what?" Ethan said. "Like sleeping with eighteen-year-olds? How many have there been? Surely Tyler and I aren't the only ones. Do you pick one a year? Or maybe more? Are they lining up?" He felt an intense cruelty he had never experienced before. He hated himself for saying these grotesque things, but he was tired of her manipulation.

"Don't you dare say that! There haven't been others. What we have is special, Ethan. And you, too, Todd. I have loved you two—like my own children. You've been such friends to me . . . I don't know how I would have gotten through the year without you."

Ethan and Todd sat in silence as they listened to Hannah's justifications. She stood up and started clearing the table, her voice brightening, as if she had suddenly switched personas. "Come on, let's focus on something happy! Let's talk about the summer—"

"You're insane," Ethan said. "Making up this stuff about me and Todd living with you. It's not going to happen. It's never going to happen. It's over." He got up, shoving the table a few inches forward. "Todd, we're leaving."

"Don't go—stay for dessert," Hannah said, as she rushed to the kitchen. "I've got a blueberry cobbler—it's warm—and I have vanilla ice cream—"

"Forget about your blueberry cobbler," Ethan yelled. "You and your stupid desserts! Go and lure someone else into your little games! We've had enough."

Tears started welling up in Hannah's eyes.

Todd's voice quavered. "Ethan—come on, you're being too hard on her. She was just trying—"

Hannah was sobbing now. She rushed toward Ethan, but he backed away from her. "You can't do this to me! You can't leave me. I won't let you."

"Stay away from me. Stay away from me, and stay away from Todd."

"Please, Ethan. Don't leave. I'll do anything."

"Hannah, forget it. Just forget it."

She threw herself down on the couch and continued to wail. As she screamed into the pillows, she made a sound that wasn't human, an animal sound that Ethan imagined a mother bear would make if its leg were caught in a trap. He wondered if anyone could hear, if there were couples on the golf course, people out walking.

"You're pathetic," he said. "You're totally pathetic."

It hurt him to say it, for he feared that he, too, had been pathetic. By staying with her. By trusting her. By not looking out for himself.

"No—" she said quietly, her voice lowering to a whisper.

"Don't do this to me. Don't leave me. You're just like all the others. Everyone leaves me. Please, Ethan. Please. Todd. Please."

She got up from the couch and ran toward Ethan, grabbing him.

"Get off me!" he screamed.

He shook her off, and she stumbled backward, falling against the dining table and giving it a violent jolt. A dish slid off and shattered on the floor. Hannah knelt down and started picking up the broken shards as she sobbed.

Ethan took Todd by the hand and they walked to the door.

"Hannah, it's over. You're on your own."

With an unsteady hand, Ethan opened the front door, felt a rush of crisp dark air, and stepped through.

IV

END OF TERM

CHAPTER 25

That night, after taking three sleeping pills, Todd dreamt of a flood that had washed over the Berkley campus. At first he had been on a raft made from his bed, he and Ethan, floating, from the dormitory to the library to the dining hall. Then he was alone, without the raft, without Ethan, drowning, barely able to breathe. Underneath it all, he wanted to forget everything that had happened, for things to go back to the way they had been before.

He woke up soaked in his own urine.

Todd stared at the ceiling for several minutes, not believing this had happened. He gingerly stepped out of bed, removing his shorts and wrapping them up in his bedding. He caught himself for a moment in the mirror on his closet door, stared at his naked body in the early morning light. He raised his arms above his head, scratched at his armpits, looked down his sinewy body to his tangle of pubic hair, his swollen penis, the blond curls of hair on his legs. He had all the outer trappings of a man, but he felt like a little boy. A little boy soaked in piss.

He stuffed everything into the laundry bag at the back of his closet. It would sit there, festering all day, until he had a chance to do his wash; it would reek of the feelings he couldn't express. Guilt. Shame. Disgust.

He tried to remind himself that he had nothing to feel guilty about, save for one thing. When Hannah had suggested that the three of them—four, if he included the imaginary baby—could live together, he had, just for a moment, thought it was a good idea.

Ethan was already eating breakfast at their usual table in the corner of the dining hall, near the entrance, when Todd joined him. For Ethan, the previous evening felt like a lurid nightmare. As they had walked away from the house, Todd had wanted to talk about what happened, but Ethan had nothing to say. Now he felt like he had killed someone, someone who had given him so much. He had felt so sure of it last night, but now that it was done, it was fading into distant memory: his reasons, everything that had been wrong with her.

They sat silently that morning eating their breakfast, gummy French toast drenched in watery syrup.

Ethan looked up and saw Hannah walk into the dining hall. She looked the same as she always did: calm, pretty, serene.

"Should we say something?" Todd asked. "Should we—"

Ethan held out his hand, motioning for Todd to keep quiet. There was nothing to say, nothing that could make things better.

Hannah walked right by their table, but appeared not to notice them.

That evening, Ethan went out to the golf course behind the school. He sat on an embankment and looked at Hannah's place nestled in the woods on the edge of the green. All of her lights were on, making the pale house float in the darkness. Ethan wondered how much of life, of love, was simply imagination. Maybe there were no connections between people at all, just brief illusions, temporary salves to ease the pain of living. Maybe that was all love was: a series of shared delusions.

He heard someone behind him. It was Todd, glowing in a pair of blue and white seersucker shorts and a T-shirt. He sat down next to Ethan.

"Did we really know her?" he asked Ethan, as they both looked at the house. "Did we really know her at all?"

A day later, a painting of Ethan's showed up in the art studio. It was the painting he had given to Hannah a few weeks earlier, after Ms. Hedge had mounted his little show, the picture of the witch leading the two children to her house, beckoning to them with candies and sweets. He examined the image: the witch's hair, the two children, their backs to the viewer, the gingerbread house, laden with crystallized fruit, peppermints, chocolate drops. He was saddened by it, not because she had returned his gift, but because he felt no desire to paint anymore. Something in him had shut off.

They didn't talk to her for the next several days. They would see her across the dining hall, in morning chapel, but she had become distant, like a minor character in a book, someone they could watch from afar but would never really know.

They took all their meals in the dining hall. The food was exceedingly bland, nothing like her cooking, her cassoulet or her croque monsieur. The desserts prepared in the school's kitchen were like cardboard; the cakes tasted like sponges, the frosting crumbled like chalk. Ethan ate them despondently, certain that with each bite she would fade further from his life.

CHAPTER 26

When Hannah McClellan left Berkley Academy, some said she had a mysterious illness. Others guessed it was a family emergency. A few suggested that she had come into money and no longer needed to work. Ethan couldn't help feeling guilty, that she was leaving because of his threats, because of the horrible evening that had transpired. He justified it in his mind, the idea that she should have been fired long ago; there was, after all, that peculiar clause in the *Bluebook* that applied to all members of the community, about *compromising the School's good name*. Now that she had left, he didn't want anyone to know about what had happened; he only wanted to get through the year intact.

On the afternoon when Ethan learned the news, he ran down to her house, across the golf course and through the trees, toward her front porch.

A few weeds had sprung up in the garden; the front railing needed painting. There were cobwebs on the lamp near the door. A shingle was missing on the roof; one of the front windows had a crack in it. The porch was littered with dead mosquitoes. It had only been a few days since he had last been here; had he not noticed any of this before?

He pushed open the front door and stepped in. All her furniture, all her things, were gone. Balls of dust and hair collected at his feet as he walked through the living room. Even her bookshelves were empty, faded dirty reminders of what they once held. Ethan knew it didn't matter. Her books had never given him any answers.

He stepped into her study. In this room, she had let her imagination run free. He stared up at the ceiling they had painted together, traced the layers of sky, the fluffy clouds. He let them form into animals until they abutted the classical statuary, the gold paint flaking off like shavings of dark chocolate on one of Hannah's cakes.

She was going back to France. The official story was that she had accepted a teaching position at a boys' school outside Paris. But as before, the rumors Ethan had always heard would spring up again, sprouting dozens of permutations. She was going to marry a count. She was opening a bakery. She was chasing down her ex-husband. The fictions became more real than the truth, as they were whispered before morning chapel, told across sandwiches in the dining hall, mulled over on senior grass.

Ethan wondered if he was solely responsible for her leaving, if she might still be at the school if they hadn't walked out of her house that evening, if she hadn't told them the story of Bertrand's death, if he hadn't implied that she should be fired. He wondered if she had been telling the truth about what had happened in Paris, or if it was something worse. He didn't know what was true anymore, as the rumors swirled around him, the stories about Hannah, about the house, about what had happened to him.

After a few weeks, the gossip stopped. People moved on to other concerns, stopped caring about a woman and a house and a student who may or may not have had a relationship with her. As the year came to a close, everything happening in the present became more important. It was the only thing, Ethan realized, that kept them going.

CHAPTER 27

A few weeks before their graduation, Todd and Ethan's English class went for an afternoon trek in the woods. They were reading Thoreau, and Ms. Davis had wanted to bring the class into nature, to let them observe and write about the wilderness as the philosopher had seen Walden. Everyone spread out in different directions, some down to the stream, some toward the cabins, some to the lake. Todd normally would have followed Ethan, comforted by the ever-present chatter he could bestow upon his friend. But today he wanted to be quiet. He walked by himself for several minutes, listening to the birds chirping, the splashing of water, the papery rustling of leaves. He came to a clearing and sat down on an old log, enjoying the sunlight on his face before turning to his journal.

He had received good news that morning. His college adviser, Mr. Riley, had pulled him aside in the hallway and informed him that he had been taken off the wait list at Brown. "You're a very lucky young man," his adviser had said, which annoyed Todd a bit. Had someone in the development office realized that Jackie could easily make a sizable contribution if he were a student there? No, he would not believe it was that. They didn't accept just anyone at Brown. He had put together a strong application. He would show them he deserved to be there; he would excel in a way he never had before.

After writing for a few minutes, he heard some movement on the trail. Todd turned and saw that it was Jeremy Cohen. He tensed up and then let himself relax. He had to stop being so cruel. Not only to Jeremy, but to himself.

"I'm sorry," Jeremy said, as he entered the clearing. "I didn't mean to interrupt."

"It's okay," Todd said. "You can sit here if you want."

Jeremy gingerly sat down next to Todd, as if the log might crumble under his hundred and twenty pounds.

Todd looked at Jeremy's eye. It was mostly healed, though there was still a slight bruise, a quiet ring of yellow where he had been hit. The fact that he had survived the assault, the fact that he hadn't gone to the administration: Todd felt something for him that bordered on admiration.

"Your eye looks better," Todd said.

Jeremy nodded. "It doesn't hurt anymore."

"You shouldn't have let Cren do that to you," Todd said. "He's an asshole."

"I couldn't do anything about it. It just sort of happened."

"Let me see." Todd held his finger up to Jeremy's eye, to the area around his temple.

"Be careful. It's still a little tender."

Todd remembered when it was purple and swollen, when Jeremy had come into his room, wanting to talk. Now Todd traced it with his index finger. Jeremy flinched, just a bit. Todd was so close to him, he could see the soft down on his temples, the places where his hair was lighter, where the sun had made it blond.

"Hey," Todd said, "if it ever happens again, will you give me a call?"

Jeremy smiled sadly. "I don't think it'll happen again. We only have two weeks left of school."

"Still. Where are you going to college?"

"Rhode Island School of Design."

Todd grinned. "I'm going to Brown. I got off the wait list today. We'll be near each other."

For a moment, Todd imagined what it would be like to be with Jeremy, to fold into his body.

"We'd better get back," Todd said.

He patted Jeremy on the shoulder. Todd felt an electric charge transfer from his hand to the slight boy, and he hoped it would imbue him with strength.

Everything in the last few weeks of the year was happy, unbearably happy: classes were almost over, the dress code had been relaxed. People were excited about their summer plans. Ethan had visited Yale, staying with Tamara Schwartz's older brother, Jonathan. He had felt that weekend as if he belonged there—not the uncertain temptation Berkley had offered him a year ago, but the impression that he could thrive among these Gothic spires and flagstone paths, that he might find others like him.

Berkley Academy had, in its own inexorable way, done exactly to Ethan what it had been doing to its students for more than a hundred years: it had broken him down, and then built him back up again. Just barely, just enough so he could make his way out of its gates.

But something didn't make sense to Ethan. How could a person have entered his life, have become so inextricably a part of it, only to disappear? Wasn't there a connection, a bond, that would last?

He realized, slowly, as the days inched toward his graduation, that if he hadn't known Hannah while she was around, there was no way he could know her now.

V

EPILOGUE

There was a knock at the door of Ethan's suite in Silliman, the sprawling residential college that bordered the north side of Yale's main campus. Outside, the air was brisk, as it had been for most of the fall.

He had resisted at first, but slowly, in those initial few weeks, Ethan had found himself drawn into the student life of the college. He wasn't happy, not exactly, but he was content. He had made some friends; he would eat with his roommates in the dining hall, laughing at their jokes, accepting their invitations to go out for ice cream or to parties. The work was intense, but he enjoyed it; he didn't mind the solitude it afforded him, the monastic existence of living between classes and books and assignments. And there were girls, girls who were more like him—one in particular from his literature class. He had asked her out for coffee twice; they had had a good time, and she had invited him to a dance at her residential college that would take place the next night. He didn't have the wild escapades of hookups and partying that his peers did, but something in him had shifted, a sense of ease, something that told him he could find a home here.

His heart still felt raw, scraped clean. A breakup, he imagined, no matter how it happened, was like a series of puncture wounds. He didn't know how long they would take to heal, if it would take another person to assuage the pain, or if they would turn into scar tissue, hardened and gamey. The important thing was that he was nearly certain, as the days went by, that those wounds, those memories, would mend themselves, and he would emerge, strong and whole. Yes, he wanted it, that delirious feeling, but he could wait.

Though he was consumed by his daily schedule, by his new friends, even by the burgeoning possibilities of dating, he saw her face in women he passed on the street; he fantasized that she would come to visit him. It was possible, he realized, to live in both the present and the past. As much as he tried not to, he imagined her teaching English to young Parisian boys, boys who were sixteen, seventeen, eighteen years old. He imagined her walking up to one of them, giving the boy a book, inviting him to her apartment for a plate of cobbler. Ethan's stomach turned as he thought of her sitting on her couch, wearing a sexy pair of American jeans, legs curled under her like a cat. He thought of finding her, of making things right. He knew she was crazy, possibly even a monster, that he was, unquestionably, better off without her. Still, he wondered if anyone would ever love him the way she did (she had never, he recalled, said those words, and yet he knew she loved him, in that simple way one knows things unspoken). He wanted her to remember him, wanted what they had shared to be unique. He hoped she would write about him, about Todd, about their little family, strange as it was. And he hoped, as the weeks went on, as anger gave way to regret and then something akin to forgiveness, that she would find a man who wouldn't leave her.

Sometimes, he had faith that this would happen. Other times, he could only think about what had happened to Louisa Berkley and how, in Hannah's novel, she, too, had spent her final days in Paris.

He would daydream, occasionally, that Hannah really had been pregnant, that the two of them had created a child through some sort of miracle. He pictured her wandering the streets of Paris, her belly distended with a child that was partly his. But no, he would shake his head as he walked to Commons for breakfast, shuffling along the granite stones of Beinecke Plaza, he knew that could not be.

Six weeks after Ethan had returned home to Palo Alto for the summer, his mother passed away. It had happened quickly, just a few days in the hospital, and then she was gone. He was able to spend those last weeks with her, though it wasn't clear until her final days how close they were to the end. It didn't make up for the nine months he had been away. But she assured him that he had done the right thing, that leaving home had been the best decision, that she had felt better knowing he was making his way in the world.

He never told her about Hannah, not the specifics, at least. It was not for fear that she might disapprove; he sensed she knew something had happened, and simply had the discretion, or the lack of awareness—he didn't know which—not to ask. His mother had never believed in ambiguity, in mixing relationships with work. All she had to know was that he had loved someone, and lost her. As she lay in her bed, surrounded by art monographs (her vision had gotten so bad, she couldn't read anymore), she assured her son that he would be fine, that in time, he would find someone else to love, a person who loved him. There was some comfort in hearing this, for he realized that right now, at this moment, she was the only woman in his life whom he could trust.

* * *

A few weeks after classes began, Ethan had picked up a package from the parcel window at Yale Station. He tore it open to find his Berkley yearbook, its blue cover stamped with gold. When he got back to his room, he flipped through the pages. There were people smiling, laughing, posing with their friends. Pictures of athletic teams, clubs and activities, school plays. He couldn't find a single picture of himself or of Hannah. It was as if neither of them had been there at all.

Now, sitting in his room at Yale on this Friday afternoon, Ethan got up to answer the door. He imagined it was one of his roommates who had forgotten his key; the three of them were a boisterous bunch, and though they were Ethan's age, he often felt like the dorm parent, the one responsible for taking messages and making sure no one was locked out of the suite.

Instead, standing at the threshold was Todd. The two hadn't spoken since the last senior party, two days after graduation. Ethan had wanted to distance himself from his time at Berkley, and he hadn't made any effort to contact his friend. Todd had tried to get in touch with him, writing him several e-mails and leaving two messages at his house, but Ethan had never returned them. He had used his mother's death as an excuse, but he knew that wasn't the only reason. He wanted a fresh start; calling Todd would only remind him of everything that had happened.

His friend was dressed smartly in a pair of jeans and a suede leather jacket. His blond hair was cut short and spiked up. Even though he was dressed like an adult, standing beneath Silliman's stone arches, Todd seemed smaller than Ethan had remembered him, like a child playing dress-up. He was proud, though, of his friend, at how clearly he had adapted to his new life.

Ethan smiled, opening the door for him to come in. "What are you doing here?" he asked.

"I wanted to visit you."

Ethan looked at Todd quizzically. "You came all the way from Providence just to see me?"

"I was headed home for the weekend. I thought—I thought it might be nice to catch up."

Ethan nodded, still surprised at the visit. "You want to get some slices?"

He grabbed his coat and they walked together across the courtyard toward a large wooden door that led onto the street. Next to the college was a pizza place, Naples, that was filled with dark wooden booths and the smell of freshly baked pies. The two of them stepped up to the counter and ordered sodas and slices. Todd reached for his wallet.

"I've got it," Ethan said.

They carried the hot slices to a booth near the window. The restaurant was suffused with an amber light, sun shining through stained glass, the haze of grease and stale beer.

Todd took a sip of his Coke. "Jeremy says hello."

"I didn't know he was at Brown."

"He's over at RISD. We've sort of—we've sort of been hanging out."

"Hanging out?"

Todd's ears colored. "I guess you could call it dating."

Ethan looked at his friend, not surprised. "That's great," he said. "I'm happy for you."

"It felt good to, you know, figure that out. Feel some certainty about it. I mean, it's not like it's not an issue anymore, but it's just—it's not the same as it was before."

Ethan looked down at his pizza. He wanted so much for Todd to inspire some of the familiarity, the comfort, that he'd had only six months ago. While Todd didn't provide that, Ethan was still grateful for his visit. Those brief nine months at Berkley might have been the closest they would ever be to each other; going forward, they might only grow apart. Still, they could write, or visit, or send Christmas cards. Yes, their lives were different, but Ethan hoped to stay in touch from now on, not to let their shifting circumstances keep them apart. It was what happened with people, he had observed; it was happening with most of his classmates from Berkley. People drifted into each other's lives because they were thrown together by time or proximity, and just as easily, they drifted away again.

The table between them was carved with decades of undergraduate markings. Ethan ran his fingers through the deep grooves formed by the words, the hearts and arrows, the pluses and zeroes.

"Did you ever hear from . . ." Todd paused, as if afraid to say her name.

"No." Ethan took a bite of his pizza.

"Did you ever think—I know this sounds odd, but do you ever think that maybe she planned the whole thing? That she wanted to leave Berkley, but she couldn't? It's messed up, but maybe she was trapped there, trapped in her own inertia. Maybe she needed us, needed you, to release her, to give her a reason to leave. To go back to France. If that's where she is."

"I don't know," Ethan said. "I don't want to believe it wasn't real. But I have no idea. I suppose it's possible."

Ethan feared the exploration of this topic, for there was something he was hiding. A few days ago, he had looked into what it would cost to buy a plane ticket to Paris. He had his mother's credit card number—still valid, as his father hadn't gotten around to canceling it. He could buy a round-trip ticket, leaving on a Friday afternoon, an afternoon very much like this one, and make it back in time for his first class on Monday morning. He imagined the plane: the Air France flight from JFK left at ten thirty at night, arriving in Paris at eleven the next morning; it would be filled with strangers and mystery, people speaking in foreign accents and reading paperback novels and clutching cartons of duty-free cigarettes.

He told himself it wouldn't matter if he couldn't find her. He would look, of course—he had been able to convince Sarge to get him the address of the school where she had supposedly taken a job—but knowing Hannah, it could all be a lie. She could be in another country, in another part of the world. It wasn't finding her that was important. It was the chance to put it to rest, not to let it linger. He wanted to bury her memory, to do what his father had not yet done with his mother, leaving the urn containing her ashes in a bookcase in her study, tucked next to the four books she had written and two battered shoe boxes full of photographs. He didn't know if he would be doing the right thing by going to look for her. He only knew that he needed to shut a door, and this would be one way to do it.

He looked at Todd, who was chewing thoughtfully on his last bite of pizza crust. He envied him for having found someone, even if it was a guy, even if it was the scrawny Jeremy Cohen. Ethan had put so much faith in Hannah and then, nothing. He knew he needed other people, just as his parents had needed each other, just as Todd and Hannah had needed him.

But something else was pulling at him, the idea that he could never get to know another soul, that just when he had started to understand someone's core, they could turn on him and reveal themselves to be something else. Either that, or he would realize he was not the person he thought he was. Even Todd, too, was different now, was not the person he had met only a year ago.

"I'm sorry I didn't write or call," Ethan said. "I needed some time to myself, after everything."

"You mean with . . ."

"Yeah, and other stuff."

Todd took in a quick breath. "Your mother. I'm so sorry."

There was something Ethan needed to say, something he had been grasping at for weeks, for months. It felt like the right time. "I never thanked you," he said. "It was weird, and I know you were going through a lot of stuff, but I never thanked you. For being there that night. You could have walked away, but you didn't."

"It's okay," Todd said. "I'd do it again if I had to." He looked at his watch. "I should be getting to the train station. My mom's having one of her dinner parties. You know, she asks about you. She said you can come stay whenever you want, if you need a place to crash in the city."

Ethan smiled. "Thanks—that's sweet of her. Maybe we could do it together sometime."

The two of them got up from the booth, and Ethan gave Todd a pat on the shoulder as they walked through the doorway onto York Street, into the twilight.

He had a box of things he had saved; they were stowed in the file drawer in his room, their placement in his cheap, laminated student-issue desk an unworthy repository for them. Cards she had given him. Stories she had commented on. Notes she had written. He had saved it all, for it was the only evidence he had of their time together.

He took all of this, and added to it the information he had printed out about flights to Paris, the address of her school. Someday, he would go to Paris, not for her, but for himself. Now his life was in New Haven, with his friends, at the dance the following night, in classes, in the library. He carried the pile from his room, out into the courtyard. At this hour, everyone was in the dining hall. He went to one of the entryways near the garbage area, and dumped it all on the stone walkway, a pile of detritus representing the last year of his life. Ethan lit the edge of an envelope, the one that held the card she had given him at Christmas, with a match, and watched the pile as it slowly began to burn. When the papers had disappeared beneath the sputtering flames, he stomped on them until they were nothing but a blackened pile of ash.

Several days later, he had the urge to paint again. He hadn't touched a brush, had not even sketched in a pad, since last spring. He would go to the art studios, would start working in his free time. He would put it all down.

ACKNOWLEDGMENTS

I am enormously grateful to everyone who has supported me during this novel's creation.

Thanks to my agents, Kate Lee and Richard Abate at ICM, for their wise counsel.

To my editor, John Scognamiglio, for his patience and vision. Thanks also to his assistant, Peter Senftleben.

To my publicist, Scott Manning, and his assistants, Dawn Hope in particular, for all their hard work.

To my assistant, Susanne Filkins, and to Halle Petro and Danielle Grabianowski, who have allowed me the time to write.

To my readers, who provided invaluable guidance: Sarah Kate Levy, Shelly Lowenkopf, Stewart Lewis, Tom Williams, David Ebershoff, Zach Udko, Michael Selleck, Melanie Fleishman, and Adam Plotkin.

To Lisa Ludwig and Matilda Kunin, for sharing with me their personal stories of loss so that I might enrich this narrative.

To everyone who has generously given me places to work over the years: Marcia and Bill Levy, Monte Albers de Leon, The Village Quill, David Epstein, Bill Candelaria, and Rudy Vela.

To my friends and teachers at the Hotchkiss School, who inspired in me a love of writing and reading that made this novel possible. It is a school that, among its many virtues, also has a keen interest in its own history, and I am grateful for its support of such books as Ernest Kolowrat's *Hotchkiss: A Chronicle of an American School* for giving me insight into the inner workings of a boarding school beyond my own experience.

I am particularly grateful to Walter DeMelle, director of the Edsel Ford Library, who is a friend to all Hotchkiss authors, and to Peter Rawson, who allowed me to peruse the school's photo archives when my publisher asked for visual inspiration for the cover.

To all my friends, who believed in this book, sight unseen, every step of the way, and to my fellow novelists, mentors, and heroes, who have been there for advice and encouragement: you know who you are.

To my family for their love and support.

Finally, I will be grateful, always, in more ways than I can count, to Drew Frist, a singular reader with a sharp eye, who helped me carry this book down the final stretch.